BLOOD RISE

A LONDON CARTER NOVEL
(BOOK 6)

BY

BJ BOURG

WWW.BJBOURG.COM

TITLES BY BJ BOURG

LONDON CARTER MYSTERY SERIES

James 516

Proving Grounds

Silent Trigger

Bullet Drop

Elevation

Blood Rise

CLINT WOLF MYSTERY SERIES

But Not Forgotten

But Not Forgiven

But Not Forsaken

But Not Forever

But Not For Naught

But Not Forbidden

But Not Forlorn

But Not Formidable

BLOOD RISE
A London Carter Novel by BJ Bourg

This book is a work of fiction.
All names, characters, locations, and incidents are products of the
author's imagination, or have been used fictitiously.
Any resemblance to actual persons living or dead, locales, or events
is entirely coincidental.

CHAPTER 1

Fifteen years earlier…
Bourbon Street, New Orleans

Virgil Brunner loved his wife, Skylar, but he didn't like her anymore. They'd only been married two years and she'd already stopped being the fun-loving girl he'd fallen in love with several years ago. Had they met in a library or a church, he might've had different expectations and wouldn't have gone forward with the marriage, but she had advertised one thing and delivered something else. So, here he was, out on Bourbon Street—or Sin City—alone, because she refused to go out with him anymore.

Virgil grinned as he stared down into the glassy eyes of the young blonde who was grinding against him on the dance floor. *Not exactly alone,* he thought. If he remembered right, this beauty's name was Amber and she was from Alabama. He thought she said something about being in college, but he didn't really care. He didn't want her number and he didn't want to see her again. He simply wanted someone to hang out with tonight.

"Are you having fun, Amber?" he asked, yelling to be heard over the loud music and raucous crowd in the tight bar.

She bobbed her head up and down, her long hair plastered to the side of her sweaty pale face. "It's the best Mardi Gras ever!"

He placed his hand firmly against the small of her back and pulled her closer, smiling with anticipation when he felt the firmness of her breasts against his chest. "Want to get out of here?"

Her eyes twinkling, she nodded and shoved her cold hands up under the back of his shirt. "What do you have in mind, Cajun Man?"

"Where's the craziest place you ever had sex?" It was a bold move, he knew, but Virgil thought she was ready for it. She'd complimented him on his dark and toned frame and had been running her fingers through his dark hair all night, and they'd even made out on the dance floor three or four times. She also hadn't protested when he cupped one of her breasts during a slow song.

She giggled. "I don't know…in the forest, maybe?"

"Well, I'm going to take you to the jungle!" Virgil grabbed her hand and gently led her toward the door. She didn't resist and even ran ahead of him as they busted out onto the crowded streets. The parade was making its way down Bourbon and they stopped to watch an approaching float. People were jockeying for position and a few fights broke out every time something cool flew from the hands of one of the crew members on the floats. Sirens screamed from somewhere toward the back of the floats and Amber had to lean close to him.

"I want a bead!" she screamed into Virgil's ear. "Help me get something cool to take back home!"

Virgil pushed his way through the drunken crowd, making a hole for Amber. Once they were standing beside the large float, which was lumbering by and rocking back and forth to the beat of its dancing crew, Virgil began yelling up at them. "Throw me something, mister!"

Amber began yelling with him and they waved their hands in the air, but they were invisible amongst the legions of other parade-goers.

"There's one trick that's always guaranteed to work," Virgil shouted in Amber's ear. "Want to try it?"

"Sure!" she shouted back, her breath warm on his ear.

Virgil slipped behind Amber and reached for the bottom of her shirt. He felt her stomach quiver as his fingers brushed against her soft and smooth skin. "Are you ready?" he asked.

She took a deep breath and looked up over her shoulder at him. He saw her bite her lower lip and nod, a mischievous grin playing at the corners of her mouth.

Virgil jerked her shirt upward, snagging his fingers against her bra on his way up, exposing her plump breasts for the world to see. It immediately got the attention of several crew members. They broke out exotic beads, stuffed bears, and roses, allowing them to rain down on Amber and Virgil.

Amber shrieked in joy and quickly pulled her shirt back down, taking a second to adjust her bra before collecting a stuffed bear and a rose from the wet pavement. Promising Amber they'd return for more loot, Virgil guided her away from the parade and toward the back of the crowd. He led the way down the sidewalk and then hooked a right onto St. Peter Street. As they walked farther down the street, the sounds of the parade grew lighter behind them.

"Where are you taking me?" Amber asked, bumping playfully into Virgil.

"To a special place," he said, wrapping his arm around her waist. As they continued walking down the dark street, lights from a doorway loomed ahead and Virgil realized they were approaching the bar where he'd proposed to Skylar four years ago. It had been their third date and he was certain she was the one. He frowned as he remembered how they had hit it off when they'd first met, and how different he thought his life would be with her.

He'd met her in a local bar while visiting his dad back home. They'd spent about thirty minutes talking before he asked if she wanted to ditch her friends and go someplace quiet. She'd readily agreed and they ended up at his dad's shop, where he convinced her to go for a boat ride. They rode around on the water until he found a stretch of bayou that was dark and secluded, and they had sex on the hard bottom of the boat. From that moment on, they were hooked on having sex outdoors.

Their third date, which was the night they got engaged, had been one of the best, albeit not the most adventurous. They'd spent the night on Bourbon Street before stumbling into a little dive on a side street where he'd gotten up on the bar and proposed to her in front of God and everyone. Immediately afterward, they'd found a nearby alley where they stripped off their clothes and began having sex against some boxes—until a New Orleans cop shined his bright light in their direction.

The cop had been cool and kept walking, but it ruined the moment. They later found a quiet and dark spot down by the Mississippi River to finish their love-making session and to celebrate their engagement. Drunk and tired, they'd passed out under the stars and woke up naked in each other's arms early the next morning, a group of tourists laughing and pointing at them from the River Walk above.

That was the beginning of what he thought the rest of his life would look like, but he was wrong.

While their relationship centered around sex mostly, they also enjoyed doing other things together, like bar-hopping, dancing, and hosting parties. It didn't matter the occasion, they always made up a reason to party and they often left their guests behind to find a place to have sex. Well, that was until about a year ago when Skylar started talking about having kids and moving back home to be closer to their parents. She suddenly didn't want to have friends over to party, she didn't want to drink as much, and she didn't think it was appropriate to have daredevil sex everywhere they went. She talked about conceiving a child in a loving and healthy environment, and she started nagging Virgil anytime he smoked cigarettes or had a drink.

"Drinking alcohol lowers your sperm count," Skylar would complain, "and smoking reduces the quality of sperm. I want our baby to be healthy and happy."

CHAPTER 2

"Hey, why aren't you talking anymore?" Amber asked, her Alabama accent breaking through Virgil's thoughts. "Are you too old to keep up with me?"

Shaking off the guilt that began tugging at his chest, Virgil grunted and pulled on Amber's hand, nearly dragging her down the street. "We're almost there."

When they reached the narrow alley where he and Skylar had engaged in proposal sex, he looked up and down the street to make sure no one would see them ducking into it. Other than the spooky glow from the street lamps and the distant drone of the rocking parade, nothing moved.

Virgil nodded and stepped into the deep shadows between the two buildings and picked his way toward the far end, which opened up onto Pinewood Street. They were halfway down the alley when he heard some voices up ahead. He felt Amber's nails dig into the flesh of his forearm.

"Do you hear that?" she asked, hissing her words. "We're not alone."

Virgil peered through the darkness and—against the glow from Pinewood Street—could see the shadows of two men standing near the far opening to the alley. They were leaning forward, as though they were looking down at something, and movement at the men's feet confirmed for Virgil that there was a man hunched over.

"Stay here," he whispered to Amber.

"Why? What are you going to do?"

"I just want to get closer to see what's going on."

Virgil stepped silently forward and finally got close enough to hear what was happening.

"...know you got the loot," the man closest to Virgil was saying. "Now hand it over before I beat your ass."

"I don't have anything," a weak and tired voice said. "I swear...I didn't get anything all day."

"That's bullshit," said the man farthest from Virgil, kicking the homeless man in the ribs. The homeless man folded over with a grunt. "I saw people throw money in your box—now hand it over!"

Virgil sighed. He worked as a detective in a neighboring parish and had pounded his share of assholes, but he preferred to spend his off-duty time loving rather than fighting. He stole a glance into the darkness behind him, where Amber was waiting. He could see her porcelain skin glowing in the night, and thought about returning to her.

"I'm not going to say it again," hollered one of the men. "Give...me...the...money."

With each word, Virgil heard a sickening thump and the homeless man wailed in pain. He cursed silently. There were two of them and one of him, which meant he could pull his gun—*if* he had it. He didn't believe in mixing alcohol and firearms, so he never took his pistol out partying, but he was wishing for it now. Still, he stood a better chance against two thugs than some helpless homeless guy, so he sighed and stepped forward. When he had moved close enough to be seen in the dim light, he whistled sharply.

The man nearest him spun around and took up a fighting stance. The man wore an oversized red T-shirt, baggy jeans, and orange shoes. His hands were clenched into fists and Virgil could see a row of tattoos down his forearms. One was a middle finger followed by the words, *All of you.*

"Who the hell are you?" Middle Finger asked, his voice low and menacing.

"That's my boy you're kicking." Virgil tried not to sound too aggressive. "Why don't you get the hell out of here before you piss off me and my friends?"

The second man, who wore a green long sleeved shirt, tight jeans, and white sneakers, also turned to face Virgil. Virgil scowled when the light illuminated the man's face, wondering what he'd just stumbled upon. Atop the second man's head, there was a baseball cap displaying a New Orleans Police Department badge.

"What friends?" asked the Badge, tilting his head to see beyond Virgil. "I see nothing but a scared little girl."

Out of the corner of his eye, Virgil could see the homeless man scooting toward the opening to the alley, dragging his body one inch at a time. If he made it out the alley, Virgil could disengage and everything should be fine. He just needed to buy some time.

"My buddies are right behind me," Virgil said, "and they don't play around."

Middle Finger suddenly sprang forward and hit Virgil right in the face. The move was so sudden and unexpected, it caught him off guard, and he stumbled backward. His upper lip burned something awful and blood poured down his face. Before he could regain his balance, the Badge closed in on him and hit him in the stomach. Virgil had been punched in the stomach many times in his life, but he'd never felt the air leave his lungs like it did just then.

He struck out blindly, trying to suck air through his mouth as he did. He managed only to choke on his own blood. Shadows and flashes of light whirled around as he moved frantically in the tight quarters. His right hand, which was his strong hand, connected with someone's face and he heard an angry grunt. He felt contact against his torso and a burning pain seared through his flesh.

"Help! Help me!" called a voice from somewhere ahead of him. "My friend's being stabbed!"

It was only then that Virgil fully understood the source of his pain and shortness of breath. *I'm being stabbed!*

As people began to shout from the sidewalk, Badge and Middle Finger quickly backed away and disappeared around the corner. Virgil stepped toward Pinewood Street, where a crowd of onlookers had gathered to see the commotion. He couldn't get air into his lungs and felt drowsy. He glanced down and saw blood all over his shirt. He lifted the shirt and dabbed at the hole on the left side of his chest. Blood and bubbles sprayed from the hole with each breath he took.

A figure suddenly appeared by his side and steadied him. "You need to lie down."

Virgil recognized the voice as that of the homeless man who'd been getting his ass beat.

"Dear Lord, is he going to be okay?" Amber asked from the alley behind him.

Virgil allowed himself to be lowered to the ground. As panic began to set in, he felt around with his hands. The concrete was wet and sticky. He didn't know if it was from his blood or the stale beer and rancid urine that tortured his nostrils.

"Help me," he said, wheezing. "I don't want to die like this."

"Take off your bra and press it firmly against that cut," the homeless man said to Amber, pointing to the wound he wanted her to address. Virgil thought he saw a tattoo on the homeless man's inner forearm that looked like a doctor's symbol—two serpents wrapped around a stick with wings—and that confused him even more.

This guy must be an angel, he thought. *God's giving me a second chance!*

The homeless man hollered at someone in the crowd to hand him a plastic bag or a rain coat. When they did, he pressed it against the sucking wound in Virgil's chest and he began to breathe a little better.

Scared and desperate, Virgil looked around until he found Amber's eyes. He clutched at her arm. "Please…take my phone and…and call…please call my wife." He stopped to take a breath. "Tell her I love her…and that…and that I'm sorry."

"You have a wife?" Amber jerked her arm away from Virgil and jumped to her feet. "You're an asshole!"

CHAPTER 3

7:35 a.m., Saturday, August 16
Present day Magnolia Parish

"Blue Summit Mountain Rentals," answered a lady in a Tennessee mountain twang. "How can I help you?"

"Yes, ma'am, this is London Carter," I said over the phone, keeping my voice low so Dawn couldn't hear me. "I reserved a cabin for seven nights and I just wanted to confirm that I'll be arriving tomorrow afternoon at three."

The woman on the other end paused for a few seconds and I could hear some papers rustling. When she got back on the phone, she said, "I have you right here...London Carter, checking in August seventeenth, checking out August twenty-fourth. I see you're coming from Louisiana. Don't forget we're in a different time zone, so you'll lose an hour once you get through Georgia. If you're not here by four-thirty, we'll text you a code to retrieve your key in the night locker."

After asking a few more questions, I thanked her and hung up. I then peeked through the kitchen window. Dawn was sitting at the table cleaning her pistol. All she knew was that we were going on vacation where there'd be bears—hence the readying of her pistol—and we'd have to drive for eleven hours. It had been fourteen months since the attempt on the vice president's life and, thankfully, everything had returned to normal in Magnolia Parish. While we still carried heavy case loads at work, the year had been filled with burglaries and thefts mostly, with a few armed robberies, two kidnappings, and one domestic murder. All in all, it had been a typical year in our southern Louisiana parish, but we both needed a vacation.

Dawn's Glock was still in pieces in front of her, so I knew I had time for another phone call. But I'd have to make it quick. Somehow, I had managed to keep everything a secret from her up to this point, but I was worried I'd find a way to blow it in these last hours.

I searched through my contacts and found the number for the photographer I'd chosen in Tennessee and pressed the button. She answered after four rings and immediately recognized my voice.

"Mr. Carter! How nice to speak with you again. Are you excited?"

I shuffled my feet and walked to the far edge of the back porch. "I'm scared to death," I admitted. "What if she says no?"

"Well, it is possible," she said slowly. "I see it all the time in my line of work. In fact, I've got dozens of pictures of men down on one knee crying in shame."

"Wait—what?" My heart dropped to my boots. "Do you really think she'll say no?"

The photographer began laughing hysterically and I grunted, knowing I'd been played—and I deserved it, too. When I'd first called to request her services, I told her I needed a photographer to follow me and a client to a desolate part of the mountains for a photo shoot. When she asked for the occasion, I told her I was planning on murdering him and I needed to record it for my mob boss.

"It's hard to kill someone while you're holding a camera," I'd joked, "so that's where you come in."

She had gasped and was about to hang up when I quickly told her I was joking. I had admitted it was a bad joke and apologized, explaining how nervous I was about proposing to Dawn. She'd taken it in stride and was good-natured about it, but I never suspected she'd exact revenge.

"Good job," I said, appreciating her humor. When she stopped laughing, I asked if she received my payment.

"I did, but you didn't have to leave such a large tip," she said. "I get paid by the hour, regardless if I have to hike or stand still."

"Well, I'm just surprised you're willing to do it."

"Are you kidding? You're paying me to hike to the most beautiful waterfall in the Smoky Mountains and do the one thing I love most in life—photography." She laughed again. "I feel like I should be paying you."

I thanked her again and we agreed she'd be at the trailhead to Abrams Falls for nine o'clock on Monday morning. While the photographer would be driving to the trailhead, Dawn and I would be hiking halfway around the eleven-mile Cades Cove Loop Road to get there. I'd never hiked the Loop Road or the trail to the waterfall, but I'd seen pictures online and I knew instantly it was where I wanted to drop down on one knee and propose to Dawn.

Jerry Allemand, the second in command of the sniper team I run for the Magnolia Sheriff's Office, had questioned the wisdom behind making Dawn hike over five miles of pavement and then two and a half miles of rough mountainous terrain before proposing.

"That's a lot of work and it doesn't seem very romantic," he'd said at sniper training last week when I explained my plan and showed him the ring I bought for her. "Why don't you just go to the beach or a fancy restaurant like a normal person?"

"Did you think I'd just let Dawn be my fiancée for free?" I had joked, and then shook my head. "No, sir, she'll have to earn this ring."

While I initially thought it was a great plan, Jerry's reaction had stayed with me all week, and now the photographer's joke was starting to make me doubt myself. What if she didn't like—

"Hey, what are you doing out here?"

"Crap!" I jerked in my skin when Dawn's voice suddenly sounded behind me. "I didn't hear you walk up behind me."

I wasn't the type to startle and Dawn knew it. Her eyes narrowed in suspicion and she glanced down at the phone in my hand, chewing on her lower lip as she tapped her bare foot on the porch. "What were you doing back here?"

I couldn't lie to her about anything, so I didn't even try. I looked right into her brown eyes and said, "If you just trust me and don't ask any questions, you'll find out soon enough."

She grunted. "It'd better be good—like a new ragtop for my Jeep or a palomino pony."

"Right," I said, as I took her hand and walked inside. While her hand was soft, her grip was firm. At five-foot, three inches tall, and 125 pounds, she was small, but tough as nails. I was about seven inches taller than her and outweighed her by more than sixty pounds, but she gave me a run for my money when we wrestled for fun on the living room floor. I never liked wrestling before I met Dawn, but the wrestling always led to other things, and for that I was grateful.

"Are you all packed up?" I asked when we stepped into the kitchen.

She nodded and closed her gun cleaning kit. "I cleaned my Glock, because I don't plan on being killed by a bear while on vacation."

As she tidied up the table, I carried my bags to her Jeep and tossed them in the back. She was right about needing a new ragtop. Some assholes had sliced it up a couple of months ago in Arkansas and I had wanted to get her a new one, but I didn't even know how to go about ordering it. She had purchased a patch kit and we'd done our best to fix it well enough to keep the water out. It worked, but it was far from perfect.

I returned inside, grabbed her bags, and loaded them, too, and then stood there waiting for her to join me. She stopped to lock the door and bounded off the steps, throwing me the keys as she approached. "I'm riding shotgun first," she said, "since I was awake all night wrapping up that burglary report."

I didn't argue. I loved driving her Jeep and had mentioned several times that I wanted one of my own.

"Why do we need two Jeeps?" she'd asked. "We can keep this one until it gets too old and then trade it in for a new one."

That one statement, uttered casually one evening not long ago, had given me the confidence I needed to set up the proposal, but not much more. While I could face down any threat and not waver one bit, I was scared to death to ask her to marry me.

As I cranked up the Jeep and pulled out of the driveway, I stole a glance at her. She was wearing blue jean cut-offs and a loose T-shirt that flapped in the wind. She hadn't put on any shoes and kicked her feet up on the dash. She brushed a tuft of brown hair off of her cheek and closed her eyes, settling in for the long drive.

I reached for the radio knob and flipped on my favorite country music station, which played old country songs on Saturdays. As I pulled out of the driveway and headed north, *Seven Spanish Angels* by Willie Nelson and Ray Charles blared over the speakers. I smiled and settled in to enjoy the wind in my hair and the music in my ears. *This is going to be a great vacation,* I thought, *and it's just the first of many for Dawn and me.*

CHAPTER 4

8:00 a.m.

Deputy Abraham Wilson was racing north on Highway Eighty, the lights on his marked police cruiser flashing and his siren blaring. Traffic was nonexistent at that time of the morning, and it was a good thing because he was in a hurry. Three boys had just returned home from checking their catfish lines in Plymouth East and claimed to have seen a woman's body suspended from the sky. One of the boys' mothers had called it in and she told the dispatcher the boys had seen the body around sunrise, but didn't immediately tell her because they didn't think it was real.

Slowing down just enough to make the turn up ahead, Abraham turned smoothly to the right and onto Plymouth Highway, heading east along the country road.

Boasting a population just north of 1,000 people, Plymouth East was a small community in central Magnolia Parish that was made up of mostly fishermen, hunters, and cane farmers. There was only one store, which also served as the gas station, two locally-owned restaurants, a church, a community center, a post office, and a volunteer fire department amongst the smattering of houses that made up the whole of the township. There was no local government and, although the residents didn't always like it, they fell under the authority of the Magnolia Parish Council and under the jurisdiction of the sheriff's office.

Abraham had visited the area a dozen times as a kid—usually for parades—and he'd been back there only three or four times since graduating from the police academy early last year, but those were for minor complaints. What he knew about the place, he loved. The community was at least four miles from the highway, and expansive forest lands and rows upon flowing rows of sugarcane fields separated it from the rest of the world. Since Plymouth Highway was the only way in or out, the residents rarely saw strangers.

As Abraham sped down Plymouth Highway—the wind making a mess of his thick brown hair—he gripped the steering wheel firmly in his hands. The road was bumpy and the shoulder nonexistent, so a wrong move could send him plunging into one of the large drainage canals on either side of the road, and that would certainly ruin his day.

The fields to his left and right were thick with tall cane and it was impossible to see around the bends in the road. Remembering what his police academy instructor—a former detective named Brandon Berger—had told him about driving only as fast as he safely could, he backed off of the accelerator and slowed to a speed that didn't scare him as much.

Once Abraham drove past the fields, he was swallowed up by the dark shadows of the thick woodlands that followed. It suddenly became dark on the highway and he shoved his sunglasses high on his forehead. He must've driven another two miles before he finally saw the first sign of civilization—an old barn on the left side of the road that marked the entrance to the community.

As he slowed to the speed limit, Abraham began to wonder what he would find once he arrived at the complaint. What if it really was a body? It would be his first death scene as a deputy, and that made him a little nervous. He wasn't sure if he would remember everything he'd learned about crime scenes in the police academy. He knew the general order of business was to eliminate any threats that might be present, render aid to the injured, secure the scene, and then make notifications.

He considered this as he drove. If there was a threat, that would mean someone injured or killed the woman. *This might be my first murder scene,* he thought.

He swallowed hard and glanced in his rearview mirror. He hadn't seen a car since entering Plymouth Highway. It was the only way in or out of this place, so it would be hard for a would-be murderer to escape by automobile. Of course, the kids had waited to tell their parents, so the suspect could've driven off long before he turned onto the road. As he took in his surroundings, Abraham figured it might be easier to disappear by hitting the woods, but there were a dozen things that could kill a person out there, so justice would probably be swift and final.

"Headquarters to 231," called the dispatcher over the police radio. "Are you there yet?"

"Negative," he said, glancing down at the notepad attached to his dashboard. The address showed 1711 Plymouth Highway and he had just passed 1658. "I'll be arriving shortly."

He studied the addresses and frowned when the numbers began skipping around. He had to stop to look at the opposite sides of a few mailboxes, but finally found the right address. The house was located at the end of a very long driveway and it was at least half a mile from Plymouth Highway.

"Just walking to the mailbox would be a great daily workout," he mused aloud as he coasted toward the gray house. There was a two-car garage attached to the left side of the house, but the doors were closed. He wondered if the woman who called it in was still inside or if they'd returned to the area where the boys thought they saw the body. His question was quickly answered when he stopped his cruiser in the driveway and the front door burst open. A woman and three boys rushed out onto the wooden porch. They stood huddled together and watched as Abraham gathered up his notebook and stepped out.

Abraham ran his hand through his hair in an attempt to tame the wind-beaten mess, but it was no use. He could feel a tuft sticking up. Shrugging, he approached the bricked-in steps and stopped when he was halfway up. He nodded his greeting. After introducing himself, he asked the woman if she had called in a complaint about a possible body being found.

"I'm the one who saw it," blurted a boy with bushy blond hair. His face and hands were dirty and his eyes were wide. "It was a lady and she was a witch and she was just hanging in the sky like it was magic or something."

"Jayce!" said the woman, who wore a long blue jean skirt and a thick blouse. "I already told you not to exaggerate. Now, when this officer asks what you witnessed, you tell him what you saw and stick to the facts. Don't say things you don't know."

She turned to Abraham and smiled, her clear complexion lighting up. "I'm Margery Russo, his mom. Please forgive him. When he gets excited he tends to make things a little larger than they are, but he's an honest young man otherwise."

Jayce stomped his foot. He couldn't have been more than eleven. "But I know what I saw!"

Abraham smiled to reassure the kid. "It's okay, little man, just start by telling me where this happened."

Jayce turned and pointed over his shoulder, toward the back of his house. "I was in the little bayou checking my catfish lines with Bentley and Ian"—he shot his thumbs toward the boys who flanked him—"and we were walking back when I saw the woman."

"What time was this?"

"At sun rise," Jayce said. "I check my lines every morning before the sun comes up and it's usually coming up when I'm walking back. That's when I saw her."

"As I understand it, you waited to tell your mom," Abraham said gently. "Why's that?"

"Because she never believes me when I tell her things." Jayce glared sideways at his mother, but he wiped the look off his face when she raised a single eyebrow in a menacing manner.

"I didn't see anything," Ian said, joining in. He had thick red hair and his face was littered with freckles. "The sun was shining in my eyes, though, and the trees were kind of thick, so it was hard to see. I thought Jayce was just joking at first, but I think he could be telling the truth."

Bentley shrugged his shoulders. He had a Mohawk haircut that Abraham knew couldn't have been middle school compliant. "I think I saw something. It looked like an angel in the air and I'm pretty sure it was a woman, because…" His face reddened as his voice trailed off.

"What is it?" Abraham asked. "What'd you see that embarrassed you?"

"The lady didn't have a shirt on." He lowered his head and a slight grin spread across his face. "She was naked on the top."

Abraham scowled. "What about on the bottom?"

Bentley shrugged again. "I couldn't see her good because of the sun and trees. But I'm sure she didn't have a shirt on."

"She wasn't naked," Jayce said. "So stop saying she was. You didn't even see her. I did."

As he studied the three boys and Margery, Abraham wondered if this was some kind of prank or just a case of overactive imaginations gone wild. He remembered thinking there were savages with spears living in the swamps behind his house when he was a kid, and this sounded a lot like that kind of fantasy. Nonetheless, he'd have to check it out. He nodded toward Jayce. "Can you show me where you found this woman?"

Margery wrapped her arms protectively around Jayce's chest from where she stood behind him. "I'm sorry, Deputy Wilson, but I don't want my son going back out there until everything is safe."

"Why not?" Jayce asked. "I'm the only one who saw her and I'm the only one who knows where she's at."

"No," Bentley argued. "I saw her, too, and I saw her naked."

"I already told you she wasn't naked!" Jayce's eyes narrowed as he squared off with his friend. "You just want to be the hero—"

"Boys!" Margery scolded. "That's enough."

"It's okay," Abraham said, handing his notebook and pen to Jayce. "Draw me a map and I'll find it on my own."

"You don't need a map," Jayce explained. "Just go straight to the back of our property and when you reach the canal, look toward the left through the trees. It's hard to see, but she's floating there in the sky—unless she flew away already."

Abraham tucked his notebook into the front of his gun belt and radioed dispatch to let them know he was going to be on foot. He then asked Margery to keep the boys handy while he investigated the sighting. "I might have more questions for them when I get back, so I'd appreciate it if y'all hung around."

CHAPTER 5

Abraham walked around the house and strode through the back yard, heading south toward the canal seven hundred yards away. He noticed the sun had climbed higher in the sky. The temperature must've been approaching ninety degrees already and sweat pooled on his forehead, dripping down his face and into his eyes. He could even feel it leaking down the center of his back. He scowled. The only thing he didn't like about being a patrol deputy was the polyester uniform. He shifted the heavy leather gun belt on his hips and pulled the top of the ballistic vest away from his chest to allow some air inside. The sweat made the fabric on his pant legs stick to his skin and he didn't like the way it felt.

"Maybe I'll apply for the next detective position that opens up," he grumbled as he walked over uneven ground with at least a month's growth of weeds. "They get to wear blue jeans and pull-over shirts to their callouts and slacks and polo shirts during the day." He then wondered if jeans would be worse because of the thickness. At least the polyester was thin and water seemed to dry pretty quickly.

After walking for about a hundred yards, Abraham came to a barbed wire fence that surrounded a large pond. He fiddled with the latch to the gate and finally got it open, then continued to the opposite side of the fenced area, where he slipped through a break in the fencing.

The tract of land Abraham was following measured about a hundred feet wide and was bordered on each side by barbed wire fences that separated it from the adjoining property. The tract of land to the west was mostly open fields occupied by grazing cattle, and the tract to the east consisted of thick forestlands. It was the property to the east that Abraham scanned as he walked, searching for the slightest hint of a woman suspended from the air. He could only think of one or two logical explanations for a kid seeing a woman suspended from the air, and a flying witch wasn't one of them. Whatever—or whoever—they saw had to still be out here somewhere, and Abraham was determined to find it.

The closer Abraham drew to the canal, the thicker the grass and weeds became on the Russo's tract of land. Lone trees began to spring up here and there until he reached a thin patch of woods. It was easy to find the path the boys had taken through the trees, because tall grass had been smashed and boot prints deposited in mud holes along the way.

There was a warm breeze blowing and it carried the stench of the canal to Abraham long before he saw the water. It was at this point that he moved as close as he could to the tract of land to the east, walking slower and peering through the thick branches overheard. Try as he could, he wasn't able to penetrate the umbrella that hovered above. He didn't have permission to enter the property to the east, so he couldn't jump the fence for a better view unless he saw something in plain view that would negate the need for a warrant.

Abraham wiped a stream of sweat from his face and swatted at a mosquito, stopping at the water's edge to survey his surroundings. Green lily pads floated on the surface of the water, blanketing nearly the entire opposite side of the canal. The white blooms were in stark contrast to the dark green background of the water and the surrounding foliage.

Everything was deathly quiet, except for the gentle plopping of water every time a bass hit the surface for food. An uneasy feeling came over Abraham and he inched his hand closer to the pistol in his holster. He glanced over his shoulder. Nothing. He moved eastward along the canal, searching above him and straight ahead. Once he reached the barbed wire fence that separated the Russo property from the eastern tract of land, he began slowly moving north one step at a time, pausing to peer through the leaves.

After taking about a dozen steps toward the north, he suddenly stopped and caught his breath. The wind had pushed a large branch aside and he caught a fleeting glimpse of something through the trees. It appeared to be on the other side of the trees, which made it nearly impossible to see, but it could've definitely been a human figure.

Thinking quickly, he figured this could amount to an emergency situation, so he took a step back and then bounded over the barbed wire fence. He landed smoothly on the ground, twigs and dried leaves crunching underfoot. Not taking a chance, he drew his pistol and slinked forward, using the nearest tree as cover. He peeked from behind the tree and stared in the approximate direction he'd seen the figure. The trees didn't part again, so he was forced to continue moving.

He stepped from behind the first tree and covered a few feet of open space before leaning against another tree, this one a giant oak with low-lying branches. He moved twice more before he saw the figure again.

"What is that?" He squinted, trying to comprehend what he was seeing. From that distance it didn't look real—hell, it couldn't be real—and he had a hard time catching a view of the entire figure. Gripping his pistol in both hands and keeping his head on a swivel, he moved forward, feeling his way with his feet. He'd learned a thing or two about stalking through the woods while trapped in the Blue Summit Mountains, and he called upon those skills right now.

When he was a dozen yards from the tree line, something rustled in the dry leaves to his right and he spun in that direction, the muzzle of his pistol moving in unison with his gaze. Nothing was there. A chill reverberated up the back of his spine and he thought he could feel someone behind him. He spun back in that direction, but he was alone.

Damn it, Abe, get a grip, he thought, wondering how much of the mountain terror had come back with him. He could still feel the hand come over his mouth—

"Stop it!" he hissed aloud, trying to shake off the feeling of apprehension. He pushed forward once more and when he reached the tree line he was able to clearly see the object. It was located in the middle of a field on the next tract of land. His hand trembled as he jerked his portable radio from his belt and keyed it up.

"231 to Headquarters," he called in a shaky voice. "I need a supervisor and detectives out here pronto. It's…it's not good."

CHAPTER 6

"Don't answer that," I said when Dawn's phone rang. We were just driving over Lake Pontchartrain and hadn't been on the road for much more than an hour. "I know it's the office."

Dawn pulled her phone from the glove compartment and checked the screen. She held it so I could see. "How'd you know it was the office?"

"My phone's been vibrating in my pocket for the past fifteen minutes."

"Why won't you answer it?"

Because I don't want anything to interfere with me proposing to you—that's why! I wanted to say. Instead, I said, "We're on vacation and I don't want them bothering us."

She playfully dangled the phone in front of my face. "Aren't you just a little bit curious?"

I shook my head stubbornly. "Not a bit."

"Well, I am." With a flip of her thumb, she connected the call. "This is Dawn…"

I winced when I heard the sheriff's familiar voice blaring through the tiny speaker in her smart phone. "Where the hell's London?"

"Um, he's right here," Dawn said slowly. While we hadn't gone through great lengths to hide our relationship, we certainly never publicized the fact that we were dating.

"Why hasn't he answered his phone? I must've called him a hundred times. I need both of you out here right away. We've got a body and it's serious!"

"Well, we're east of New Orleans at the moment."

"That's okay. Just get here as fast as you can."

Dawn looked at me for help, but I only grunted and shoved my elbow on the window frame, leaning as far from her as I could. I wasn't happy she answered the phone and I wanted her to know it.

"I don't know if you remember or not, Sheriff, but we took the week off for vacation."

There was a brief moment of silence from the other end. Finally, I heard his muffled response. "Sorry, I forgot. Are y'all going anywhere special? Or can it wait? I really need the both of you here."

"To be honest, I don't know where we're going." Dawn pursed her lips and glared pointedly at me. "But I guess it can wait. Where do you need us?"

"Start heading to Plymouth East. You'll see our cars in the driveway."

"What's the situation?"

"You'll need to see it to believe it. Just hurry." I thought he had disconnected the call, but then his voice came back on. "Dawn, is there something I should know about you and London?"

I shot a glance in her direction and watched as her face burned red like a turnip. She stammered for a second, but quickly recovered. "Yes, sir—we're the best damn detectives you have."

He didn't even laugh, and that made me think they'd discovered something really bad. "Good, now get your asses over here before I have you replaced."

"Why'd you have to answer the phone?" I asked when she ended the call. "We have to get to—"

I clamped my mouth shut.

"Get to where?" she asked. "You won't even tell me where we're going, so how do I know I even want to be there?"

I didn't want to argue with Dawn, so I grumbled silently to myself and took the first exit after we got off of the Twin Span. Before long, we were heading back across Lake Pontchartrain on our way to Plymouth East. I didn't know what they'd found, and I didn't really care. I'd made important plans—probably the most important of my life—and I'd be pissed off if I had to cancel them. With luck, we could handle whatever needed handling and then head to Tennessee afterward. As long as we left tonight, we'd be fine.

Whatever they found, I thought, *it'd better be damn good—or bad—because I'm not cancelling this proposal over some bullshit.*

CHAPTER 7

Ninety minutes later

"Jesus Christ!"

"Don't talk like that, London," Dawn said idly, her mouth agape.

"I don't mean disrespect." I pointed and shook my head. "I'm saying she looks like Jesus Christ."

Abraham Wilson nodded from where he was leaning against a nearby tree. His uniform shirt was dark from sweat and the front of his hair was plastered to his forehead. "I thought the same thing," he said. "Forgive my French, Ms. Dawn, but it scared the living crap out of me."

"Not only have I heard worse," Dawn said, "but I've actually said worse."

Abraham chuckled and handed Dawn a piece of legal paper that was folded neatly.

"Is this the search warrant for the property?" she asked.

"No, ma'am, it's a consent form," he explained. "I found the land owner and he granted permission to search his property."

"Did you tell him anything about this?" I asked.

Abraham shook his head. "I only told him there had been a crime of violence back here and we needed to process the scene for evidence."

I ran my hand across my face and walked closer to the finding, trying to wrap my mind around what I was seeing. I'd been exposed to a lot of death and destruction in my career and thought I'd nearly seen it all, but this shocked me to my core. Someone had stripped this woman naked and crucified her—straight up nailed her to a wooden cross and planted her in the middle of a large field in the back of Plymouth East.

I checked for shoe impressions in the dirt as Dawn and I approached the woman, but there was none. When I was a few feet from the cross, I shielded my eyes against the afternoon sun and tried to look at the woman's face to see if I recognized her. We needed to identify her and we needed to do it in a hurry.

"It's bad enough to kill her by crucifixion," I mused, "but why strip her naked?"

"Humiliation," Dawn offered. "If you strip a woman naked and expose her, it's usually to embarrass her—and it's usually some sort of payback. Think of those pricks who engage in revenge porn. They post pictures of their former lovers naked to humiliate them for making the right choice to leave their sorry asses."

"So, you think this is for revenge?" I asked, studying Dawn's face.

"At this moment, any guess is as good as the next, but I think the humiliation aspect points to some sort of payback or punishment."

I was thoughtful. "If the purpose is to embarrass her, why not place the cross in a more public place?"

"Because they'd get caught."

That made sense. If the killer would've tried to erect a cross anywhere near civilization, it would've gotten lots of attention. Plymouth East was so small the people here couldn't have sex without the neighbors reading about it in the community newsletter.

I turned my attention back to our victim. The woman's eyes were closed and her mouth hung open as though she had fought hard for her last breath. Dawn moved a step to my left and we each began visually inspecting the victim inch by inch, looking for any clues that might help us figure out her identity. She didn't have any tattoos that I could see, but there was a scar across her belly. I pointed to it.

Dawn nodded and snapped a picture of it. "Caesarean section…she's a mother."

The woman had curves, but she appeared fit, as though she exercised on a regular basis. Although she was pale in death, it was clear she had a bronze complexion.

Dawn moved closer to the cross and took a picture of the woman's feet. The left foot had been folded over the right foot and a large rusty railroad spike had been hammered through both of them. Dawn shook her head in disbelief. "Who would do something this crazy?"

I didn't have an answer for her, so I just kept looking for clues and jotting my observations in my notebook. Railroad spikes had been hammered through each of her wrists, as well, and there were trails of dried blood leading from each of the wounds. It had dripped down the splintered boards of the cross and pooled on the ground far beneath each of the spikes. Dawn set out to collect samples from each pool of blood.

I snatched a measuring tape from my crime scene box and measured the height of the vertical board, which was a piece of six-by-six treated lumber that had been out in the weather for a while. It was just over eight feet high. The horizontal board was about five feet long. The center of each board had been notched to allow the two to be merged together, and the cuts in the notch were fresh.

I stepped back and glanced around. "There's no way the killer nailed this woman to the cross after erecting it."

Dawn nodded her agreement. "It would've been much easier to nail her in place while it was on the ground, and then hoist it into the air afterward."

There was a pile of dirt packed high around the base of the cross. Judging by the amount, the hole must've been four feet deep. When I stepped around the cross and examined the ground behind it, I was able to detect a faint impression of the cross in the short grass that grew in the field. It wasn't as tall as the grass on the adjacent property, so I figured cattle must graze in this area intermittently.

Dawn saw where I was looking and she moved to inspect the ground where the cross board would've been resting. She waved me over. When I was standing over her, she pointed to specs of blood spatter sprayed across the blades of grass.

"This is where she was hammered to the cross," Dawn said, and then shuddered. "It just sounds so weird to say it out loud." She pointed toward the canal. "He must've come by boat, because there's no way to get back here by vehicle."

I nodded idly and studied our surroundings. "How'd the killer get the cross up into its stand? I don't know anyone strong enough to single-handedly walk it up and drop it into the hole with a body attached to it. Unless…"

"Unless what?" Dawn asked when I didn't say anything more. Instead of answering her, I walked toward where Sheriff Corey Chiasson was sitting in the shade of a large oak tree about fifty feet from the front of the cross. I glanced at him and scowled. He was pale and looked like he was going to be sick.

"Are you okay, Sheriff?"

He shook his head. "I'm not going to lie to you, London…this has got me shaken. For someone to kill another human being in the same manner that Jesus was killed…"

His voice trailed off, but he didn't need to say more. We were all freaked out by it and knew we were in the presence of pure evil.

I moved past him and examined the trunk of the tree carefully, looking for any holes or scars on the bark. Finally, I located a tiny hole about three feet from the ground, and then another several feet above that one and to the right of it. Higher and higher the holes zigzagged and I followed them with my eyes until I saw a large branch with some scuff marks. It appeared a chain had been wrapped around the branch. Several feet to the right of it were more scuff marks. I nodded and turned to face the cross.

"He secured a couple of come-alongs to that branch above us, and used them to hoist the cross into the air. As it rose, the foot of the cross slowly slid into the hole and fell into place."

The sheriff glanced overhead. "But how'd he get up in the tree?"

I pointed out the tiny holes in the trunk. "He used screw-in tree steps to climb up there and the rest was easy."

"Now that we know *how* this crazy person did it," Dawn said, "we need to figure out *who* did it…and *why*."

I stared at the woman and nodded, trying to imagine the terror and torture she endured in her last minutes on earth. I could think of but a few individuals who were deserving of such treatment, but they were bad men who hurt children and women. A warm breeze blew across the field and something caught my eye above the woman's head.

"What's that?" I asked, approaching the cross again so I could get a closer look. Something was flapping just above her head, but I had missed it earlier because of her thick blonde hair. "It looks like a note of some kind."

"Do you think the killer left a clue?" Abraham asked from his perch beside Sheriff Chiasson. "Maybe a taunting message?"

"I'm not sure." I strode to my crime scene bag and pulled out the binoculars I kept there. Once I moved to a place where I could get a clear view of the entire page, I peered through one of the lenses and adjusted the focus. I grunted when I read the single word scribbled in dark ink on the page.

"What is it?" Dawn asked. "What's it say?"

"Sinner…it just says, *Sinner*."

CHAPTER 8

While we were thoroughly examining the cross and surrounding area, we mulled over the meaning of the message attached above the woman's head, and we began trying to figure out how to lower the cross.

"We could do it in reverse order," I suggested, pointing to the branch above us. "Get a couple of come-alongs, attach them to the branch, and wrap the end of the cable around the cross. We would then start digging into the back of the hole at the base of the cross and make a trench going in the opposite direction. It would free up the back of the cross. We could then start giving the cable some slack while pushing the cross backward. If everything works as I think it should, we would slowly lower the cross onto its back, and we'll be able to free the victim."

The sheriff slapped his knee and stood to walk away. "I'll work on getting you everything you need."

I asked him to wait while I wrote out a list of other tools and items we'd need. He snarled dryly when I handed it to him. "It's longer than my wife's grocery lists."

Once he disappeared into the thick trees of the adjacent tract of land, Dawn pursed her lips. "I've never seen him like this."

"Yeah," I said. "He's really disturbed. Of course, this is enough to disturb anyone."

Abraham, Dawn, and I then set out to scour every inch of the field while waiting for the sheriff to send someone with tools. We didn't find anything that brought us any closer to finding the killer or identifying our victim. After we'd been at it for nearly two hours, the chopping sound of helicopter blades greeted us like a hot meal on a cold day.

"It's Ben," I said when the chopper came into view.

Ben Baxter, our department's helicopter pilot, landed his bird in the open field several dozen yards away and Detective Rachael Bowler, who was also on my sniper team, jumped out when he stopped. She was followed by Detective Melvin Ford, and each of them carried a large come-along in their hands.

"There's an extension ladder secured to the helicopter skids," Melvin said when he reached us. "The sheriff said you needed to get up in a tree. We also have some shovels."

I nodded gratefully and hurried to retrieve the ladder. I stopped to say a few words to Ben—after all, I owed him my life—and then lugged the ladder to the oak tree. Once I'd scaled up the tree and secured the come-alongs in place, we each grabbed a shovel and began digging out the back of the cross.

The heat from the sun was relentless and it was so humid it felt like we were being water boarded. Thankfully, Ben had also loaded a case of bottled water and a box of chicken, and we stopped often to drink and once to eat.

On any given day at any given crime scene, someone would've made a joke about something by now, but we were all numb from the grisly discovery and kept to our own thoughts, speaking only when we had to.

Even with the lunch break, it didn't take long for us to dig a long trench behind the cross that was a little wider than the treated board, and at least six feet long. When we had all stepped back, I gave the cross a gentle push and it strained against the cable that held it in place. It was ready to fall over. We just needed to provide some slack from the come-alongs.

Rachael climbed the ladder first and crawled out onto a large tree branch. From her perch, she was able to access the come-along on the left side and she gave a nod when she was ready. Abraham climbed the ladder next and shimmied onto a branch on the right side, where the second come-along was located.

Dawn, Melvin, and I stood in front of the cross and—wearing several layers of latex gloves—gave it a gentle push. As we applied constant pressure, Rachael and Abraham began releasing the slack in the come-along cables. The gears clicked loudly in the otherwise stillness of the sweltering afternoon as Rachael and Abraham worked the release switch little by little. With each click, the cross lowered a few inches at a time. It was a painstaking process, but the head of the cross was soon several feet from the ground. The base had stabbed into the earth because of the steep angle and the depth of the hole, so we had to gather around and lift the cross into the air and drag it from the hole.

Although the weight of the body and cross were distributed among four of us, I could feel how heavy it was. Once we had set the cross onto the flat ground, we all took a breath and stepped back.

Rachael was pale. "The sheriff told us what was going on, but this is not what I expected it to look like—it's much more horrible than anything I could've imagined."

"Yeah," Melvin acknowledged, averting his eyes. "I thought I was going to lose my breakfast when I first saw her. I just keep imagining it happening to my wife or my mom and it makes me sick."

I didn't want to imagine anything bad happening to Dawn again, so I focused on the task at hand. The sooner we solved the case and brought the killer to justice, the safer our parish would be.

I knelt beside the woman and gently pushed her eyelids open. Her eyes were cloudy, but I could tell they were green.

"What's that?" Dawn asked, pointing to her left cheek.

I leaned close and examined what looked like snail tracks across her face. "It's saliva!" I said. "Someone spat in her face."

"It shows contempt, disrespect, or anger," Dawn said, pulling out a DNA swab kit, "but that one act of raw emotion might help us catch the killer."

After Dawn swabbed the saliva sample and secured the evidence, we determined the victim's height to be five-seven and she appeared to be about a hundred and forty-five pounds. Next, I tried to bend one of her toes. It didn't budge. I checked her hands, as well, but they were also stiff.

"She's been dead over six hours." I turned to Abraham. "What time did you get the call?"

"Nine minutes before eight," he said without hesitation. "I arrived at eight-oh-four."

I liked how sure he was of his information and how precise. While time of death estimations were not exact, she was most likely dead by seven that morning.

I continued my examination, noting how the holes in her wrists and feet were a jagged mess. I'd played with railroad spikes as a kid and, as I recalled, they weren't sharp. Whoever nailed these blunt fingers of death into this poor woman had inflicted a heap of pain upon her and she suffered greatly before she died—and death had come slow.

I moved the hair from her face so Dawn could get a good identifying photograph. If no one reported her missing, we might need to get an artist to recreate her image in a less grotesque state for dissemination to the media.

"She looks young, maybe forty-one or forty-two," I said to Dawn, "but that might be because she's taken good care of herself. She might be a little older."

"I'd put her closer to fifty," Dawn said, pointing to her eyes and neck. "These lines tell a different story to us women."

I knew better than to argue. I copied all of the identifiable information we had complied onto a separate sheet of paper and handed it to Abraham. "Can you check with dispatch to see if anyone fitting her description has been reported missing?"

He nodded and hurried to the helicopter, where Ben was sitting with the doors open, and used one of the satellite phones in the chopper. Even from that distance I could see how wet the front of Ben's shirt was, but he just sat there, patiently waiting for us to finish processing the scene. Since we couldn't get a coroner's wagon back where we were, we would have to transport the body by helicopter, so he was stuck there until we were done.

While Dawn collected blood swabs and recovered the handwritten note from above the victim's head, I retrieved some tools from the helicopter and prepared to remove the spikes from the woman's feet and hands. I would've preferred to cut away the portion of the board that was attached to the nail, but we couldn't do it without risking damage to the woman's limbs.

When Dawn was done with her duties, she helped me spread white butcher's paper under the cross in the area of the hands and feet, so it could catch any microscopic evidence that would break away once we removed the spikes.

I then grabbed a crowbar and a block of wood and set out to remove the large spikes from our victim's hands and feet.

CHAPTER 9

I loaded the last of our crime scene boxes into the back of my truck and watched as Dawn signed the release paperwork for the coroner's investigator. Ben had made several trips from the crime scene to the complainant's home, transporting the body, the large treated boards, and then our gear. After waving his goodbyes, he disappeared into the afternoon sky, where the sun was lazily dipping to the west.

It was six o'clock and, while our counterparts had knocked off of work an hour ago, Dawn and I were just getting started. Abraham had notified us that there were no missing person cases filed within the last few days in Magnolia or any of the surrounding parishes, so we would have to pound the pavement.

After securing all of the evidence we'd recovered into the evidence cage at the detective bureau in Payneville, we worked late into the night canvassing the neighborhoods in Plymouth East that were within a few miles of the scene. We began with the landowner upon whose property the body had been found, but they hadn't heard or seen anything suspicious. The man who owned the property hadn't gone to the back of his property in several days, but when he was there everything had been normal.

The neighbors who lived along the highway to the east and west also didn't see or hear anything, nor did they know of anyone who was missing. When we ran out of people to interview, we headed home for the night. The autopsy had been scheduled for first thing the next morning and we both planned on attending, so we needed to get some sleep.

Our clothes were stiff from grime and sweat and we disrobed in the laundry room and dropped everything straight into the washer, slipping extra detergent pods with the load. Next, we showered together, but we didn't fool around and we didn't talk much. After we'd eaten and crawled into bed, Dawn leaned into me and placed her cool hand on my chest.

"I can't get the image of that woman out of my head," she whispered hoarsely. "She's all I see now. I see her when my eyes are open and I see her when they're closed."

I stared up into the darkness and nodded. Everything I was thinking had already been spoken throughout the day out at the scene, so I just said we needed to catch the evil person or persons who did it before they struck again.

"And if we don't?"

"Then I hope this was a one-time incident." I sighed. "If not, God help his next victim."

CHAPTER 10

3:10 a.m., Sunday, August 17

I quietly rolled out of bed, careful not to stir Dawn from her sleep. I'd lain wide awake for the last few hours just staring into the darkness, so I figured I'd get up and move around. I grabbed my laptop and sat on the sofa to research death by crucifixion. What I already knew about it wasn't good—it was a slow and excruciating death, often taking several days, and the cause of death was usually exhaustion or asphyxiation.

Our victim had been dead since at least seven o'clock Saturday morning, but she had been hanging on that cross for much longer. The temperatures had reached the triple digits every day for the past three weeks, and this weekend was no exception. The cross had been erected in the direct sunlight and that might have contributed to an accelerated death, but it wouldn't have been any less painful.

I searched through some old historic articles and even turned to the Bible to see what it had to say about the method of punishment, and everything I read confirmed it was a form of humiliation killing that was often used to dissuade others from behaving in the same manner as the one crucified.

I leaned back against the sofa and pondered this nugget of information. Someone had affixed a sign calling the victim a sinner, but what was her alleged sin? If she had committed some sort of sin, was it possible someone was trying to use her as an example to dissuade others from committing that same sin?

"We need to find her sin," I said out loud.

"Whose sin?"

I turned to see Dawn standing in the doorway to the living room, wearing nothing but one of my long T-shirts. Her eyes were half closed and she leaned heavily against the doorframe.

"What're you doing up?" I asked, placing my laptop on the sofa and hurrying to her side. She fell into my arms and held up her phone.

"We're getting called out again," she mumbled, her moist lips dancing against my neck as she spoke. "It seems they found an abandoned car shoved between some cane field rows on the shortcut road to Plymouth East."

That got my attention. "Who's it registered to?"

"I don't know. I just got the text message and started reading it when I realized you weren't in bed." She rubbed her eyes and held her phone a few inches from her face, squinting to read the entire thing. "Some woman named Kathleen Bertrand—"

Dawn's eyes widened and she was suddenly wide awake. "This might be our victim!"

"How so?"

"She's five-seven, a hundred forty-eight pounds, short dirty blonde hair, green eyes, and dark complexion." Dawn looked at me and nodded her head slowly. "This has got to be her."

"Well, let's go."

Dawn and I dressed as quickly as we could—pulling on jeans and collared T-shirts—and raced to the Plymouth East shortcut road. Although it was formally named Plymouth East Access Road and many people referred to it as a "shortcut", it didn't come close to reaching Plymouth East. Instead, it was simply a loop between Highway Eighty and Plymouth Highway and was mostly used by the cane farmers who worked the fields in that area.

When we turned off of Plymouth Highway onto the shortcut road, we saw the deputy's strobe lights flashing brilliantly up ahead.

"I still can't believe no one's reported her missing," Dawn said when I pulled my truck to a stop behind the patrol cruiser.

"Are you thinking what I'm thinking?" I asked.

She nodded. "Where in the hell's her husband or children and why haven't they missed her yet?"

We dropped from the truck and walked around to the front of the patrol cruiser, where Abraham Wilson was standing near a four-by-four truck speaking with a young boy and girl. They looked to be high school age and both had dark hair. The girl was standing with her hands wrapped around her shoulders and, although it had to be in the low eighties, she was shivering. The mud on the tires and the time of morning told the rest of the story—these kids had been sneaking off for a romp in the fields.

Abraham instructed the young couple to wait in their truck and he turned to Dawn and me.

"Why are you out so early?" I asked, wondering if he was also having problems sleeping. I didn't have to wonder for long.

"I couldn't sleep, so I came on shift early." He shot his thumb toward the truck. "These lovebirds were trying to find a place to practice procreation and stumbled upon an abandoned vehicle." He reached into the open window of his cruiser and handed me a printout from his onboard computer. "This is the DL photo of the registered owner. I think she's the victim from yesterday."

I pursed my lips and held the picture so Dawn could see. The woman was smiling and she'd worn makeup for her driver's license photo, but there was no doubt it was our victim. Dawn took the printout from me and stood staring at it in the flashing lights, her face expressionless.

I turned back to Abraham. "Can you show us the vehicle?"

After telling the two kids to stay put, Abraham led us down a wet and muddy cane field road. It had rained during the night and, while it didn't help cool off the place, it sopped up the ground and gave the mosquitoes something to cheer about.

There were two sets of tire tracks leading to and from the heart of the road. I shined my light on the ground and compared the tracks. They were the same. "Did you check the tires on the couple's truck?"

I saw Abraham's head move up and down as he walked. "They appear to match. I'm guessing the victim's car was driven here some time before the rain, because there's no sign of tracks matching her tires."

As we continued walking, we stayed to the right side of the road where clumps of grass formed small islands of semi-solid ground, but it wasn't long before warm water seeped into my boots and saturated my socks. I heard Dawn silently curse in front of me, and I knew her feet were wet, too.

The cane was tall—at least nine feet high—and it was so dark in the shadows along the road that the moonlight didn't dare reach that low. Even our tactical flashlights seemed weak against the sheer depth of blackness that surrounded us.

"It's right up ahead," Abraham called after a few minutes of trudging along.

Sweat dripped down my face, but it was nothing compared to the tiny needles from the mosquitoes drilling for blood along my exposed neck, arms, and face. I didn't even bother swatting them away, because legions more would take their places.

Even after Abraham pointed it out, I had to look hard to see where the car was hidden. Someone had driven it right between two rows of cane, but there wasn't as much damage to the ground as I would've expected. Upon closer inspection, I saw deep ruts and damaged cane along both rows, but stalks of cane had been propped up to conceal the damage.

"How in the hell did those kids find this?" I asked, beginning to wonder if they had some knowledge of the case.

Abraham shook his flashlight and it reflected off the taillights. "When the fellow turned his truck around right here it caught the taillights."

Dawn nodded. "That makes sense."

I examined the ground between the rows. The mud was wet and there was standing water along the packed earth between the rows, but there were no shoe impressions. I aimed my light deep between the rows and shook my head. Whoever drove it must've hit the gap at a nice clip, because the car had plunged at least twenty feet into the field.

Abraham showed us the route he took to get to the car—between the rows to the left—and we followed him through the narrow opening. The sharp leaves of the cane sliced at our arms and necks as we walked, leaving behind an annoying burning sensation, but we didn't pay it much attention. We were all focused on finding out what had happened to our victim and we were hoping this vehicle would offer some clues.

I stepped through a spider's web just as we reached the driver's door. I tried to wipe all of it from my face, but to no avail. I finally gave up and, along with Abraham and Dawn, shined my light into the windows. It was a little black SUV and it was fully loaded. The seats were leather and everything was power-activated, even the rearview mirror.

"I didn't touch anything," Abraham explained. "I used my light to search through the windows to make sure there were no other victims. Once I realized it was clear, I backed out and called for y'all."

I thanked him and told him he had done a great job. He seemed pleased, but even more so when Dawn added that his dad, who was a former Magnolia Parish detective, would be proud.

I turned to Dawn and shined my light in her face. "Want to toss it here or have it towed to the motor pool?"

She smacked at a mosquito on her face—leaving a giant splotch of blood—and cocked her head to the side. "What do you think?"

I laughed and wiped the blood from her face, and then we retraced our steps back to the vehicles to wait for a wrecker truck.

While we waited, we interviewed the young boy and girl. They were both from Gracetown and had just entered their senior year of high school. They didn't want to admit why they were back there, and I didn't press them. They were both of age and consenting, so I simply asked about the SUV.

"We didn't even know what kind of car it was," the boy said. "We just saw red taillights deep in the cane and knew there was something wrong."

"Yeah," the girl said. "We figured it had to be that woman's car."

"What woman?" Dawn asked.

"The one who was crucified."

"How'd you know about that?" Dawn asked.

The girl shrugged. "Everyone knows."

I frowned in Dawn's direction. "Sheriff Chiasson's not going to like this."

CHAPTER 11

Two hours later

Once the wrecker truck had finally left the motor pool and Dawn and I had dropped the large garage door, we set about processing the vehicle. We photographed it, sketched it out, and visually examined it first. Once we had documented everything, we began processing it for prints, DNA, and fibers, and then inventoried the entire interior.

Kathleen Bertrand's purse was on the front passenger's floorboard seemingly undisturbed when Dawn located it. She checked the contents and shook her head. "I don't know what she had in here, but it doesn't seem that anything has been disturbed." She held up a wad of cash. "I'm surprised to see this still here."

I frowned. "The killer didn't even rifle through her stuff?"

Dawn shook her head. "It doesn't seem so."

"That's odd." I pointed to an identification card attached to the lanyard that held her keys. It was shoved into a protective sleeve, so only part of it was exposed. "Where'd she work?"

Dawn pulled it out and whistled, holding it up with her gloved hand. "She's a lawyer."

"Does she work for a firm?" I asked, even more shocked than ever that she hadn't been reported missing yet. "Or is she on her own?"

"I'm not sure," Dawn said, turning the card over. "This is her access card for the courthouse in Chateau, but I bet she has a business card."

She paused and began digging deeper into the purse. After a few seconds, she produced a metal business card holder. She pressed the release button and waited impatiently as the fancy lid slowly rose. When she could reach inside, she dug out a card and held it up to the nearby shop light.

"Ash and Kat Law," Dawn said. "The address for the firm is in Chateau. It says here she's a partner."

"Is her cell phone in her purse?"

Dawn nodded and handed it over.

"We need to know who she communicated with during her last hours." I turned it on and waited. When it glowed to life I cursed out loud. "It's been wiped clean."

Dawn began chewing on her lower lip, and that usually meant she was thinking or angry. In this case, I was certain she was thinking.

"The only reason a killer would try to cover up a victim's tracks is if it led to him or her."

I nodded my agreement and bagged the phone. "We'll have the crime lab take a crack at this. They might be able to recover some data."

Before calling the inventory of the car complete, I went back inside to make a final sweep of everything. I ran my hands in the cracks of the cushions again, under the dash, between the console and the seats, under the floor mat, and even behind the flap of the glove compartment. I used my light to see in the dark spaces, but it seemed we had accounted for everything.

I was sweeping the underside of the seat one last time when my light splashed against something shiny from deep in the entanglement of wire amidst the seat motors. I brought my light back to the spot and tried to make out what was causing the shine, but I couldn't. I reached under the tight space between the floor and seat and tried to force my hand through the wires and motors, but it was no use. I grunted and dragged my hand back out.

I asked Dawn to try and squeeze her hand in the small space and she playfully pushed me aside.

"Get out the way, you big gorilla," she joked. "And let the expert through."

She dropped to her knees outside the door and snaked her hand under the seat. She made weird faces—they were cute, but weird— and grunted a bit, but finally gave a triumphant whistle. When she slowly pulled her hand back, she turned and held up the object. It was a one hundred dollar poker chip and it had the name, *Dark Sands Casino* imprinted on the rounded edges.

"Isn't that in Mississippi?" I asked.

"How should I know? I don't gamble."

I took the chip from Dawn and rolled it through my fingers, as though hoping it would talk to me. It could be something, or it could be nothing. Shrugging, I bagged it as evidence and made one last walk through just to make sure there were no other surprises hanging around.

Once we were done, we sealed the car with evidence tape, locked it in the private bay area, and then headed to the detective bureau in Payneville to secure the evidence in lockers and fill out the crime lab submittal forms.

CHAPTER 12

The sun was shining brightly through the door of the detective bureau by the time Dawn and I finished with all the evidence. We both needed a shower, but we didn't have time for one. We had an autopsy to attend and we needed to find out why Kathleen's husband—we'd learned he was a local carpenter named Joey—hadn't noticed his wife missing yet.

After getting breakfast on the road and eating it in my truck, we headed for the Magnolia Parish Coroner's Office and got there right at nine o'clock. The coroner, Doctor Ally Fitch, was visibly disturbed when she first saw Kathleen Bertrand's body.

"In all my years of working at the coroner's office," she said, "I've never seen something as horrific as this."

I just nodded and stood silently by while she did her job. There were no surprises with regard to the cause and manner of death. Cause of death was heart failure due to heat exposure, and manner of death was homicide. But the surprise came when Doctor Fitch completed a sex crimes kit.

"There's no evidence of sexual assault," she said, a bit puzzled. "As violent as this event was, I really thought it would include a sexual element."

Dawn and I traded glances.

"No theft and no sexual assault," I said. "So, what's the motive? Could it be someone wanted to punish and humiliate her for something?"

"I still can't wrap my head around the *way* she was killed," Dawn said, "much less *why* it happened."

We collected known samples of the victim's DNA and retrieved the sex crimes kit for processing. We then headed for Payneville.

Once we'd delivered the items from the autopsy to the evidence custodian and signed all of the lab forms, we stopped in at the sheriff's office down the hall.

He waved us in when he saw us standing outside the door and pointed to the two chairs across his desk. He was on the phone and it was clear he was speaking with a reporter.

"No, we don't have a serial killer operating in our parish," he was saying. "Look, it's an ongoing investigation and I'm not at liberty to say more about it... Right... You know me... Yes, you'll be the first person I call when I have more information... Goodbye."

He slammed the phone down. "This shit's spreading faster than a wild fire across the dry marsh in front of a hundred-mile wind."

I winked at Dawn to let her know I was right.

"Please tell me you've got something," he said. "I'll need to feed the media beast soon and I'm hoping you're coming here to tell me you're closing in on the suspect and that he'll be in custody in time for you two love birds to finish your little honeymoon, or whatever it was y'all were doing."

I silently cursed myself for forgetting about our plans. I needed to call the cabin people and the photographer as soon as I could break free from Dawn. I glanced coyly at her and saw that her cheeks were rosy red. She started stammering, but I quickly rescued her, knowing the sheriff was only joking and that he had no clue we were seeing each other. It's not like we were intentionally keeping it from him, but it was our private business.

"I'm sorry, but we don't have a suspect yet."

He started grumbling, but stopped when I slid a picture of our victim's business card across his desk.

"She's an attorney and she's married, so we've got some leads. We're going to locate her husband first and find out why he hasn't reported her missing yet and—"

"Then why the hell are you still sitting in my office?" he asked in feigned anger, running his hand through his hair as he spoke. "Get your ass out there and wrap this case up before I lose even more of my luscious mane. I'll have to get one of them muskrat toupees before long if this keeps up."

Dawn and I laughed on the way out the door, but she whirled around and dug her nails into my arm when we were out in the parking lot. "Do you think he knows about us?" she asked. "He called us *love birds* and talked about a honey moon!"

"He was just saying that because we're always working

together," I said, trying to convince her not to worry about anything. "I heard him say the same thing to Melvin and Warren one day. You know how dry his humor is. Trust me, it's nothing."

Melvin Ford and Warren Lafont were two of the detectives who worked in the bureau with us, and they were often partnered up on major cases. The information seemed to calm Dawn's nerves a little, so I took that opportunity to escape and make my phone calls.

"Want to start my truck?" I asked, tossing her the keys. She caught them with one hand. "I need a bathroom break."

She nodded and stomped to my truck, still wondering if the sheriff was on to us.

When I was safely inside the bathroom, I locked the door and moved near the window to get cell service. I certainly didn't need one of my nosy colleagues overhearing my conversation. Only a few of our trusted friends knew for sure that Dawn and I were seeing each other—the rest of them only suspected it. Those who weren't in the "know" would have to wait to find out the truth. Until then, it was none of their business.

First, I called Blue Summit Mountain Rentals and told them we might be late. I'd already made the payment in full, so it didn't matter to them if we arrived or not—they were still getting their money. The woman was very polite and told me she was wishing we would make it.

Next, I called the photographer and asked if we could push the photo shoot to later in the week.

"I have an opening on Thursday," she said. "Is that good for you?"

"I sure hope so." I said. "I sure hope so."

CHAPTER 13

It was almost noon when Dawn and I drove by 1711 Plymouth Highway on our way to Kathleen Bertrand's residence. We both instinctively looked toward the field where our victim was found murdered, and I knew it would become a habit. There were a few such unmarked and tragic locations in the parish that always got my attention when I passed by, and this would certainly join the growing list.

I turned my eyes back toward the road and reduced my speed. "Isn't that the address up ahead?"

Dawn glanced down at her notes and then at the approaching mailbox. "Yeah...damn, we knocked on that door last night but no one answered."

I coasted to a slow roll and turned right onto the long and winding asphalt driveway, zigzagging along its path until we reached the large brick home. There was an expansive workshop attached to the side of the house, and Dawn pointed to the large concrete driveway extending off of it, where a man was bent over a large table saw. He was guiding a sheet of three-quarter-inch plywood along the rip fence assembly of the table saw and seemed oblivious to our presence, as he hadn't looked up when we parked and stepped out of my truck.

The large blade buzzed loudly as it ripped easily through the plywood, sending sawdust raining down on the man. The shavings clung like giant snowflakes to the thick black hairs on his arms and a pile had gathered on his shoulders, but he didn't seem to notice. *He's in his bubble,* I thought.

Once the man had finished pushing the plywood through the

blade, he allowed one piece to fall to the ground and caught the other. He used his hip to shut off the saw and turned away holding the piece he had just cut.

"Damn it!" he exclaimed when he saw Dawn and me standing there. "I didn't hear y'all drive up."

I apologized and waited while he put his board down and removed his clear safety goggles. He was average height—about five-nine—and his belly extended out over his belt. Judging by the crushed beer cans strewn about, his could probably be described as a "beer belly". He tried to brush the sawdust off of his arms and out of the thinning hair on his head, but only succeeded in smearing most of it into the sweat on his flesh.

His face was square and his jaw thick. Although he seemed nice enough, there was a permanent scowl on his face. He wiped his hand on his jeans and extended it. "Joey Bertrand. What can I do for you two?"

I reluctantly shook his wet mitt and noticed how Dawn sauntered casually toward the table saw to avoid having to shake his hand. "Pretty powerful blade," she commented. "It sliced through that board like it was butter."

"It's a DeWalt—it's supposed to do that." After watching Dawn run her fingers across the saw, he turned his gazed back toward me. "Is there something I can do for you? I've got a deadline here and I really need to get back to work."

I had spent all morning mentally rehearsing what I was going to say to this man once I saw him, and each time I went over my speech, it came out a different way. There was no easy way to tell a man his wife had been found crucified, but I had to consider the possibility that he already knew about it because he had done it. Still, I didn't want to risk inflicting more psychological trauma than necessary, just in case he happened to be innocent.

After providing him with our names, I asked if he knew where his wife was.

"Of course, I do," he said, smirking.

Out of the corner of my eye, I saw Dawn stop admiring the table saw and turn to stare sideways at Joey, waiting to see what he would say next.

"Why?" Joey asked. "Does she have another outstanding parking ticket or something? I swear, her friend down at the DA's office keeps saying he'll fix a ticket for her, but then he forgets and they issue a warrant for—"

I raised my hand. "No, sir, it's not about a parking ticket. Can you please tell me where I can find her?"

"If it's not about a parking ticket, then what's it about?"

"I just need to know where she is."

Joey studied my face, his eyes narrowing in suspicion. "She's at a conference in Dark Sands, Mississippi. Why are you looking for her?"

"How long's she been gone?"

"She left Wednesday night after church." Joey squared his feet and crossed his arms in front of his chest. "Now, that's the last question I'm answering until you tell me what the hell is going on."

I sighed. "Mr. Bertrand, I hate to be the one to break this to you, but we have reason to believe your wife has been involved in a very bad incident."

"Involved? Like…she would've done something wrong?"

"No, sir." I shook my head somberly. "I'm sorry to tell you this, but your wife was found just down the road yesterday and she had been—"

Joey's eyes slowly rolled back in his head and his arms dropped straight down. He spilled forward in a limp heap and I immediately lurched toward him, reaching him just in time to save his head from bouncing off the concrete. Dawn joined me and we lowered him to the ground, where he immediately took a breath and looked wildly about.

"What happened?"

"You passed out," I explained slowly. "I was telling you about your wife."

Joey's mouth fell open and he let out a guttural wail that sent shivers down my spine. Tears flooded his eyes and rained down his face. "Oh, Dear Lord, no!" he cried. "Not my Kathleen!"

CHAPTER 14

It took Dawn and me twenty minutes to get Joey Bertrand calmed down enough to have an intelligible conversation with him. We had helped him into his house and stretched him out on his sofa. Dawn offered to get him a wet towel for his head and, when he nodded his agreement, she disappeared farther into the house. She returned about five minutes later with a cool wash cloth.

Although Joey could speak coherently, he was still quite shaken and we had to ask him to repeat himself several times during the initial part of the interview. He had heard about the woman who was found on the cross and had immediately tried to call Kathleen when he found out. While he was worried when she didn't answer, it wasn't unusual.

"She often keeps her phone off during conference and then forgets to turn it on later," he said, his voice growing a little stronger as he spoke. "I just figured it was one of those times. To be honest, when I saw the badges on your belts, the worst feeling of dread came over me and I just knew why you were here, but I didn't want to believe it. I kept telling myself it couldn't be true. I mean, who would want to do that to anyone—especially my wife?"

I nodded and frowned, wondering if he was a good actor or if he was being sincere. His reaction appeared genuine, but one could never know.

"We came over last night," I said. "But no one answered."

"If it was after nine, I was sleeping. I don't hear the door when I'm sleeping."

I studied the man for a long moment. His eyes were blank as he stared at the floor. "Mr. Bertrand, can I ask you what time Kathleen left home Wednesday night?"

"Um, it was early evening, I guess. She gets out of church around eight, so it was right afterward. She didn't have to be there until Thursday morning, but she usually leaves Wednesday night so she doesn't have to be on the road so early in the morning."

"Usually?" I asked. "Does she do this often?"

"She goes up once a month and has a conference with her firm's partners in Mississippi. They meet for an extended weekend and she's usually home by Sunday night." Joey glanced at his watch. "She would've been home this evening sometime, anywhere between five and nine."

"Why didn't her law partners call when she never made it to Mississippi?" I wanted to know.

Joey shrugged. "I don't get involved with her business. She's an independent woman, you know? She doesn't like me meddling in her affairs."

I started to frame another question when Joey asked if he would get to see his wife's body. "I need to see her—to be sure."

"Absolutely," I said. "We can take you there as soon as we're done talking."

He nodded and wiped his unkempt hair with the damp towel. "Is it true what everyone's saying about how she died?"

I didn't want to lie and I didn't want to admit it was true, so I ignored the question. "I don't like to ask this kind of thing, but I'm just following procedures. It's routine that we find out if there have been any problems in the marriage."

"I understand." He shook his head. "We argue about things like every other couple"—he pointed to the missing crown molding overhead and the staircase that still needed spindles—"but nothing major."

"I've always heard a carpenter doesn't like to come home to more carpenter work," I said. "I guess that's true."

"It is. And Kathleen didn't like talking law when she was off. Every time we had family gatherings someone would invariably start asking her legal questions. How to draft a will, what to do if someone got hurt on their property, could they sue the neighbor for the dog always knocking over the garbage—it was endless." He stopped talking and his eyes clouded over. "I can't believe she's gone."

I frowned. "We're really sorry for your loss. We're going to do everything we can to catch whoever's responsible."

"I appreciate you saying that." He wiped his eyes and sat up. "What happened to her car?"

I didn't want to give away too many of the finer details, so I just told him it had been located in Magnolia Parish.

"Do you have any leads?" he asked.

"Not at this time." I hesitated, never liking this part. "Again, this is routine and I don't want to offend you, but was there any infidelity in the relationship? If she was unfaithful, that would be an avenue we would definitely want to explore, because a boyfriend would be a most likely suspect in a case such as this."

"No, she wasn't unfaithful. She was a God-fearing woman who went to church every Sunday and Wednesday."

"Which church?"

"The only one in town...the Second Temple Fellowship."

I nodded, thinking back to an earlier statement he'd made. "She goes every Sunday?"

"Religiously." He nodded for emphasis. "She never misses."

"If she gets home between five and nine, how does she make the services every Sunday? You said earlier that the services end around eight."

"The sermon starts at six-thirty. If she gets home at five, she'll leave from here to go to church. If she's late, she'll go straight to church and I'll see her afterward, which is usually between eight and nine, depending on how long she stays and visits."

A thought seemed to suddenly occur to him and he fixed me with level eyes. "I watch all the crime shows, so I know where this is going. I'm automatically a suspect, ain't that right?"

"Well, no one is actually a suspect at this point," I explained. "When authorities use the phrase, 'Everyone's a suspect,' it doesn't mean they suspect everyone. It simply means they shouldn't rule anyone out until all the evidence has been collected and the case has been thoroughly investigated." I pointed to Joey. "I don't have a shred of evidence suggesting you did this, so you're not a suspect. However, you haven't been cleared yet, either, because we haven't finished processing all of the evidence and the investigation is just getting started."

He nodded his understanding. "I just want you to catch the evil bastard who killed my wife. She didn't deserve this."

"Of course she didn't." I was thoughtful, and then asked if he knew if Kathleen had any enemies. "Anyone who might want her dead?"

"None at all. She was loved by everyone."

"What about friends?"

Joey shrugged. "She hangs out with some of her coworkers and the ladies from church every now and then, but that's about it. She's too busy with work to socialize much."

"Do you know who her friends are?"

"Her partner is Ashley LaCroix. They're pretty close. And she has a friend from church named Shelby Rove. They've been friends since they were kids."

"Speaking of kids—do you two have any?"

"We have two grown boys, Nathan and Sirus, but they both live away and we don't see then much anymore except for holidays…" He got choked up and began bawling again. "How in the hell am I supposed to tell them what happened to their mom? How do you explain something like that?"

CHAPTER 15

I couldn't imagine the pain Joey was enduring, so we waited patiently until he had calmed down enough to speak again. When he nodded his head that he was okay, we asked about his sons and whether or not they might have been in touch with Kathleen since Thursday.

"Nathan lives in Morgan City. He's nineteen and still has a bit of a wild streak, so we don't hear from him much. When he's not working offshore, he's usually partying with his friends or hanging with the girlfriend of the week. We hear from him once or twice a month, but we have to initiate the contact." He paused to take a quivering breath. "Sirus is twenty-two. He just started med school in Houston and we don't expect to see him until Thanksgiving. He doesn't call much either, but it's because he's so busy studying. I think Kathleen spoke with him last weekend."

"What about parents and siblings?"

"Her parents live in New Orleans. She talks to her mom pretty often." He stopped and shook his head. "This is going to kill her dad. She's got one brother and one sister, but they both moved out of state. Kathleen's the only one who stayed close, so she sees their parents more often. If she leaves the conference early enough, she usually stops in for a quick visit on her way home."

When he finished talking, I jotted down some notes and hesitated again, but then went for it. "In order to move the investigation forward, do you mind giving us permission to search your wife's financial records, cell phone records, internet history…things like that?"

"I'd love to, but I don't have access to any of it. We keep our finances separated." He stood, but grabbed onto the sofa to steady himself.

Dawn quickly moved toward him. "Are you okay?"

He nodded, pausing for a second to get his legs under him. "I'd like to see my wife now—if that's okay."

I glanced toward a doorway that led to an office. There was a large mahogany desk at the center of the room and a desktop computer was centered above it. It must be Kathleen's home office and I wanted to be in there turning over every sheet of paper, but I needed permission or a warrant.

"Do you mind if I go through her office before we leave?" I asked, taking one more shot at it. "Just to see if it'll offer any clues as to her disappearance."

"I mean, I wouldn't necessarily be opposed to it, but it would be a waste of time," Joey said. "And right now I'd like to be with my wife."

"Certainly." I cursed under my breath and put on a fake smile. "We'll take you there as soon as you're ready."

While we waited for Joey to change his clothes, Dawn leaned close and told me she'd *accidentally* wandered into a couple of bedrooms while searching for the bathroom to get Joey a towel. "They had to be guest rooms because they didn't look lived in, but everything I saw was in pristine condition. If there was a struggle in this house, he sure cleaned up his mess, because nothing's out of place."

I mulled over her information and our conversation with Joey. I finally asked Dawn if she thought we had enough for a search warrant.

"It's not a crime scene and he's not a suspect," she said. "I don't think we've got a leg to stand on."

I begrudgingly agreed about the house, but I knew we could get a warrant to search her cell phone records and bank accounts. I quickly shot a text message to Detective Melvin Ford and asked him to get Kathleen's purse from evidence and obtain the account numbers on her credit cards and checking account and prepare a search warrant for each.

I also wanted a search warrant for her cell phone, but I didn't know the subscriber information. Keeping my voice low, I asked, "How are we going to get the information on her cell phone service provider? If he's involved, he won't give it to us."

She lifted a finger and winked, and then called out to Joey.

"I'll be right there," he hollered from the master bedroom, which was positioned deep in the house. "I'm almost done."

Dawn pulled out her phone and pretended to be playing with it when Joey appeared in the hallway. He had changed into dress jeans and a button-down shirt. Although it was wrinkled, it was better than the torn shirt he wore earlier.

"My phone doesn't seem to be connecting," Dawn said, slapping it against her hand. "What service provider do y'all use out here? Maybe that's the problem."

"We never have problems," Joey said. "We use Ring-Tele. I know my neighbors had to switch to Ring-Tele when they moved out here last summer."

Ring-Tele was a local telephone company that provided services for land lines and cell phones, as well as internet and cable service. I was relieved, because I had dealt with the company before and their managers were always quick to honor our search warrants and court orders.

While Dawn made small talk with Joey on the way to my truck, I shot a follow-up message to Melvin and gave him the information. I also asked him to have Kathleen's cell phone forensically examined. I wanted to know what she had been up to in the days leading up to her murder.

CHAPTER 16

3:00 p.m.
Magnolia Parish Coroner's Office

"This officer will see to it that you get home safely," I told Joey Bertrand after he had finished spending time with his wife and we had walked outside to meet Lieutenant Jim Marshall. I handed Joey my card. "If you need anything—anything at all—don't hesitate to call."

He nodded weakly and slipped into the front seat of Lieutenant Marshall's cruiser. Dawn and I stood and watched them drive away.

Joey had said all the right things and he was as emotional as I expected I'd be if that was Dawn lying on the morgue slab, but I still wasn't sure about him. Something he'd said earlier was bothering me and I couldn't wait to mention it to Dawn.

"Earlier, at his house," I began, "Joey said Kathleen didn't deserve what happened to her."

"I remember."

"That strikes me as odd."

"Why?" she asked. "Do you think Kathleen deserved it?"

"No, I don't think anyone deserved it, and that's what makes the comment odd to me."

Dawn leaned back against my truck, her eyes tired and droopy. "Care to explain yourself? I'm too exhausted to play mental ninja at the moment."

"If something terrible happened to you, I wouldn't say you didn't deserve it—"

"Gee, thanks a lot," she interrupted.

"Well, because it's completely unnecessary. Of course you don't deserve to be crucified. When we heard the news of that boy getting his arm bit off by a shark, we didn't say he didn't deserve it—because it's already *understood*. Now, if you did something wrong and I've been wishing mean things on you, but I thought *this* punishment was too severe, I might say you didn't deserve it because of the guilt I felt for wishing mean things on you."

I could almost see the wheels in her head turning. "So, you think she might've done something wrong and he wished some evil on her, but this was much worse than anything he would've hoped for her and now he feels guilty for wishing her ill?"

I pointed at her. "You nailed it."

She shrugged. "It seems weak."

"We need to get to her law firm first thing in the morning and find out everything her partner knows about her."

Dawn glanced at her phone. "What are we going to do until then?"

"Head to New Orleans to visit with Kathleen's parents and then go to church."

Dawn shuddered and I nodded my understanding. "I can go alone if you like."

She shook her head. "I'll be fine."

CHAPTER 17

6:00 p.m.
Second Temple Fellowship, Plymouth East, Louisiana

"This is different," Dawn said when I parked at the far end of the asphalt parking lot to the Second Temple Fellowship Church. She was referring to the simple and modest construction of the building. There were no fancy picture windows or large mahogany doors or massive concrete steps leading to the place of worship—it was a plain rectangular building wrapped in wooden siding. The building was white with brown trim and there was an overhang that offered a little shade over the doorway. A squat steeple topped with a crucifix stood proudly above the roof of the church. It appeared dark and ominous against the waning daylight, as though serving as a reminder of the horror that had befallen Kathleen Bertrand.

"If he's taking his parishioners' money," Dawn said, drawing my attention from the crucifix, "he sure isn't putting it back into the building."

I nodded but didn't say anything, because I was fully aware how troubled Dawn had been when she and Brandon Berger had handled the case with the Magnolia Life Church.

I stepped out of my truck and we walked across the parking lot, where she and I waited in line to get inside. It was a small place, but there was a long line waiting to enter.

Upon leaving the coroner's office, I had received a call from Joey Bertrand saying his in-laws had gotten word about Kathleen's murder and they were en route from New Orleans. While waiting for them to arrive in town, Dawn and I had eaten lunch and checked on the status of the search warrants Melvin had prepared for us. Not thrilled about working on a Sunday, but happy to be helping on the case, Melvin had gotten all three warrants signed by a district judge and he had faxed them to the legal departments of the appropriate companies. He said he was waiting to hear back from the technicians, but they said it might be a few days.

Joey had called again when Kathleen's parents arrived in town and we met them at the Bertrand residence. A family friend had driven them down because they were too distraught to drive, but they gutted through the interview and answered all of our questions. When we left, we were no closer to finding Kathleen's killer and were leaning further away from Joey as a suspect. According to his in-laws, he was a good son-in-law and he and their daughter had enjoyed a healthy relationship.

"Kathleen adores that boy," her dad had said, "and he adores her. They raised two fine young men and, now that they're empty nesters, they finally have more time to themselves. Kathleen was saying just the other day how she feels closer to Joey now than ever."

Dawn and I had wrapped up the interview just in time to run home to change and then return to Plymouth East for the church sermon. Now, we stood there wondering if we'd ever make it inside.

"Does everyone in Plymouth East go to this church?" I asked Dawn out of the corner of my mouth, keeping my voice low.

She nodded, as though certain. "It's a residential requirement. If you don't attend at least one session per week, they show up at your house with a mob and drag you from the town."

Several elderly women who were standing in front of us began whispering amongst each other. One of them pointed in our direction, but quickly turned her head when our eyes met.

The crowd shuffled forward a little at a time and we finally made our way through the entrance, where a man stood on each side of the door and they were greeting the crowd as they entered. When they reached Dawn and me, who were last in line, they welcomed us and pointed toward the last pew.

"Since when is there assigned seating in church?" Dawn grumbled.

Before I could answer, the doors slammed shut behind us and several musicians took to the stage.

I scanned my surroundings. Other than the double doors we'd entered, there was one more exterior door at the front of the building to the left, and a door that went deeper into the structure toward the right. There were four windows on the left wall, four on the right wall, and two on the rear wall.

I was impressed with the size of the crowd. If every person in each pew would've slid over a few inches, they might've been able to squeeze a dozen more people, but not much more than that. As it was, I felt like I was in the pocket of the lady to my right, and Dawn was nearly in my lap. When I stole a glance at the woman beside me, I noticed she had some sort of cloth on her head. I looked around and realized all of the women had one. I knew enough about religion to know that some Christian faiths used to require women to cover their heads during worship as a symbol of man's authority over them, but I didn't know it was still being practiced in modern day. If a man told Dawn to put a cloth over her head as a symbol of authority over her, she'd drop-kick him into the next parish.

The drummer slammed his sticks together and then the band started playing what sounded like Christian rock. Everyone in the church jumped to their feet and began dancing and singing. The floor shook from the combined weight of the congregation jumping up and down on the wooden boards. Dawn and I just stood there watching— waiting for it to end—but it wasn't an unpleasant experience. The lyrics to some of the songs were really cool and the beat was uplifting.

Once the music stopped, a man who had been dancing in the corner of the stage walked to the lectern and adjusted the microphone. He stood for a few seconds with his eyes half closed, staring out over the heads of the church members.

While he did whatever it was he was doing, I scanned all the faces I could see, wondering which one was Shelby Rove. Joey had described her as short and cute with black hair and an infectious smile.

"Her whole face lights up when she smiles," he had said, "and it makes you want to smile, too…even when you're having a horrible day."

A few of the people in the church fit that description, so I figured it would be a long night. As my eyes roved over the faces in the crowd, I caught sight of a man staring in our direction. Our eyes locked for a brief moment and, when I wouldn't look away, he averted his gaze. He looked to be in his mid-forties (which I didn't consider old anymore, since I was approaching thirty-six) and he combed his hair like he was stuck in the seventies. It was slicked back and—except for a white patch over his forehead—glowed jet black under the weight of the grease. He had a thick moustache, but the rest of his face was clean shaven.

I nudged Dawn and nodded in Moustache's direction with my head. Just as I did so, he leaned over and said something to the man sitting beside him, and they both looked at us. The man next to Moustache had thinning hair that was short cropped and sticking straight up. His nose and lips were thick and his eyes beady. He glanced briefly at us, but then turned his attention back to the preacher, staring up at him like a child watching a super hero in action.

"Why's that moustache looking at us?" I asked Dawn. "We're just sitting here blending in with the rest of the good folks in this town."

"He's looking at you," she said. "I'm blending, but you look like an obvious cop who's about to kick somebody's ass."

I grunted and scanned the rest of the crowd. They all wore a similar expression as the guy sitting next to Moustache, as though waiting with bated breath for the words that would soon spill from the golden mouth of their leader. Moustache was the only one who seemed distracted.

I turned my attention to the preacher, who had begun talking. His dark hair was combed neatly to the side and his tone was smooth. "Brothers and sisters in the Lord, welcome to our house of worship. For those who don't know me, I'm Father Nehemiah Masters and I will be bringing you more of the Lord's word."

He paused when a few "amens" reverberated from the crowd, and then he continued.

"Last week, we talked about the evil women in our midst and why Christian men should avoid them. Proverbs Five tells us that a strange woman's mouth is smoother than oil, but her end is as bitter as wormwood. These she-devils bring temptation down on Godly men and cause them to falter. We must rebuke these temptresses and let their feet take hold in hell, for the wages of sin is *what*?"

The crowd chanted, "Death!"

"That's right, my children," Nehemiah continued, "the wages of sin is death and these evil women will find their places in the pits of hell…"

Dawn pushed her lips up against my ear and whispered, "If this bastard doesn't start talking about evil men in a hurry, I'm going to march up that stage and kick his ass!"

Although she kept her voice low, it carried somewhat and I heard someone behind us gasp.

I chuckled to myself, but then stopped dead. I leaned forward and began to listen carefully as Nehemiah Masters preached out against women. He spoke with such venom that it could only have come from a place of deep betrayal. I craned my neck to see the front of the church, where I imagined a preacher's family would sit.

The front pew to the right was occupied by three couples and a few small children, so I turned to the left pew. It was crowded, but there was a woman sitting against the wall to the left and she was dressed more conservatively than most of the women in the church. There were three small children lined up beside her on the pew and they all had blonde hair like she did. Two of them were boys and their hair was parted to the side just like Nehemiah's. They looked like little clones.

As the words of rebuke flowed from Nehemiah's lips, I studied his wife's face carefully. When she wasn't whispering a correction to one of the kids, she was staring down at her feet. I couldn't be positive, but she looked embarrassed and angry.

You bastard, I thought. *Are you publicly calling out your wife?*

CHAPTER 18

When the sermon was over, most of the congregation applauded, and nearly every man gave a standing ovation. Nehemiah never once rebuked any of the men in the church, and everyone seemed fine with it. I moved over so I could catch a glimpse of Mrs. Masters. She just sat there with her head hanging.

I turned to Dawn, whose face was red with fury, and pointed out the wife. "I think his whole sermon was aimed at her."

"Well, if I'd be her, I'd slice off his balls and drop them in a garbage disposal."

I laughed out loud and nodded my agreement. I was about to ask her what she thought about the head coverings when someone tapped me on the shoulder. I turned to see Nehemiah Masters standing there, a polite smile on his face.

"Welcome to Second Temple Fellowship," he said in his smooth voice. "While we always encourage people from the outside to visit our place of worship, we ask that all visitors abide by a few simple rules when entering the house of the Lord."

Dawn stepped forward and looked up at him. "And what rule might that be?"

Nehemiah regarded Dawn with a curt smile and then turned back toward me. "As I was saying, we require that you have your wife wear a head cover while in the presence of the—"

"Can you read?" Dawn asked, shoving her badge in his face. "Because I'm about to require that your ass be hauled down to the station for questioning."

Nehemiah's eyes widened ever so slightly. "I'm very sorry, detective. I did not realize this was a formal visit. I imagined you two were wishing to attend services here. I do apologize for the confusion."

"You can call me Sergeant Luke," Dawn said curtly. "Now, I need you to point me to Shelby Rove. As you might've heard, one of your church members was murdered yesterday. It seems she and Shelby were good friends."

Nehemiah's eyes fell and his face tensed up. "I did receive the news about Sister Kathleen. I was so heartbroken to learn of her passing. We are in the process of preparing a celebration of life in her honor and—"

"Her *passing*?" Dawn bellowed, catching the attention of several church members who were pushing past us in the crowd. "She was murdered, Nehemiah. Tortured and killed—I'd hardly consider that a *passing*."

"I apologize for my poor choice of words, Sergeant Luke." Nehemiah bowed his head. "Sister Kathleen is the first of my flock that I have lost."

Dawn studied him for a few moments. "I take it you don't like women very much, do you?"

"I love all of God's children."

"Then what's with the sermon about evil women?"

"I was moved by the Spirit last week to deliver a message about sin and adultery. Tonight's message was merely a continuation of that lesson."

"Did the Spirit have anyone in mind when it moved you to deliver this message?" Dawn wanted to know. It was obvious she had also noticed the way Nehemiah's wife was behaving during the sermon. If he didn't know about his wife's infidelity, he was a fool, because we could read it all over her.

"I am often inspired to deliver a message to my flock, but I am not always enlightened as to whose lives have been touched by the teachings of the Lord." He smiled and raised his hands at his side. "I am but a vessel to deliver a message from God, and I am not all-knowing like the Father."

Dawn nodded idly and looked around the room. People were milling about talking and none of them appeared to be in a hurry to leave. I caught a glimpse of Nehemiah's wife sitting in the corner alone, staring into empty space. Dawn saw her, too, and I could tell she wanted to walk over and talk to her.

When Dawn turned back toward Nehemiah, I noticed her expression had softened. He might've been caught off guard by it, but I knew she was acting.

"I think I was wrong about this place," she said. "Everyone seems so happy here, so you must be doing something right."

"They have the joy of the Lord in their hearts," he explained. "With it comes peace, love, and happiness."

"Most churches take an exorbitant amount of money from their parishioners and the preachers buy big ole houses and fancy cars for themselves to drive, but not you." She waved her arms around. "Is this where you live?"

Nehemiah nodded. "I am the church and the church is with me."

"Well, Father Masters," Dawn said, extending her hand. "I apologize for being wrong about you and I appreciate your time. Now, if you could point us to Shelby Rove, we'll be out of your hair."

Nehemiah looked around and then raised his hand and waved it in the air. "Sister Shelby...can you come here, please?" He shook his head and waved his hand dismissively. "She can't hear me. I'll go fetch her for you."

CHAPTER 19

While Nehemiah walked down the aisle to get Shelby, Dawn spun toward me. "We're coming back here when that son of a bitch isn't around and we're going to see what his wife has to say about his little bitch session. That was all about her!"

I nodded my agreement, shooting another glance in his wife's direction. She hadn't moved and she seemed completely demoralized. I felt bad for her and wanted to walk over and offer to free her from this hell, but I knew she was probably so indoctrinated that she thought she deserved the public rebuke she'd received.

"Heads up," Dawn said quietly. "They're coming."

Nehemiah approached with a petite woman following close behind him. I lost sight of her a few times as they worked their way through the crowd, but I saw enough of her to see that her face was troubled. When she reached us she stared into Dawn's eyes, frowning as they clouded over.

"I guess you're here to talk about Kathleen. I knew I'd be hearing from someone sooner or later."

Dawn nodded and extended her hand. "I'm so sorry for the loss of your friend. We'd like to have a word with you"—she looked up at Nehemiah—"in private, if that's okay with you, Father?"

I stifled a chuckle. Nehemiah was so self-absorbed that he didn't consider for a second that Dawn was patronizing him.

"Of course," he said, turning to Shelby and nodding his permission. Someone called out his name and he turned away, leaving us alone with Shelby.

"Would you like to follow me home?" Shelby asked. "I live just down the road and it's really scary now that this has happened to

Kathleen. I've been terrified to be alone ever since I heard the news."

"We'd be happy to follow you," Dawn said, stepping aside to allow Shelby to lead the way through the crowd and out into the parking lot. She stopped and peered nervously out into the darkness. "I don't know why I get here so late every evening. I need to start arriving earlier so I can get a good parking spot."

Dawn nodded her agreement and we walked Shelby to her car. Once she was inside, Dawn pointed to where my truck was parked and told her we'd be close behind her. We started walking toward my truck and hadn't gone far when a redheaded woman hollered Dawn's name from across the parking lot. The woman was standing near a gray Nissan Sentra with a man who looked a bit younger than she did, and she was waving almost hysterically.

Dawn looked up and gave a short nod, but kept walking. I sensed there was some tension between her and the woman, but I didn't ask about it.

I fired up my truck and got behind Shelby, who was waiting to pull onto the highway. We followed her to her house—a small trailer at the end of a narrow street—and then joined her at the kitchen table.

After asking some initial questions about how their relationship began, Dawn asked Shelby if she had heard any details surrounding Kathleen's murder.

"I heard that she was…I don't even know if I can say it." Shelby covered her mouth with a hand and her eyes misted over. "I heard she was…um…crucified. At first, I didn't believe it. I mean, I *couldn't*. That kind of thing doesn't happen. I mean, maybe back in biblical days, but not in modern times."

"Who'd you hear it from that first time?" Dawn asked.

"It was someone at the grocery store, but I didn't know who she was. Before long, it was circulating all over town. My husband heard about it from the young boy who cuts our grass, and I think he heard it from his dad who's a volunteer fireman."

"Did you hear anything regarding the condition of her body?"

I knew Dawn wasn't going to provide any details Shelby didn't already possess, and I was curious myself to see how much Shelby knew. It was obvious word traveled fast in this small community, but I didn't know how much had gotten out.

"Well…" Shelby cupped her hands over her face, thinking. "I heard she was found totally naked, I heard they think the husband did it, and I heard there was a note saying she was a sinner."

The skin tightened ever so slightly around Dawn's eyes.

"Who told you about this note?"

"I really don't remember. It must've been someone at the grocery store."

"It's very important that you remember who mentioned the note." Dawn leaned across the flimsy table and looked deep into Shelby's eyes. "Think back to the moment you were having that conversation. Picture the faces of everyone in the group. Who mentioned the note?"

After a couple minutes of deep thought, Shelby shook her head. "I...I just don't remember. I don't think it was someone I knew."

"What's the name of the grocery store?"

"Plymouth Shop. It's the only grocery store in town. There's also a gas station attached to it."

"Where were you standing when you had the conversation?"

Shelby's brow furrowed. "Where was I standing?"

"If the store has cameras, we might be able to identify the people you were talking to," Dawn explained. "It might help us track down who mentioned the note."

"Oh, I was standing in the front by the registers. There're only three registers, and I was standing at the first one on the right as you're facing the front of the store."

Dawn nodded and jotted down the information. I knew where she was going with this line of questioning. The "sinner" message had been a closely-guarded secret. Other than the sheriff, Abraham, Rachael, Melvin, Dawn, Ben, and me, no one knew about it—well, except for the killer. If the information was getting out, it was because the killer was talking, so we needed to trace the comment back to its original source.

When Dawn looked up from her notepad, she asked Shelby if Kathleen had any enemies.

"No, everyone loved her. She was always very agreeable and she was kind to everyone she met. I don't think she's ever even been involved in an argument with anyone. I'm serious...she was as nice as they came."

"What about marital problems?"

Shelby hesitated for a split second. "I mean, when two people from two different backgrounds get together, there're bound to be issues that come up. She has complained to me a few times about Joey. She said when he gets home from work he just sits around watching football and drinking beer. Of course, that's *if* he decides to go to work. Most days he just hangs around the house drinking. She said he never wants to go places with her. He wouldn't even take her out to dinner. The worst of it, though, was that he refused to attend church with her."

"Did she mention any boyfriends?" Dawn watched Shelby closely for reaction.

Shelby sighed. "She never mentioned a boyfriend, but she did say she was thinking about divorcing Joey."

"When was this?"

"Oh, about three months ago, I reckon."

"What'd you say to her when she mentioned wanting a divorce?"

"I told her what the Bible says about divorce—that if you divorce your husband and then marry another man, you've committed adultery and you've made the man commit adultery."

Because I knew her intimately, I could tell Dawn was struggling with Shelby's belief system, but she was doing a good job of hiding her true feelings.

"Did that convince Kathleen to stay with her husband?"

"I don't believe it did. She doubted what I said about the scripture, so I pulled out my Bible and showed it to her. She then pointed to the scripture that says we should not be unequally yoked with nonbelievers. At that point, neither one of us knew what was right, so I suggested she turn to Father Masters for counseling."

"Did she meet with Nehemiah?" Dawn asked, intentionally calling him by his first name.

"I don't really know. After advising her to speak with the Father, she didn't bring it up again and I didn't ask about it. Each time we spoke after that night, she seemed to be in good spirits, as though her conscience had been cleared."

Dawn leaned back and regarded Shelby with a curious expression. "Are there a lot of evil women in your church?"

Shelby cocked her head to the side. "Excuse me?"

"Nehemiah spent an entire evening trashing what he calls *evil women*," Dawn said coolly. "I was wondering what necessitated such a speech. I mean, if there aren't any evil women in your midst, why would he give a speech like that?"

"His sermons are ordained by the Lord," Shelby explained. "Whatever message God impresses upon him is what he teaches."

"Let me ask it another way. Do you know of any women in the church who are committing adultery?"

Shelby hesitated again, but then shook her head.

"I noticed that Nehemiah's wife didn't look too happy with his speech." Dawn snapped her fingers. "What'd he say her name was again…?"

"Her name is Gretchen."

"Gretchen, right. Who's she banging?"

Shelby began to look extremely uncomfortable, turning her head from side to side as though someone might be listening. "I'd like you to leave now."

"I'd like you to tell me who's screwing the preacher's wife."

"No one…and she would be offended if she heard you ask such a question."

"You do know lying is a sin, don't you?" Dawn asked. "And the wages of sin is…"

"Death," I said when Dawn allowed her voice to trail off.

"Do I have to continue answering your questions?" Shelby's eyes were wide and she was clutching at her collar. "I don't feel comfortable answering these types of questions and I'd really like to get to bed now, so if you don't mind…"

"Just remember your friend was murdered in the most heinous way possible," Dawn said. "And the killer's out there right now looking for the next sinner to crucify, so if you know something—anything at all—you'd better spill it."

"Please leave," Shelby said with a sternness that seemed out of character for her.

CHAPTER 20

12:30 a.m., Monday, August 18

Debbie Brister lay wide awake. She'd been staring in the darkness toward ceiling for over an hour, trying not to move until her husband, Gerard, fell asleep. When he finally started snoring, she eased the covers off and slid her feet to the floor. She paused, but there was no break in his snoring.

Guilt tugged at her heart as the words from Father Masters' sermon haunted her, and she was tempted to stay in bed. *Is he really a prophet?* she wondered. *Is it true that God speaks to him?*

True or not, it felt like he was looking directly at her during his sermon. All the talk about evil women and adultery had struck a chord so loud that she'd almost broken down and confessed to Gerard on the drive home. But she hadn't, and it was only because she didn't want to hurt him.

If I don't want to hurt him, then why do I mess around?

She sighed, listening to the steady snores of the man beside her. She'd met him at a church in Seasville soon after separating from her husband of thirteen years. Having been married for that long, she was terrified to get back out in the dating world, and Gerard just sort of plopped into her lap one day at church—literally. She had been sitting at the end of a pew with her daughter and they were listening to the church service when a man walked down the aisle and took a seat right on top of her. She had screeched and he had apologized profusely, explaining that he meant to sit in the pew behind her, which was empty, but he wasn't paying attention.

The incident had created quite a disturbance to the service, but no one seemed to mind and she and Gerard hit it off from there. They became good friends and she was happy to have someone to talk to, but it wasn't long before Gerard wanted more than friendship. She didn't feel the same about Gerard and, when she expressed that sentiment, their friendship stalled. While she would never admit it out loud, she still loved her ex-husband and she was hoping they could reconcile. But when the divorce became final a few months later, she was faced with a terrifying reality—it was possible she could spend the rest of her life alone.

She was honest enough with herself to realize she'd made some mistakes during the year of separation, but it was only out of desperation over losing control of the only man she had ever loved. She had apologized profusely to her ex and to her daughter, but, nonetheless, her actions had caused her daughter not to want to spend time with her anymore. That was a crushing blow, but it was nothing compared to watching her estranged husband move on with another woman—someone younger and prettier. It was in that low and lonely moment she turned to Gerard, who always loved her far more than she deserved.

Trying to push back the flood of guilt, she stood carefully to her feet, but paused when there was a break in Gerard's snoring. She held her breath, waiting for him to adjust his position and settle in once more. When his mouth slid open and he fell back into a deep sleep, she stole silently across the floor, her feet padding lightly against the thick carpet. She slipped through the door and made her way quietly to the bathroom, where she shrugged out of her night shirt. She pulled on some shorts, slipped into her sandals, and pulled on a T-shirt. She didn't even bother putting on a bra, because she'd only have to take it off again in a few minutes.

She then dropped to her knees and reached behind the toilet, where a piece of base molding was propped up against the wall. She pulled the molding free and slid her hand into the crack behind it and, using two of her fingers, pulled out a small black cellular phone. She turned it on and waited nervously for the display screen to light up. When it did, she sent a simple text message to the only contact on the phone: *On my way.*

Clutching the cell phone in her hands, she pushed her ear to the bathroom door before opening it. She sighed as the sound of steady snores continued from her bedroom. *I'm home free!*

When Debbie slipped out the back door, she was instantly attacked by an army of mosquitoes. She waved them off and hurried to her car. It was a Nissan and it didn't make much noise, so she wasn't worried about Gerard waking up at that point. She cranked up the engine and backed smoothly out of the driveway and then headed west on Plymouth Highway.

She checked her cell phone, but hadn't received a response yet, so she dropped it between her legs and put both hands on the steering wheel, watching the narrow road carefully. She couldn't afford to get in a wreck, because that would be a bit difficult to explain.

"The wages of sin is death!"

The words from Father Masters' sermon popped into her head just as she drove past the property where Kathleen Bertrand's body was found crucified, and she jerked in her skin. Someone at church said a note had been found over Kathleen's head claiming she was a sinner, and someone speculated she had been punished for committing adultery.

"That should be a lesson to every adulterous woman in this town," Gerard had said on the way home from church just a few hours earlier. "Like Father Masters said, the wages of sin is death, and, if you ask me, that temptress got what she deserved."

The venom in Gerard's voice had surprised Debbie, but she had elected to sit quietly and not respond, because she felt as though anything she said would drip with guilt. She had stared out the window wondering if he knew what she had been doing. While he hated confrontation, she didn't believe he could keep quiet if he suspected her of infidelity—

"What the hell?" Lights flashed in the rearview mirror and Debbie instantly glanced down at her speedometer. "Poop!"

She had just hit the last curve heading out of Plymouth East and hadn't slowed down when the speed limit dropped to thirty-five. She was going forty-eight. Tapping her brakes to let the officer know she was aware of the pending traffic stop, she continued coasting until she found a spot where the shoulder was wide enough to fit her car. The Nissan jostled as she guided it onto the rough and uneven surface and she slid her window down when she came to a complete stop.

After quickly grabbing her driver's license from her purse and the registration and insurance card from the glove compartment, she folded her arms across her breasts, silently cursing herself for not wearing a bra. She had only planned to drive down the highway to Kim Berry's house, spend an hour with him, and then get back home before Gerard woke up. She'd done it many times and had never even seen a vehicle on the road at this hour, much less a cop.

"What the hell is a patrol deputy doing out here at this time, anyway?" she said aloud. "They never come back here unless they're called."

That's when it dawned on her—they must be running extra patrols because of the murder. She was suddenly glad to see the deputy. It made her feel safer out here all alone. Of course, how would she explain to Gerard that she got a ticket at that hour? Maybe she'd tell him she wanted a midnight snack and they didn't have any milk. That was plausible. The only store in the area that was open twenty-four hours was in Gracetown, so she would have to go get the milk to establish her alibi and then—

"Step out of the car, ma'am."

Startled, Debbie screeched and threw her hands in the air, losing her driver's license in the process. She hadn't realized the officer had approached the car, and apologized as she felt around on the floor for the license. When she found it, she looked up to hand it to the officer, but was blinded by a flashlight.

"Wow, is that really necessary?" she asked, shoving her documents toward the bright light. "I'm not the Taliban."

"Ma'am, step out of the car and do it now," came the terse and authoritative reply.

"Look, I really have to get home, so could you please just write the ticket and let me be on my—"

"Woman, do what you're told," said the officer, jerking the door open.

"Do you know who my ex-husband is?" Debbie demanded, lifting her arm to shield it from the light. "I know what you can and can't do, and you definitely can't—"

"Shut your mouth, you filthy whore!"

A hand reached from the light and grabbed Debbie by the throat. She tried to resist, but the officer wrenched her from the front seat like a sack of flour and tossed her to the side of the road. She fell hard to her face, but quickly rolled to her back and looked up as the figure approached at a slow walk.

"You can't do this," she said weakly. "You're an officer of the law. There are rules—"

The light that was blinding her suddenly turned toward the figure and she wet herself when she realized this was not an officer.

"What do you want?" she asked, her voice trembling as tears poured from her eyes. "Why did you stop me?"

"It's time for you to pay for your sins."

CHAPTER 21

8:30 a.m., Chateau, Louisiana

I scowled as I glanced at the clock on my truck's dash. Dawn and I were originally supposed to be in front of Abrams Falls in thirty minutes, where I would've dropped down to one knee to ask for her hand in marriage. Instead, we were pulling up to the Ash and Kat Law Firm in downtown Chateau to speak with Ashley LaCroix.

"What's wrong with you?" Dawn asked as I shoved the gearshift in *park* and pushed my door open.

"I'm a little bummed about our vacation."

Dawn eyed me suspiciously. "We're still going when this is over, right?"

"Yeah, but it won't be the same."

"Why not?" she pressed.

"For one, the same cabin won't be available."

She shrugged. "It doesn't matter to me where we stay—as long as you're there."

I smiled, but it quickly faded when I thought again about the conversation I'd had with the photographer earlier in the morning. She had called to tell me she'd made a mistake and she wouldn't be available Thursday.

I stepped out and Dawn followed me down the sidewalk. Cars lined both sides of the streets and people rushed by us, everyone in a hurry to get somewhere. The courthouse was on the next block and they were always busy on Mondays. When we reached the front door to Ash and Kat Law, I opened the door and stepped back for Dawn to enter.

She smiled coyly. "You'd better not stop doing that when we get old."

My chest swelled. *She'll definitely say yes.*

Dawn stepped to the sliding glass window and dinged the bell that rested on the counter. Within seconds, the glass slid open and a familiar face peered through.

"Miss Dawn! Mr. London!"

We both smiled as Lily Pierce jumped to her feet and rushed around to open the door. She was one of my former snipers' daughters and she found herself all alone when her dad and brother were killed three years ago. Things had been rough for her, but she had gutted through the evil cards life had dealt her and was on her way to being a successful and productive young lady. She was pursuing a degree in political science and planned to attend law school once she graduated next year.

When she stepped out into the lobby, Lily threw her arms around Dawn first and then me, and asked how we were doing.

"We're great," Dawn said. "What about you? How long have you worked here?"

"A few months." She was beaming, and it made me feel good to see her happy. "I work here between classes and I volunteer at the animal shelter on the weekends."

We caught up for a few minutes and then she asked if we needed something or if we were there to visit.

"We actually need to speak with Ashley LaCroix," I said. "It's about her partner, Kathleen Bertrand."

Lily's face fell and she leaned close. "She's taking it really hard. I mean, we're all a little freaked out about everything, but she's taking it the hardest. They were more than partners—they were best friends."

"Is she in?" I asked.

Lily nodded. "I'll let her know you're here."

We waited in the lobby for a couple of minutes.

"She looks amazing," Dawn whispered. "I'm so glad she's doing well."

"Me, too." I smiled, knowing her dad, Dean, would've been proud. I only wished he could be here to see her all grown up and taking life by the horns.

When Lily returned to the lobby, she waved for us to follow her. "Mrs. LaCroix has to be in court for nine, so she said she can meet for about ten minutes."

We thanked Lily when she opened the door to Ashley LaCroix's office and let us in. I made the introductions and we took a seat across from Ashley, who was a thin blonde with an Alabama accent. Her eyes were puffy from crying the night before—and probably ever since she heard the news about Kathleen—but her jaw was bravely set and she looked determined to make it through the interview without showing emotion.

"Kathleen was more than a friend and partner," she began slowly. "She was family."

"I'm so sorry for your loss," I said soothingly. "And I hate that we have to bother you with questions."

"Do you have any leads?"

I frowned. "We're working on it, but, so far…"

"Her husband did it."

I raised an eyebrow. "Joey?"

"Yeah, he's been freaking out ever since Kathleen began reclaiming her independence." She took a breath and continued. "Joey, he'd rather sit at home in front of a television with one hand shoved in the front of his pants and the other holding a beer. Kathleen had dreams, she was adventurous. She wanted to travel and see the world, but Joey didn't let."

"He didn't *let*?" I asked. "How could he stop her?"

"When they first met, Joey was a hard worker, or that's what Kathleen thought. He supported her all through law school. He paid the bills, paid for her gas to drive back and forth, paid for her meals, bought all of her clothes—everything. Since she didn't have an income for three years, everything was in his name. The credit cards, bank accounts, vehicles, the house, utilities. He controlled all of it.

"Once she graduated from law school and started working, she left things as they were. Her checks were direct deposited into the checking account Joey had always managed and she let him continue to take care of the bills. That's when things started to change."

"How do you mean?" I asked.

"Now that Kathleen was working, Joey figured he could take it easy. He would go weeks without working—he'd just sit around the house and drink—and when Kathleen began questioning him, he'd get angry and tell her he had supported her all through law school and it was time for her to support him.

"They began arguing all the time about the finances. If Kathleen needed money, she'd have to ask him for some. He didn't want her to have a checkbook or a debit card, because he said there were bills to pay and he didn't want her spending more than they had. She came in to work crying more than a few times. She felt weak and foolish."

Ashley shook her head. "She trusted him and he totally betrayed her. While she thought he was loving and supportive, he was actually manipulating her and using her. He saw her as a cash cow and he only supported her because she would make a nice living as a lawyer. He knew how generous and kind she was, and he knew he would be able to guilt her into doing whatever he wanted her to do later."

After Ashley provided more back story, I asked why she suspected Joey.

"He was losing his livelihood and he didn't like it. Kathleen was taking steps to divorce him, and he knew it. She opened her own checking account, diverted her paycheck to it, and told him he'd have to start carrying some of the bills. And then—*BOOM!*—she's dead. It doesn't take a detective to figure this one out."

I nodded slowly, studying Ashley. Her face was red with passion and I wondered if she would lie to protect her friend.

"There's no good way to ask this...was Kathleen cheating on Joey?"

"If she was, she never told me."

"Did you ever suspect her of cheating on him?"

Ashley shook her head.

"What about at the conferences? Did she ever get friendly with anyone when y'all were there or take anyone back to her room?"

Ashley cocked her head to the side. "What conferences?"

"The conferences in Dark Sands, Mississippi. Joey said Kathleen told him y'all meet once a month with the partners for an extended weekend..."

I allowed my voice to trail off as I watched the blank expression on Ashley's face.

"There are no conferences, are there?" I asked.

"Joey's lying. We don't have any partners in Dark Sands—or anywhere else for that matter." Ashley said it with confidence, but I got the sense she was starting to wonder if her friend kept some secrets from her. "Kathleen and I take a four-day weekend each month, and this past weekend was her turn. As far as I know, she stayed home and did some yard work. Joey probably lied about the conference to cover his ass for not reporting her missing."

I nodded, thoughtful. "So, there's nothing in Dark Sands for us to see?"

"Not to my knowledge."

After asking a few more questions, I turned to Dawn. "Anything?"

"Ashley, if Kathleen was having an affair, do you think she

would've told you?"

"I doubt it. She knows the best way to get caught doing something wrong is to run your mouth, so she probably would've kept it to herself." She grunted. "I wouldn't tell her if I was having an affair—I wouldn't tell anyone and I'd deny it to my grave."

Dawn thanked her and we stood to leave. Ashley walked us to the door and watched us walk down the short hallway. As we passed by Lily's work station, she jumped up and hurried around her desk. She reached me first and threw her arms around my neck.

"It was so good to see you again, Mr. London," she said, sliding her hand down the back of my forearm as she backed away. Before releasing me, she pressed something into the palm of my hand. She turned to Dawn and hugged her, too.

I slipped my hand into my pocket and waited until we were out on the sidewalk before pulling it out.

"What's that?" Dawn asked when I began unfolding the small piece of paper.

"It's a note—Lily gave it to me as we were leaving."

CHAPTER 22

9:00 a.m., Mathport, Louisiana

Abraham Wilson sat on the back porch of the tiny apartment he shared with Joy Vincent and stared out at the calm waters of Bayou Magnolia. His apartment was within a mile of the top of the lane where he used to live with his mom and dad, but sometimes it felt much closer than it was.

He'd been watching an alligator stalk an egret for at least twenty minutes while waiting for Joy to get dressed for school. She was attending the state university in Chateau and was heading to the college to sign out her books and get a parking pass for the year.

"What did your mom want?" Joy asked when she joined him on the porch and kissed the top of his head.

"Oh, the usual: *You and Joy shouldn't be living together, that's a sin,*" he said in his best mom impression. "*Have you found a better job yet? I just never imagined you'd want to do what your dad did. It's just so dangerous and I worry so much about you. I wish you'd get a normal job like Brett…yada, yada.*"

Joy laughed, tucking a strand of long black hair behind her ear. "What'd you tell her?"

"I told her I loved her, too, and I had to go to work."

Joy's mouth dropped open. "You lied to your mom?"

"Of course not."

"But you don't go back on shift again until Wednesday."

"I want to check something out in Plymouth East."

Joy plopped in his lap and wrapped her arms around his neck. "That case has got you upset, hasn't it?"

Abraham nodded his head, swallowing hard. "I'm having nightmares about that lady. I keep seeing her stretched out on that cross and I feel like I need to do something to help out. I mean, the person who did this is still walking around our parish, maybe even looking for another victim. I can't just sit around waiting for my next shift to do something."

"Why don't you ask if you can be assigned to the case with the detectives?"

"I asked my shift lieutenant if I could be temporarily reassigned to the detective bureau to help out, but he turned me down. My buddy overheard him telling one of the sergeants I thought that just because my dad was a former detective here that I would be shown favoritism." He frowned. "I don't know why he would say something like that. I've never even mention my dad's name to anyone. I want to earn my way like everyone else."

Joy leaned forward and kissed his forehead. "I know you do. They'll soon realize what I already know—that you're the bomb dot com."

Abraham thanked her and then kissed her on the mouth. "Be careful on the way to school."

"Yes, father," Joy joked. "I'll drive the speed limit and won't touch my phone."

"For the first time, that's not what I meant."

Joy sobered up in a flash. "Do you really think this person's a threat?"

"They don't know who did it or why, so until they catch the person, I want you keeping your head on a swivel." He took a breath and exhaled forcefully. "I thought I lost you once…"

Joy pushed an index finger to his lips. "It's okay. I'll be careful. I promise."

Once Joy had left for school, Abraham shoved his pistol in his waistband, snatched up his police radio, and jumped into his Ford F-150. Since he wasn't on official police business, he didn't take his patrol cruiser. His lieutenant might be able to deny a request for a transfer, but he couldn't stop Abraham from driving around town in his personal vehicle. And if he stumbled upon some evidence that might prove useful, he'd simply be a private citizen doing a good deed by reporting it.

As he turned off of Highway Eighty and onto the Plymouth East shortcut road, Abraham wondered if the alligator had snatched up the egret. He also wondered if the killer was out there right now, sneaking around like the alligator and trying to catch his or her next victim. While they had never determined if the killer was male or female, he couldn't imagine a woman doing something like that to another woman.

Abraham pulled his truck to the soft shoulder of the road near where Kathleen Bertrand's car had been found. It had been nighttime then and things looked a little different now. After shutting off his truck, he stepped out into the warm morning sunlight and walked toward the ruts that had been made by the wrecker pulling the vehicle from its resting place. He stopped at the edge of each row of cane and peered deep into the shadows, trying to see if the killer had discarded anything on the way out of the area, but he didn't find anything.

He walked over every inch of the surrounding area, hoping to find something they might've missed in the dark. He had no such luck and returned to his truck hot, sweaty, and disappointed. His police academy instructor, Captain Brandon Berger, had taught him a criminal always leaves something behind—they just needed to keep searching until they found it. So, he kept looking.

Driving back to Highway Eighty, Abraham turned onto Plymouth Highway and followed the same route he'd traveled Saturday morning, except he was driving much slower and on the wrong side of the highway so he could get a better view of the ground. There wasn't much traffic on the highway, so he figured it wouldn't be a problem.

There were a few houses at the very beginning of Plymouth Highway and the grass was short-cropped and visibility was excellent, but he quickly passed them by and was soon traveling along the desolate stretch of highway, where weeds grew thick on the shoulders and large drainage ditches bordered both sides of the road.

He buzzed his window down and slowed to a crawl, carefully scanning the ground on the northern shoulder of the highway. He was searching for anything that might be even remotely related to the Kathleen Bertrand case. While he was hoping to find her clothes, because that might provide a direct link to the suspect, he would settle for anything at that point.

He hadn't travelled far when the shoulder widened into a gravel pull-off that was free of weeds. He sped up a little, but then lurched to a stop when he saw a small object resting in a crevice right at the edge of the asphalt. He pulled onto the widened shoulder and stepped out of his truck, taking his cell phone with him in case the object turned out to be something important.

Squatting low when he reached the object, he recognized it to be a cheap flip-top cell phone. "I didn't know they made these anymore," he said aloud, shooting a photo of it with the camera feature on his phone. Hurrying back to his truck, he grabbed a latex glove from the first aid kit he kept under the seat, and then gently lifted the phone from the crack. At first glance, there was no way to tell how long it had been there, but when he flipped the top open and the screen lit up, he knew it was fresh.

Abraham sighed. If it was Kathleen Bertrand's phone, the battery would've been dead by now and the phone would've been in poor shape due to the rain from Saturday night. He worked his thumb across the keypad, searching for a list of contacts, but there was only one: *Kim.*

He checked the call log, but it was empty. He then checked the text messages and located one message that was sent at twelve thirty-eight in the morning. It read, quite simply: *On my way.*

Abraham pressed every button on the phone and scrolled through every option, but—other than the one contact—he couldn't find any information that might reveal the owner's name. With nothing else to try, he dialed Kim's number.

"Hey, Honey," said a man who answered on the first ring. "Where the hell are you?"

"I'm sorry," Abraham began. "This is Abraham Wilson and I'm a deputy with the Magnolia Parish Sheriff's Office. I was calling because—"

Click!

"Hello?" Abraham pulled the phone from his ear and looked at it. "The little prick hung up on me!"

Abraham called a second time, but it went straight to voicemail. Shrugging, he contacted Headquarters and pulled a complaint number for a found item.

"I didn't know you were working today," the dispatcher said cheerfully. "The schedule says you come in Wednesday night."

He grunted, still not accustomed to the attention he received from some of the female dispatchers. "I was riding around Plymouth East and located this phone," he explained. "I just want to make a note of it in case someone reports it stolen."

"Do you know who this is?" she asked.

"Um…" He did recognize the voice, but he was afraid he'd say the wrong name. "Give me a hint."

"It's Martha." She grunted. "I can't believe you didn't remember my name. I'm like you're biggest fan. But, just because it's you, I'll forgive you."

Abraham only half listened while she continued talking, chattering excitedly about her weekend. He wanted to tell her he didn't care, but he also didn't want to be rude. Ever since news broke about the incident that took place in the Blue Summit Mountains of Tennessee two years ago, a few of the single dispatchers had shown an interest in him. While Joy was good-natured about it, she was starting to grow annoyed by the way a couple of them acted when they'd meet in public. They were overtly flirtatious toward Abraham and wouldn't even acknowledge Joy's existence. Although they had met Joy before, Abraham would re-introduce her as his girlfriend, but they'd pretend they didn't even hear him.

"Do they act that way when I'm not around?" Joy had asked upon leaving the grocery store after one such encounter.

"No," he had said. "They act worse."

That had almost sent Joy over the edge until he laughingly told her he was joking. He never took the dispatchers serious and knew they were only acting under some misguided impression that he was a celebrity. In a small town, being on national television was a big deal to some people, and news that he had been offered a book deal only made these dispatchers more intrigued.

When Martha finally stopped talking long enough to give Abraham the case number, he jotted it down and told her he had to run. He then continued down the road, determined to cover every inch of Plymouth Highway.

CHAPTER 23

Chateau, Louisiana

"What does it say?" Dawn asked as I unfolded the pink piece of paper Lily had handed me upon walking out of the Ash and Kat Law Firm. My mind was on the information we'd just learned from Ashley and I began to wonder if Joey was lying about Kathleen going to a conference. It was possible Kathleen had lied to Joey, but, at this point, I didn't know for sure who to believe.

I glanced at the note, turned it over, and then handed it to Dawn. "It's a phone message for Kathleen, and it's dated this morning."

"Vaughn Toussaint," Dawn said, reading the name at the top of the message. She tilted it toward me and pointed to the telephone number written at the top of the note. "That's a Mississippi area code. Do you think it's got something to do with this conference Joey was talking about?"

"I don't know about the conference, but Lily thought it was significant enough to sneak to us." I dug out my cell phone as we walked to my truck. "We need to find out if Kathleen ever communicated with that number—"

My phone rang in my hand and I quickly answered it. "This is London."

"Mr. London, this is Lily. Mrs. Ashley left for court and my manager is smoking, so I've got a quick minute." She was speaking in hushed tones. "That man calls for Mrs. Kathleen often. He's never left a message before, but today he sounded different…like something was wrong. He told me to have her call him as soon as she got the message. He said it was urgent."

"Did he say what it was about?"

"No, but when I first answered and he asked for her, he sounded angry. His voice was real rough. We already knew about Mrs. Kathleen, but I didn't tell him anything. I just told him she wasn't in, and that's when he told me to have her call him."

"Thank you, Lily. I really appreciate you sticking your neck out for us. No one will ever know."

When I hung up, I immediately called Melvin. When he answered, I asked about the status of the search warrants.

"The search warrants for her bank and credit card accounts have been faxed out, but I haven't heard anything back yet. The cell phone was a bust…whoever wiped it knew what they were doing. As for Ring-Tele, their technicians have been working since late last night and they'll be faxing the report within the hour." He paused and I heard him take a breath and hold it. Finally, he said, "That must be it. I hear something coming through the fax machine now."

"We'll be there in twenty," I said and ended the call. We had reached my truck and jumped inside. While I drove, Dawn got on her phone and called dispatch to request a criminal history check on this Vaughn Toussaint character. She jotted some information down and then asked for a driver's license inquiry and a registration check. After waiting and then talking for about ten minutes, she hung up and turned toward me.

"What a hell of a coincidence…Vaughn Toussaint lives in Dark Sands, Mississippi."

I grunted. "I guess Joey was telling the truth and Ashley was kept in the dark."

"Yep, it seems Kathleen was having a private conference with Mr. Toussaint."

"If we believe Ashley, then Joey might have a motive to kill Kathleen—even if he didn't know about the affair."

"And if he did know, that'll be damning for him."

"Do you have Vaughn's address?" I asked.

"I have more than that," Dawn said when her cell phone dinged. She opened a text message and held it so I could see. "I've got his DL picture."

"Does he have a record?"

"I'm glad you asked." Reading from her notes, Dawn said she would start with the small stuff. "He's got a few convictions for minor traffic offenses dating back ten years and two recent wildlife offenses relating to shrimp season violations. There's also a shrimp boat registered in his name, so he might be a fisherman." She tapped her notebook. "Now for the good stuff...he's got three convictions for domestic abuse battery that date back five years. They were all in a span of a few months, so it was probably the same woman. It seems he straightened up for a few years and didn't get another felony charge until last year, when he was arrested for sexual battery."

In Mississippi, sexual battery involved sexual penetration and was a serious offense. I mulled over this new information and tried to figure out how Vaughn Toussaint might relate to the case. Was it possible he came to Louisiana and killed Kathleen? If so, what would be his motivation? Sexual battery is one thing—mutilation and murder is something altogether different. Besides, Doctor Fitch concluded there had been no sexual assault.

If Vaughn was calling for Kathleen and he sounded angry, it was quite possible he had no clue she was dead. Joey did say Kathleen was on her way to Dark Sands, and her vehicle was found heading out of Plymouth East, so one could safely assume she was heading to meet Vaughn. If she never showed up, that might anger Vaughn, but it didn't seem reason enough for him to drive to Louisiana and nail her to a cross.

I ran my thoughts by Dawn. She listened intently and nodded her head slowly after I'd finished. She began chewing on her lower lip and staring off into space. Finally, she turned to me and said, "If Joey thought Kathleen was going to a conference and Vaughn thought she was heading to Dark Sands to meet him, neither man would have a reason to kill her. If neither of them did it, then someone else decided to interrupt her trip and hang her to a cross...and that someone must've been really mad at her."

"Joey might still be involved," I said. "If his wife was lying about attending conference once a month and was actually seeing this Vaughn fellow, Joey could have easily found out something was up and could've taken matters into his own hands. It would've been nothing for him to follow her and flag her down on the highway. She would've stopped, not thinking anything of it."

"He didn't even have to flag her down," Dawn said. "We might be looking at this all wrong. Other than her car being found in the cane fields, there's no evidence to suggest she was taken from the highway. Think about it—Joey could've nailed her to the cross in the comfort of his woodshop, loaded the cross in the back of his boat, and then launched the boat in a place that had access to the back of that field. He could've later ditched her car in the cane and then gone home to wait for her body to be found. He could've come up with the story about Dark Sands just to throw us off."

"If that's all true, he had to have found out about her lover in Mississippi and made up the story about the conference. Otherwise, it would be a hell of a coincidence that he mentions Dark Sands and she's got a man in Dark Sands—and I don't believe in coincidences when it comes to murder investigations."

Dawn nodded and pursed her lips. "I want more information on this Vaughn character."

CHAPTER 24

Detective Bureau, Payneville, Louisiana

"Here's everything from Kathleen Bertrand's cell phone," Melvin said when Dawn and I entered the detective bureau.

I took the thick stack of paper and followed Dawn into the conference room, where we sat to pour over it. We separated the call records from the text records and began searching for Vaughn Toussaint's number. It wasn't hard to find, because she talked to him often.

"They're definitely having an affair," Dawn said. "No one talks on the phone until four in the morning unless they're 'doing it'."

"We're 'doing it'," I said, "and we don't talk on the phone until four in the morning."

"That's because you sleep next to me, goofball."

"*Sleep* next to you? I can't sleep with all that snoring you do—"

"I don't snore!" Dawn's head jerked up from her stack of records. Her face was red and her eyes were wide. "Please tell me I haven't turned into my mom!"

I laughed and waved her off. "I can sleep through a hurricane, so it's not a problem."

She grunted and went back to scanning the documents.

I found a text message from Kathleen's phone that was sent to Vaughn on Wednesday evening at eight-eleven. I showed it to Dawn. "I wish I knew what it said."

She pointed to the GPS coordinates in the column to the far right. "Where was she when she sent it?"

I moved to the desk in the corner of the room and accessed one of the computers. I punched in the coordinates and clicked on the map that showed up. "It's a block from her house."

Dawn lifted the last page in her stack and let it fall to the table. "There's no more activity after that text message."

I drummed my fingers on the desk, lost in thought. I was going over everything we knew at that point when I remembered the poker chip. "I bet you a hundred-dollar poker chip that Kathleen and Vaughn have been going to the Dark Sands Casino together."

"I'll pass on the bet, but I'd like to see the surveillance footage from the casino."

I nodded. "We would need a roundabout date and approximate hour or we'd just be shooting in the dark and wasting a lot of time."

"I'll take care of that." Dawn pulled out her cell phone and punched in a number. When the person on the other side answered, Dawn's eyes lit up. "Hey, Lily, I hate to involve you in this case again, but I just need to know when Kathleen took her four-day weekend last month." There was a pause and then Dawn smiled. "Thank you so much, Lil!"

She lifted her notepad and turned it so I could see. It was the Fourth of July weekend, and her days off began on the second.

I turned back to the phone records and scanned the week of the Fourth. On July first at eight-fifteen, she had sent a text message to Vaughn. The coordinates were nearly identical to the coordinates from Wednesday.

"That must be her routine," I said. "She sends him a text message when she leaves the church or her house."

Dawn nodded and leaned against me to enter the next set of coordinates, which corresponded with a phone call to Vaughn two hours later. The coordinates were near the Dark Sands Resort and Casino. "Now we're getting somewhere," she said. "I think we should take a trip to the casino and then we need to find Mr. Vaughn Toussaint."

I picked up the handset from the desk phone and called the sheriff to get his approval.

CHAPTER 25

12:30 p.m., Dark Sands, Mississippi

I had never been to a casino and I had to admit I was impressed when we stepped through the lobby doors. There was a restaurant to our immediate left, where a live band was performing for the many people eating lunch, and an expansive opening to the right served as the entrance to the gaming devices. A security booth was set up in the center of the aisle and they were carding people as they walked by.

Since we were going to be out of our jurisdiction, we had called Dark Sands Police Department and requested that a detective assist us in obtaining surveillance footage from the casino's security team. During the drive to Mississippi, we received a call from Detective Richard McQuarie, who asked for the facts of our case.

"They'll want a search warrant before showing the tapes, so I'll type one up while waiting for you guys to get here," he had told me.

I'd given him the information for the affidavit and he said he'd meet us at the casino at two o'clock with the signed warrant.

I glanced at the time on my phone. We were a little early, which explained why I didn't see anyone in the immediate area who looked like a detective. The check-in counter was near the opening to the casino and McQuarie told me that's where he'd be waiting. All I saw was a long line of impatient guests waiting to get into their rooms. I heard someone behind the counter tell an elderly woman she couldn't check into her room until three, and the woman began cursing heatedly.

"What do you want to do while waiting?" I asked, side-stepping two young boys who were chasing each other with water pistols. The place was crowded with people of all ages. They were coming and going in every direction. There were lone individuals walking around, couples strolling hand-in-hand, and even families bustling about. Some of the people were dressed elegantly, while others wore casual attire, and a few were even running around in bikinis and swim shorts. Nearly everyone old enough to drink had some type of alcoholic beverage in their hands. I shot my thumb to the left. "The restaurant looks good, but there're a lot of people waiting to be seated."

Dawn pointed up ahead, where a row of shops were situated along a long corridor that led to one of the two residential towers of the luxury hotel. "If that's an ice cream shop, I want two of everything while we wait."

I looked where she pointed and saw a flashing sign displaying a large ice cream cone. There was also a picture of a pizza, and the sight alone made my stomach growl.

We slipped our way through the crowd and stood in a short line. We didn't have to wait long to order, and a short time later they called our number. Once we were seated at a small table near the counter—the large supreme pizza and two chocolate milk shakes taking up most of the tabletop—we tore into our meal. We didn't talk much, but my mind was working nonstop and I knew Dawn's was, too. I didn't know what Vaughn Toussaint would give us, but I hoped it would be a big break in the case. With every minute that passed, our chances of solving the murder grew more and more slim, and this was not a case that could go unsolved.

As I glanced around the elegant building, I tried to image Kathleen Bertrand walking around with her fisherman lover. According to his driver's license, he was a little shorter than she was, standing only five-six, and he must've had a paunchy belly, because he weighed one-eighty-five. I stared idly at some of the couples walking by, wondering if they were also cheaters. It was so busy in the resort that it would be easy to get lost in the sea of people and activities. But how did Kathleen find this fisherman, who lived so far from her—

"Do you think they ate at this pizza place?" Dawn asked, breaking through my thoughts. She had finished her pizza and was sucking on her straw. After swallowing a mouthful of milkshake, she pointed to the girl behind the counter. "Let's show her their pictures. She might remember them."

"Good idea," I said.

I had finished my own food, so I emptied the tray into a nearby trashcan and joined Dawn at the counter. She had identified herself and was pulling up a picture of Vaughn when I approached them. "This is my partner, London Carter."

"Your partner?" The young girl's face flushed. "I thought he was your husband."

It was Dawn's turn to flush. "Really? What gave you that idea?"

The girl shrugged. "I don't know. You guys just look cute together."

I smiled. "We'll take that under advisement."

"Okay, Mrs. Cupid," Dawn said, turning the screen so the girl could see Vaughn's picture. "Do you recognize him?"

"Yeah, that's Vaughn."

"You know him?"

"I don't *know* him, but I've seen him a number of times. He comes in here with this tall woman every few weeks." She leaned across the counter. "The only reason I remember him is because he gives me the creeps. And the only reason I know his name is because he tells it to me every time."

Dawn showed her Kathleen's picture and she nodded. "That's the lady."

"What is it about Vaughn that gives you the creeps?" Dawn asked.

"First off, the lady *always* pays for their food. I've never seen him take a single dollar out of his wallet and I've never heard him thank her for buying. But the main thing that makes me uncomfortable is the way he looks at me."

"How does he look at you?"

"Like a hungry dog that's about to bite."

"Why does he tell you his name?" Dawn asked. "Do you think he's flirting with you?"

"Oh, absolutely." The girl nodded her head for emphasis. "The lady always has to use the bathroom when they walk up, and I get the impression she drove a long way to get here. Anyway, since we're the only shop outside of the casino that has a bathroom, they stop here and she goes in the bathroom while he looks at the menu. He's been here so many times he knows exactly what we have, but he stares up and asks me a bunch of questions about the pizza. And he always finds a way to fit in the conversation that his name is Vaughn and he always invites me to go for a ride in his boat."

"What do you tell him?"

"I tell him I have a boyfriend, but then he tells me he has a girlfriend and that it doesn't matter."

Dawn's brow furrowed. "Does he talk that way in front of the lady?"

"No, ma'am. He always shuts up when she walks out the bathroom. He doesn't say a word to me while she's around."

"Does he ever come in here alone?"

She shook her head. "Not that I've ever seen."

Dawn thanked her and we turned to walk back to the check-in counter. We were standing there for a few minutes when my phone rang. It was Melvin.

"Hey, London, I heard back from Kathleen's bank," Melvin said. "She's spent thousands of dollars at the Dark Sands Resort and Casino over the course of the year. She's been there at least six times since January, with the last time being the Fourth of July week."

No surprises there. "Anything else?"

"Yeah, she wrote a five thousand dollar check to a divorce attorney from New Orleans. The memo section of the check calls it a retainer fee."

"Damn." I was thoughtful. "When did she write the check?"

"Last week."

CHAPTER 26

One hour later

I was watching the entrance to the casino when Detective Richard McQuarie ambled lazily through the door. He was tall and lanky, except for his lower abdomen. It sloped outward and hung over his beltline like molten lava frozen in time. He gave a slight nod of the head when he noticed us and headed in our direction, his shoulders pulled back as he walked.

He handed me a search warrant and, in a slow tone, said, "The judge signed the warrant, so we're good to go."

I thanked him and the three of us proceeded to the security annex, where we presented the warrant to the head of security. He made a show of studying the warrant to be sure everything was in order, and then he directed one of his underlings to pull some tape that corresponded to the date and time range specified in the warrant.

Dawn and I sat back and allowed McQuarie to do all of the talking, but it was painful to watch. He was a nice enough fellow, but he wasn't much on action and his words dragged. At long last, we were huddled around a bank of monitors watching the cameras that covered eight different entrances to the casino. It was Dawn who spotted Kathleen first.

Kathleen was seen walking through the main entrance a few minutes after ten o'clock on the evening of July first. Kathleen stopped momentarily in the doorway and looked around. Almost immediately, a man sprang from a bench near an indoor waterfall and rushed to her. They embraced and spoke excitedly before walking away hand-in-hand.

The security officer switched cameras and we picked them up walking toward the same pizza shop where Dawn and I had eaten. Just as the girl at the shop had described, Kathleen made her way to the bathroom and Vaughn sidled up to the counter. While we couldn't hear what was being said, the girl's body language told us all we needed to know about her feelings toward Vaughn. When Kathleen reappeared from the bathroom, Vaughn quickly straightened from the counter and put his arm around Kathleen.

We continued watching as they walked around for a while, returned to the parking garage for Kathleen's luggage, and then disappeared into a room on the eleventh floor. After about an hour, they left the room and went to the restaurant on the ground floor before spending the rest of the night in the casino.

They left the resort for a few hours the next day and returned a little after lunchtime. For the next few hours, we played the tapes in maximum speed, watching them coming and going throughout the weekend until we finally reached Sunday.

"They lived like they were married," Dawn said. "I don't understand how she can go back home after all of this and her husband not suspect a thing."

I nodded my agreement as we watched Vaughn rolling Kathleen's luggage toward the parking garage exit. I was about to turn away from the camera when something caught my eye.

"Wait!" I grabbed the security officer by the shoulder. "Back it up a little."

The officer jerked in his skin, and then cursed silently. "You scared me."

"Sorry," I said quickly, watching as he reversed the footage. When he reached the spot I wanted, I pointed. "There—look at the man standing in the doorway."

Dawn leaned close to the camera and studied the man. He was tall and thin and wore faded jeans and a tight dress T-shirt. He wore dark sunglasses and a ball cap, so it was hard to make out any facial features. "What about him?" she asked.

"Go back to Wednesday night," I told the officer, "right when Kathleen first arrived."

When he did, I pointed out a man with a similar build sitting in the corner of the room reading a newspaper. He wore the same ball cap, and the same sunglasses were dangling from his neck.

"Whoa!" McQuarie whistled. "Good eye—that's the same guy."

I made a rolling motion with my right index finger. "Fast-forward to when they go to the casino."

The security officer did as I asked and stopped when I pointed to a man sitting at a video poker machine three seats away from Kathleen. "Watch him," I said. "He's pressing buttons, but he hasn't put a single coin in the machine and he's not even watching what he's doing."

Dawn nodded, her mouth slightly open. "He looks familiar now that he's not wearing a baseball cap."

"He should," I said. "That's the same man who was scoping us out at the Second Temple Fellowship Church."

"That's right!" Dawn exclaimed. "The moustache man!"

I nodded, watching as the man got up from his chair and approached Vaughn during one of Kathleen's trips to the bathroom. They spoke briefly—until a waitress walked by in a short skirt. Virgil immediately turned away from Moustache and stopped the waitress. Since Virgil's back was now toward him, Moustache returned to his chair and resumed pretending to play the video poker machine.

"Why in the hell is he here following our victim around the casino?" Dawn asked to no one in particular.

"I don't know, but when we get back home, he's got some explaining to do." I turned to Detective McQuarie. "But before we go, I'd like to have a word with Vaughn Toussaint."

"Okay." He nodded idly and tugged the police radio from his belt clip. "I'll go ahead and run him for an address."

Dawn handed him the driver's license printout.

"Well," he said. "That was easy. Since my radio is already in my hand, I'll check him for local warrants."

We knew not all local warrants made it into NCIC (National Crime Information Center, a computerized database of criminal justice information), so we waited while he radioed his headquarters. Within a minute the radio scratched to life and the dispatcher said there were contempt of court warrants for Vaughn because he failed to appear for his arraignment on the sexual battery charge.

McQuarie scowled and returned his radio to his belt. "He's got warrants."

"That's great," I said. "He's got to come with us whether he wants to or not."

"Yeah, that's great," he mumbled, turning to lead the way out of the casino. "You guys can ride with me."

I got the sense there was someplace else he'd rather be, but I shrugged it off and followed him to the front of the casino, where he was parked in the fire zone.

CHAPTER 27

"Do you know anything about this fellow?" I asked McQuarie when we drove up to Vaughn's front doorstep. I didn't like how close he'd driven to the house, but I wasn't about to tell him how to do his job.

"Well, we know he's a local fisherman who hangs around the beaches harassing women when he's not offshore. He's out on bail for fondling a drunk lady who was passed out on the beach." He eased the gearshift in *park* and scratched his head. "That's what the contempt warrant is all about."

From the back seat of the unmarked cruiser, I kept my eyes on the front door as we stepped out and approached the house. Dawn had spread wide to the right and her hand was dangling near the baby Glock in her holster.

"Want me to cover the back?" I asked McQuarie, who was walking directly to the door.

"Sure, but I don't think it's a problem."

I made my way down a narrow pathway between the house and the neighboring chain link fence until I reached the back door. I stood poised at the corner and waited. From where I stood, I could hear McQuarie bang on the front door. His knock brought about an immediate reaction from inside as small dogs—there had to be three or four of them—went crazy and assaulted the front of the house. Footsteps soon followed the barking. While I couldn't hear what was being said, the low drone of voices at the front of the house sounded cordial.

"London, it's clear," Dawn called from the narrow walkway. When I reached her, she told me Vaughn was working on his boat.

"His mom said he's leaving to go trawling first thing in the morning, but we can catch him at the dock."

We had to wait a few minutes while McQuarie made small talk with Vaughn's mother. He finally turned and walked to his cruiser. I grumbled silently to myself, but slipped into the back seat without saying a word and sat patiently while we headed toward one of the many docks along the Gulf of Mexico. I hadn't planned on spending all day in Mississippi and McQuarie wasn't moving fast enough for me.

We needed to find out what Vaughn knew and then we needed to return to Plymouth East and identify the mystery man from the casino. We'd obtained copies of the surveillance footage, and the security officer had been gracious enough to print out a still shot of Mr. Moustache, so we could head straight to Joey Bertrand's house. If he didn't recognize the man, anyone from the church would, because it was hard to miss that large caterpillar on his lip.

At long last, McQuarie turned into a large oyster shell parking lot and stopped near three long concrete piers that extended like slender fingers over the water. We stepped out and were greeted by a warm breeze blowing in from the Gulf.

"Which boat is his?" I asked, calculating that there must be over five hundred boats along the three piers.

McQuarie pulled out his pocket notebook and nodded to himself as he studied his writings. "He calls his boat the Mr. Vaughn Damn. He's a big Jean Claude fan. His mother said his boat's docked down the pier on the end."

Each pier had to be half a mile long and there were boats docked all up and down their lengths. Large creosote pilings jutted up from the water at even intervals along both sides of each of the piers, making up individual slips for the fishermen to tie up their boats. I turned to McQuarie and shot one thumb to the left and the other to the right. "Which one is considered the pier on the *end*?"

He scratched his head again and chuckled. "That's a good question."

I pointed right. "How about Dawn and I go down the one on that end and you take the one on the other end?"

"That's sounds good." He turned and ambled toward the pier on the left and I wondered how many days it would take him to make it to the end.

"Is it just me, or does he not have a care in the world?" Dawn asked.

"He's certainly not in a hurry for anything." I shrugged. "I guess it's better than being uptight."

Seagulls screamed overhead, circling the boats and water in search of food. A few fishermen were cleaning their nets on the platforms in their individual slips, and every now and then a seagull would swoop down and snatch up a random fish or shrimp that had fallen from the nets.

We walked across the shell parking lot and stepped onto the pier. The concrete surface was damp and sticky with salt water and we had to watch our footing. As we walked, we noticed one guy, who wore a red raincoat, jeans, and black rubber boots, leaning over a large ice chest picking small fish from his catch. He would toss them overboard, to the delight of the nearby gulls, and then drop the shrimp in smaller ice chests. I approached him from behind and said hello.

He didn't even look up. "What do you want?"

"I'm looking for the Mr. Vaughn Damn."

"Slip eighteen."

I thanked him and stepped back to look for a number on the slips.

"There aren't any," Dawn said. She started counting from the parking lot. "This would be four or five, depending on which side is an even number."

We continued walking as she counted and stopped when she reached sixteen. We looked ahead, surveying the boats on either side.

"Over there," she said, pointing. "It's the white wooden boat with the blue trim. I can see the name."

I nodded to let her know I saw where she was pointing. It was twenty yards away and there was a man on the rear deck squatting beside a gray wooden box. The box appeared to be the housing for the engine, and there were tools spread out on a nearby bench. An exhaust pipe extended up from the engine and it was attached to a muffler high up in the air. I didn't know what a boat muffler was supposed to look like, but that one looked like the muffler on my pickup truck.

As we drew nearer, we walked softly and tried to appear casual in the event he turned around and saw us. We were still too far to reach him if he decided to make a run for it, so we had to be stealthy. I looked toward the opposite pier to see if it would be possible to get Detective McQuarie's attention, but the middle pier was blocking my view of where he was. He would probably hear if I yelled his name, but I didn't want to alert Vaughn.

When I looked back toward the boat, Vaughn was staring directly at us. He had stopped working and had fixed us with narrow eyes. I knew in an instant that he would run, and that's exactly what he did. Without a moment of hesitation, he dropped the tools in his hands and dove over the side of the boat, disappearing into the salt water below.

"Damn it!" I yelled.

Dawn and I bolted in Vaughn's direction and I hollered for McQuarie as we ran. I didn't know if he heard me, but I didn't have time to make sure, because Vaughn had resurfaced on the opposite side of our pier and was already half way to the center pier. He was swimming faster than I thought possible for a person in boots and clothes, and I knew he would reach the nearest slip before I had time to run back to the parking lot and down the center pier. Still, I tried.

"Stop or I'll shoot!" Dawn hollered, trying to bluff him into surrendering. It didn't work, and only motivated him to swim faster.

Pumping my arms and legs as fast as I could while trying not to slip, I turned the corner at the end of my pier and raced toward the center pier. I had finally reached it and was just starting down it when I saw Vaughn come up for air to the left of the pier. He was heading for the pier that McQuarie was on.

I switched directions and saw Dawn run by in the parking lot ahead of me. She had seen him, too, and was hollering to get McQuarie's attention. McQuarie finally heard Dawn and turned to look where she pointed. He waved that he saw Vaughn and picked up his radio. I didn't know who he was calling, but it was obvious he wasn't going to chase the fugitive and it would be up to Dawn and me to catch him.

I hit the parking lot on a dead run, my legs stretched to their limit, and began to close on Dawn, who was approaching the last pier. She turned down the pier, but I saw her lurch to a stop and whip around, pointing farther down.

"He swam under it!" she hollered. "He's still heading east!"

I kept running, trying to keep an eye on him while dodging the occasional fishermen walking around carrying supplies to and from their boats. One man didn't see me until the last second and he screeched out loud, dropping a small ice chest and a six-pack of beer. He began cursing at me, but I didn't even look back.

Once I ran past the last pier, I realized where Vaughn was heading. Just east of the shell parking lot there was a long stretch of beach. People were sunning and splashing in the water and, at first, I thought he might try to get lost in the crowd. However, it quickly occurred to me *why* he was heading in that direction. About three hundred feet from the beach was a long line of Jet Skis waiting to be rented. They were secured to an anchor rope by a short strap and a snap hook. If he reached the Jet Skis and stole one, we might never see him again.

I called upon every muscle in my body, begging for more speed. I was almost parallel to Vaughn's position, but he was still three hundred feet from the shore and only about twenty feet from the nearest Jet Ski.

Once I hit the beach, I headed straight for the water, but I lost a step because of the soft sand. Directly in my path were two women sunbathing. I didn't have time to run around them, so I hurdled right over them—they were lying on their stomachs and didn't even notice—and hit the water two steps later.

High-stepping it for the first dozen or so feet, I dove into the water when it got deeper and swam as fast as I could. I was still two hundred feet away when Vaughn climbed up the back of one of the Jet Skis and cranked it up. I hollered at him to stop, that I only wanted to talk, but he revved the engine and sped off, shooting a stream of water behind the craft as he fled.

My heart sank as I watched him growing smaller and smaller in the distance, but I continued fighting forward. After what seemed like forever, I finally crawled up the back of the Jet Ski and mounted it. I slipped the kill switch key in place and fired up the engine. I then smashed the finger throttle, nearly flying off the back of the watercraft as it shot violently forward. The only thing that saved me was my grip on the handlebars.

Once I was clipping across the water, I stood high in the saddle to get a better view of my surroundings. I raced in the direction of the tiny spot that represented Vaughn and his Jet Ski. He seemed to be growing fainter with each passing second. The speedometer indicated I was going sixty-four miles per hour. I hollered and squeezed the throttle tighter, trying to force the Jet Ski to go faster, but it was no use. It would accelerate, but then I would hit a wave and lose a few miles per hour. Water sprayed my face with each wave I hit and the salt burned my eyes, but I just blinked it away and focused like a laser on Vaughn.

After racing full-speed across the water for about ten minutes, it appeared I was gaining on him a little. I kept the throttle fully smashed and took the inside lane as we followed the shoreline, feeling encouraged.

The sense of optimism was short-lived, because I was still a long way from him when he cut left and headed for the beach. At the rate we were traveling and my distance from him, he would reach the shore about a full minute before I did, and that would give him plenty of time to run away or jump into a vehicle and disappear.

I scanned the beach as I raced forward, wondering if there were any Dark Sands police officers around. I didn't know if they had officers assigned to beach patrol, but if they did, I certainly couldn't see them. I got excited for a moment when Vaughn hit a wave at an odd angle and nearly capsized, but he righted the craft and barreled forward.

He was only about twenty feet from reaching the beach when, out of nowhere, a speedboat blew by me and nearly rocked me off my Jet Ski. I started to curse them out when I realized there were blue flashing lights mounted to a rack above the boat and a siren was blaring.

It was the Dark Sands Police Department's water patrol division! I wanted to cheer out loud at the sight of the officers closing in on Vaughn, and I immediately realized Detective McQuarie had been on his cell phone or radio calling them to action from the pier. I suddenly felt bad for how I'd initially felt about him, but there was no time for beating myself up. I needed to get to Vaughn as soon as they captured him so I could question him about—

"Oh, no!" I stared in shock as the speedboat turned sharply when it reached Vaughn and sideswiped his Jet Ski. Vaughn went airborne and seemed to skid along the surface of the water when he landed. I heard him yelling, but then his cries were cut off when he disappeared into the murky bubbles of the Gulf of Mexico.

CHAPTER 28

4:15 p.m., Plymouth East, Louisiana

Abraham pushed through the last cane row in the area where Kathleen's car had been found and wiped his face on the front of his shirt. He had been searching all day, but hadn't found anything since locating the random cell phone on the side of the highway. He had searched the patch of sugarcane where the car had been found at least three times. For his efforts, his shirt was torn, his jeans muddy and wet, his arms sliced up from the sharp sugarcane leaves, and his boots were saturated. He looked around, wondering what it was that he was missing.

"Come on," he said out loud. "There's got to be some evidence out here!"

He thought about plunging back into the cane, but he knew he had thoroughly searched every inch of the area. He had to face it— there was nothing worth finding out here. If some evidence had been left behind, it had been destroyed or the killer washed away any traces of it.

Sighing in defeat, he trudged from the muddy patch of sugarcane road and made his way to his truck. He stopped to kick the mud off of his boots and even considered taking them off, but decided against it. He could wash his truck later. As for right now, he needed to get home and spend what was left of the day with Joy. She had called him three times—once to say she was back from school and twice more to ask when he was coming home—and it seemed she was losing her patience with him.

Before Abraham could start his truck, his cell phone rang. He put it to his ear without looking and shoved the key in the ignition. "This is Abe."

"Hey, Abraham, it's Martha."

Abraham winced. "What's up?"

"I haven't heard from you all day and I was wondering if you were still in Plymouth East."

He glanced at the clock on his dash. Martha would be knocking off soon and he suddenly worried she might be taking the flirtatious behavior to another level. "I am," he said, "but I was just leaving. Joy's waiting for me at home and I've—"

"But you're still there right now?"

"Yeah, I'm on Plymouth Highway near the shortcut road," he said, trying to be patient. "But I have to go—"

"I just need you for a minute. There's a disturbance up the road from where you are and my nearest deputy is twenty minutes away on a traffic stop. Do you think you can run over there and get things under control until he breaks free from the traffic stop? We don't know exactly what's going on, but it sounded heated in the background."

Relieved, Abraham agreed. "What's the address?"

After providing the address, Martha said, "The complainant is a man named Kim Berry. He said someone's at his house wanting to fight him."

"Got it!" Abraham whipped his truck around and sped up the shortcut road toward Plymouth Highway. Once he reached it, he turned right and smashed the accelerator. As he drove, he shoved the front of his shirt tail into his jeans to expose his badge. He didn't want the complainant or the suspect to mistake him for a citizen.

He had just rounded the last bend in the highway and was traveling along the final stretch of road that led to Highway Eighty when he saw the disturbance. A man was standing in the front yard of a house to the left and he was wielding a baseball bat. Abraham was still a quarter mile away, so he couldn't hear what the man was saying, but it was obvious he was angry and screaming something toward the house.

Abraham smashed the brake pedal and coasted into the front yard, barely throwing the gear shift in *park* before jumping out. "Sheriff's Office!" he called. "Sir, I need you to put down the bat!"

The man didn't even turn toward Abraham.

"Where is she, you bastard? I know you have her!" The man smashed the bat against the side of the house and continued yelling.

Abraham stole up behind the man and announced his presence

again. Still ignoring him, the man reared back to swing the bat again, and that's when Abraham sprang into action. He leapt forward and hooked his right arm over both of the man's arms and locked them in place, controlling the bat. He then used his right leg to sweep the man's feet out from under him. The man landed on his back with a thud that knocked the wind out of him.

Abraham rolled the stunned man to his stomach and handcuffed him.

"I'm going to place you in the back seat of my truck," Abraham said calmly, helping the man to his feet and then snatching the bat from the ground. "If you act civil, there won't be any more trouble and you won't face any more charges. Is that understood?"

The man, whose face was streaked with tears, nodded and continued gasping for air.

"My name's Abraham Wilson," he said. "What's yours?"

"Gerard," the man said. "Gerard Brister. That son of a bitch has my wife and he won't tell me where she is."

Abraham turned toward the house and a chill reverberated up and down his back. *Is there another missing woman? Is this Kim Berry the suspect?*

"What do you mean, he has your wife?" Abraham asked.

"My wife left me to be with him and he knows where she is, but he won't come out and tell me."

"Oh, so he didn't kidnap her?"

"No, man, didn't you hear me? She left me!"

Relieved, Abraham exhaled the breath he was holding. "What's your wife's name?"

"Debbie."

"And how do you know this guy knows where she is?"

"Because I paid a private investigator to follow her, that's how," Gerard said. The hurt was evident in his voice and his chin quivered as he continued. "She waits until I go to sleep and then she sneaks out and comes to this house. She's come out here at least eight times in the last two months."

"I see," Abraham said thoughtfully. "Does she have a car?"

"She does. It's a gray Nissan Sentra and she usually hides it in his garage." He nodded confidently. "I know it's in there, but he won't open it so I can see."

Abraham hefted the bat in his hand. "What were you planning to do with this?"

"I just brought it for protection."

"From what?" Abraham was skeptical.

"Just in case the man tried to fight with me."

"Well, when I arrived you were the only one out here and you were swinging the bat around with bad intentions."

CHAPTER 29

After strapping Gerard into the back seat and telling him to stay put, Abraham walked toward Kim Berry's house. He had almost reached the door when a man gingerly stepped out onto the back patio.

"Is he locked up?" the man asked.

Abraham nodded. "Are you Kim Berry?"

"I am." The man rubbed sweat from his bald head and wiped his hands on his pants. "I don't know what's going on, but that man just showed up and started swearing at me and swinging a baseball bat around. He was talking crazy and saying things I couldn't understand." He paused and licked his lips. "You know, he didn't do any damage or anything, so I don't really want to press any charges. I'd be satisfied if you gave him a warning. I'd just like him to leave and not come back, if that's okay."

Abraham nodded slowly, studying the man. "So, you didn't understand anything he was saying?"

"Not really." Kim licked his lips again. "He was talking crazy, you know? I think he's got the wrong house."

"Did you understand him when he asked about his wife?"

"His wife?" Kim's brow furrowed. "I don't recall hearing anything about his wife."

"Do you know a woman named Debbie Brister?"

He shook his head. "Never heard of her."

"That's strange," Abraham said, taking a step closer to Kim's house. "Mr. Brister claims his wife has been here at least eight times in the past two months. He said she hides her car in your garage."

Kim chuckled nervously. "That's the craziest thing I ever heard."

"I have to agree...it does sound pretty farfetched." Abraham pointed casually toward the garage, which didn't have any windows. "Do you mind if I have a look inside? Just so I can prove to Mr. Brister that his wife isn't here and he can leave you alone?"

Kim hesitated.

"Is there a problem?" Abraham asked. "You're hesitating."

"I mean, I don't know what's going on. I'm the one who called the law and now you're asking to search my garage." Kim pointed to Abraham's jeans. "You're all dirty and not even wearing a uniform. For all I know, you're working with him and this is a trick to get in my house to harm me in some way."

"Right...except you called the sheriff's office and then I showed up." Abraham pulled his wallet from his back pocket and stepped forward, showing Kim his law enforcement commission. "This is me, Abraham Wilson, and I'm a patrol deputy with the Magnolia Parish Sheriff's Office."

After Kim studied the commission card and then nodded, Abraham shoved it back in his pocket. "So, what about the garage?"

Kim scowled. "I mean, you showed me your card and all, but it could be fake."

Abraham was starting to lose his patience, but a plan suddenly crept into his mind. "Mr. Berry, do you have your cell phone with you?"

Kim nodded, and Abraham detected a look of suspicion on his face.

"Why don't you walk with me to my truck so I can keep an eye on Mr. Brister?" Abraham suggested. "And then you can call the sheriff's office to verify who I am."

Kim nodded his head reluctantly and followed Abraham to his truck. While Kim stood in front of his truck and called the sheriff's office, Abraham grabbed a glove from his first aid kit and retrieved the cell phone he had located earlier in the morning. He opened it and scrolled to the only contact name on the phone. Keeping his thumb poised over the green call button, he hid the phone behind his back and walked around to the front of his truck where Kim was standing.

"Did you speak to the dispatcher?" he asked.

Kim nodded, but frowned. "She verified you are who you say you are, but I still don't want you in my house."

Abraham nodded and pressed the call button on the cell phone behind his back. Almost instantly, Kim's phone started ringing. He glanced down and then his head jerked up in bewilderment.

"That's right," Abraham said, slowly producing the cell phone. "You're busted."

The blood drained from Kim's face. "Where...where'd you get that phone?"

"You need to cut the crap and tell me what you know about Debbie Brister," Abraham said coldly. "And you can start by telling me where she is."

"I don't know."

"She texted you this morning and told you she was on her way over here, right?"

Kim nodded. "But she never showed up."

"You do realize that if something bad happened to her, you're going to be at the top of that suspect list, right?"

"Me?" Kim's eyes widened. "I didn't do anything to her!"

"Then you need to start talking and you need to help us find her."

"I have no idea where she could be. She was supposed to meet me here, but she never showed—I swear it."

"Yeah, you also told me you didn't know her, so forgive me if I'm a bit skeptical." Abraham returned to his truck to secure the phone, and Gerard Brister asked him what was going on.

"Did you find my wife?" he asked. "Where is she?"

"I'm working on it." Abraham shut his door and approached Kim. "I need to look inside your garage to make sure she's not here. If you don't let me in, I'll get a search warrant and bust through the door."

Kim exhaled, seemingly deflated. "That won't be necessary. You can search it."

Abraham followed closely behind Kim and watched as he punched in the code to open the garage. He glanced back toward his truck once and saw Gerard craning his neck in an attempt to see through the garage door, which was slowly rising.

Abraham bent over slightly as the bumper of a vehicle came into view. He frowned when he realized it was a pickup truck. Once the door was completely open, he stepped inside and glanced around. The parking bay on the right side was empty—except for a small marijuana plant under a lamp against the wall—and the pickup took up the left side.

"Is that why you didn't want me in here?" Abraham asked, pointing to the marijuana plant.

"I...I..." He clamped his mouth shut and nodded. "Yes, sir. It's for medicinal purposes. I have glaucoma."

"I'll be trading it for a misdemeanor summons before I leave."

Abraham shot a thumb toward the empty parking bay. "Is this where she parks her car when she comes over?"

Kim nodded and hung his head.

"What is it?" Abraham asked, sensing Kim was troubled about something. "What aren't you telling me?"

"It isn't like her not to show up. When she says she's coming over, she does—every single time."

"What do you think happened?"

Kim swallowed hard and licked his lips again. "Ever since that woman was killed—you know, the one they found on the cross?— Debbie has been spooked about our relationship. She said she felt like she was being followed. I thought she was just being paranoid, but when she didn't show up this morning, I started to worry they had taken her."

"Who had taken her?"

"The church."

"What makes you think the church took her?"

"She told me her preacher has been talking about evil women and saying that women who commit adultery should be killed." He wiped the sweat from his face. "I think they got to her."

Abraham scowled. "Did Debbie attend the same church as the first victim?"

"She did." Kim nodded for emphasis. "She thinks the pastor killed that Kathleen lady, because there was a sign over her head that said she was a sinner. She was afraid he would find out about us and kill her, too."

Abraham walked away from Kim and pulled out his cell phone to call Headquarters. When Martha answered, he asked her to patch him through to London Carter's cell phone.

"London?" she asked, surprised. "Why? What's going on?"

"I think we might have another crucifix victim."

CHAPTER 30

Just off the coast of Dark Sands Beach, Mississippi

I hit the reverse on the Jet Ski when I reached the spot where Vaughn Toussaint had been thrown overboard and then shut off the engine. The water patrol officers were scanning the waves that rolled gently in from the Gulf of Mexico.

"He went down right over there," one of them shouted, pointing to a spot in the water.

A Jet Ski slowed to a rocking stop beside me and I turned to see Dawn straddling it. Her wet shirt was stretched tight over her flesh and streams of salt water dripped down her face. "That was a rush," she said breathlessly. "I almost flew off the back when I first gave it the gas."

I nodded and pointed toward where a hand broke the surface of the water. It was followed quickly by Vaughn's head. His eyes were wide and he was gasping for air, choking on water.

"There he is!" I shouted.

With a quick flick of his wrist, one of the water patrol officers sent a life ring sailing through the air. It plopped into the water directly over Vaughn's head and he gratefully wrapped both arms around it. Hanging on like a wet rat on a log, he meekly allowed himself to be pulled toward the boat. While he'd appeared to be a strong swimmer, he was now exhausted and out of breath.

The officers handcuffed Vaughn and sat him in the back of the boat while Dawn and I retrieved the third Jet Ski. We guided it toward the water patrol vessel so they could tow it back to the rental company, and then we all returned to the beach.

Detective McQuarie was standing on the sidewalk beyond the beach eating an ice cream sundae. He smiled when we approached, taking in our drenched clothes. "I don't run after anybody," he said, holding up his left thumb. "I just use this to press the button on my radio, and the suspects miraculously appear—handcuffed and ready to talk."

I grunted in amusement and we followed McQuarie to his cruiser. He raised an eyebrow when we got in all wet, but he didn't say anything about it.

"We'll get you guys some dry clothes at the station," he said. "And then you can interview Mr. Toussaint before we transport him to the county jail."

I thanked him and reached for my phone to see if we'd heard anything from Magnolia, but immediately groaned.

"What is it?" Dawn asked.

I held up the slender paperweight. "It's useless. I drowned it in the water."

Dawn smiled and lifted her phone triumphantly. "You should've gotten a waterproof case."

Cursing myself for settling for the cheaper phone case, I shoved it back in my pocket and stared gloomily out the window. I didn't like wasting money on things I destroyed. When I was a little boy, and before she died, my mom used to call me *Carter the Destroyer*, because I broke all of my toys. My grandma, who raised me, kept the name going. It seemed I hadn't changed much.

CHAPTER 31

Thirty minutes later…

Once Dawn and I were in dry clothes—the shirt and pants they found for me were too tight, while Dawn's clothes were loose—we stepped into the spacious interview room and sat across from Vaughn Toussaint.

"I don't understand what you guys want from me. I've never been to that place you mentioned."

"Magnolia?" Dawn asked, leading the interview. "Maybe not, but it seems Magnolia has been coming to you."

Pulling a photo of Kathleen Bertrand from our file, Dawn slid it across the table. "Do you recognize this woman?"

Vaughn scowled. "Did something happen?"

"You tell us." Dawn leaned back and folded her arms across her chest.

"I mean, two detectives from Louisiana come all the way down to Dark Sands and nearly drown me in the ocean." He grunted and rubbed his hands through his damp hair. "Yeah, I'm guessing something happened."

"What do you think happened?" Dawn asked.

He shrugged. "If I was a betting man—and I am—I'd bet her husband and the preacher found out about us and he sent you guys here to scare me into leaving her alone. The whole, 'Stay out of my town,' kind of thing. Well, that's not legal anymore, you know. I can go wherever I want and I don't care what any church says."

Dawn leaned forward. "Why would you think her preacher sent us?"

"Kathleen said the preacher's real connected down there and he's got a lot of sway with the locals. She said once you join the church, it's hard to get out. It's like a motorcycle gang, but with Bibles." He shook his head sadly. "It's depressing to see how much they control her. Everything's a sin. She can't listen to certain kinds of music, can't watch television unless it's one of those evangelical programs, and they make her wear napkins on her head during mass. Hell, they don't even want to let her divorce that lazy bastard of a husband she's got."

Dawn glanced at me and I knew what she was thinking. She'd worked a case with Brandon Berger ten years ago involving a cultish church and things hadn't turned out so well. She was starting to think this Father Nehemiah Masters was crucifying his parishioners. At this point, I didn't know what to think, but I figured he was as likely a suspect as Joey. The only problem? We couldn't yet prove that either man knew about Kathleen's affair.

Dawn turned back to Vaughn and asked what he knew about Kathleen wanting a divorce.

"I know she wants to leave her husband, but the pastor won't let her because he says it's a sin." He shook his head. "She's terrified that the preacher finds out about us, because he said in a mass that you get the death penalty if you commit adultery…"

Vaughn's voice trailed off and when his expression fell, I knew he had finally figured out why we were there.

"Oh, no," he said, his hands beginning to tremble. "Is it Kathleen? Did something happen to her? Please tell me she's okay—please!"

"I'm so sorry," Dawn said slowly, "but Kathleen was found dead last Wednesday."

"No!" Vaughn fell to the floor and threw up.

Dawn pulled back just in time to avoid getting his vomit all over her wet boots. I wasn't so lucky. As Vaughn remained on his hands and knees retching, Dawn and I tried to calm him down. About a minute later, the door to the interview room burst open and a uniformed officer came in with a handful of paper towels. He handed them to Vaughn and the man cleaned off his mouth as he knelt there crying.

The look on his face had to be one of the most pitiful expressions I'd ever seen. Had he not been an abuser of women, I might've felt sorry for him. Instead, I knew he was crying because he would no longer be able to freeload off of Kathleen.

"Pull yourself together," I said sternly. "We've got more

questions for you."

Vaughn nodded absently and dragged himself back into the chair.

"Do you guys want to move into the interview room across the hall?" the officer asked. "I can get a prisoner to come clean up this mess."

Dawn nodded and thanked him. We stood and led Vaughn across the hall to an identical room. Before Dawn could resume her questioning, Vaughn asked, "How'd she die?"

"I don't think you're ready for details," she said. "Let's just stick to what you—"

"No! I want to know how she died or I'm not saying another word."

Dawn pursed her lips. "Very well...she was crucified."

"Dear God!" I thought Vaughn was going to puke again, but he managed to keep it down. "Are you serious?"

"Very."

"It's that preacher, I just know it! Kathleen said she was afraid of him. She said he gets this look in his eyes when he starts talking about sinful women—I think that's what she called it. It scared the shit out of her. I mean, we loved each other dearly. I'm the only man she ever truly loved. She was going to leave her husband for me, but she was just too scared to pull the trigger. With my help, she was working on it a little at a time."

"Did she talk to anyone about leaving Joey?" Dawn asked.

Vaughn nodded. "She put a down payment on a lawyer, but she said before she could file papers she'd have to find an apartment far away from Plymouth East. She said when she leaves, she'll have to leave all at once and never look back."

"Come on," Dawn said, "did she really think the church would stop her?"

"Not just stop her—she thought they would kill her. That preacher man said you get the death penalty for adultery. That's why she comes here to see me, because she's too afraid to do anything back home. She won't bring me anywhere near that place. She can't risk getting caught." He paused, but then lifted his hand. "Oh, and get this...she can't miss a single sermon or she'll face the wrath of the preacher. She comes out here on Wednesdays, but she can't leave there until after she attends the mass."

"What about vacations?" Dawn asked. "Can church members only take two- and three-day vacations?"

"I asked that same question! She said you have to get special permission from the preacher to miss a church mass."

"You might take offense at this next question," Dawn said, "but that's fine. What did a successful lawyer like Kathleen see in someone like you?"

Vaughn sneered. "She saw the real me and she didn't judge me like the rest of the world."

"Does the real you commit sexual battery on women?" Dawn asked flatly. "Did she even know about that charge? What about all the times you beat your past lovers?"

"I told Kathleen everything about me. She knew I was being railroaded and she believed in me." He stuck his chin out defiantly. "Love is blind, you know."

I was still laughing inside from when he said—with total confidence—that he was the first man Kathleen every truly loved, but this almost caused me to laugh out loud.

"Let's get back to my original question," Dawn said, ignoring the buzzing of her cell phone in her pocket. "What did she see in you?"

"I made her feel safe." Vaughn balled up his fists. "I offered to go down to Louisiana and beat the shit out of that preacher, but she didn't want any trouble. She did tell me we had to be prepared for trouble, though, when she finally made the move."

Dawn checked her notes and then pulled out the printed photo of the mystery moustache man talking to Vaughn at the casino. She slid it across the desk and asked if he knew the man.

"I do remember him." Vaughn grunted. "It's hard to forget that moustache. I thought they outlawed those things a long time ago."

"What'd y'all talk about?"

"We didn't talk. If I remember right, he asked if the machine I played was hitting. I told him no and he just moved on. We might've said a few more words, but it would've been small talk."

"Would it surprise you to know this guy goes to Kathleen's church?"

"What?" Vaughn recoiled in his chair. "They did get to her! It's the church that killed her!"

As Dawn was asking the next question, McQuarie opened the door to the interview room and waved for me to step out and follow him down a long corridor.

"What's up?" I asked when we were in the bureau section.

He pointed to a desk in the corner. "Your sheriff's on the phone. He said he tried calling your cell and Dawn's cell. He said it's an emergency."

I snatched up the phone.

"London, what's going on over there?" Sheriff Chiasson asked, his voice tense.

I gave him an update. "I don't think Vaughn's involved, but he did give us some insight into the church and how controlling the preacher is."

"Well, I need you and Dawn to get back here as fast as you can."

"Why?" I asked, a feeling of dread falling over me. "What happened?"

"Another woman's missing." He went on to tell me the details, including how Abraham Wilson had worked the case all day on his own time and put the crucial pieces together. "I'm going to transfer that kid to the bureau."

I was glad to hear it and said as much, but I couldn't help but think there was something more he wasn't saying. "Sheriff, is something else bothering you?"

"Another woman in our parish is missing—isn't that enough?"

"Come on, you know I've been doing this long enough to know when something's going on."

He sighed heavily on the other end of the phone. "It's the victim."

"What about her?"

"You're not going to believe who she is."

My heart sank when he told me. I dropped the phone in its cradle and leaned against the desk for a long moment. I knew I had to tell Dawn, but I didn't want to. It would upset her, and I didn't like seeing her in the dumps.

I was still leaning against the desk when she stepped out of the interview room. Her face fell when she saw me standing there.

"What's going on?" she asked. "It looks like someone peed in your shoes."

"Did you get anything more out of him?"

She shrugged, still studying my face. "Nothing more than you already heard. So, what's going on?"

"We have to get back to Magnolia."

"Did they find someone else crucified?"

"No, but there's another woman missing and she fits the first victim's profile—she attends the Second Temple Fellowship Church and she was having an adulterous affair."

Dawn nodded thoughtfully. "Is there something more?"

"Yeah." I frowned and stared deep into her eyes. After taking a deep breath and exhaling, I told her.

"No!" She gasped and covered her mouth with one of her hands. Her eyes filled with tears and I quickly moved to hold her. She buried her face against my neck and said, "I...she tried to tell me hello at church last night, but I totally ignored her. I was so rude to her and now she might be dead!"

I remembered the redheaded woman hollering Dawn's name from across the parking lot and the way she'd reacted to the lady. Now I knew why.

"We'll find her," I said with confidence, because I knew we would—I just couldn't promise she'd be alive.

CHAPTER 32

Less than two hours later

I had pushed my truck to its limit on the drive back to Louisiana. Dawn hadn't talked much, and I was okay with it. She'd spent most of the trip with her head pressed against the side glass staring into the darkness that blurred by. Every now and then she'd lean away from the glass and scoot closer to me and rest her head on my shoulder.

When we did talk, we considered the possibility that Nehemiah Masters was behind Kathleen's crucifixion. If he was, and if his motive was to punish evil women, then Debbie's fate was sealed unless we rescued her. If it wasn't Nehemiah, then our only other likely suspect would be Joey Bertrand. While Joey had a motive to kill Kathleen, we didn't know if he was familiar with Debbie. It was possible he might target another woman to make it look like a pattern killer was responsible for Kathleen, and thereby throwing the scent off of himself, but how would he know Debbie was also a cheater? Hell, at this point, we didn't even know if he knew Kathleen was a cheater. And, of course, there was the mysterious moustache man. Why had he followed Kathleen to Dark Sands and was he involved in her murder?

I cursed silently when I turned into the detective bureau parking lot in Payneville. "Look at all the cars."

Dawn nodded absently and I made the round of the building and parked along the shoulder of the road a block away. I shut off the engine and was about to step out when she grabbed my arm to stop me.

"Debbie used to be like family to me," she said. "Even though I don't like the person she's become, I still have that familial attachment to her. If we find her dead—if she's been crucified—I don't think I'll be able to process her body. I want to work this case and see it through to the end, but I don't want to see her like that."

I reached over and squeezed her shoulder. "It's okay, love, I'll take care of everything."

She smiled warmly, a few tears rolling down her cheeks. "Thank you for always being here for me."

I leaned over and kissed her soft lips, tasting the salt from her tears. "I'm never going anywhere."

She smiled again and turned toward the door, holding her head up strongly and pushing it open. I followed her into the bureau and squinted as the bright lights hit us. Sheriff Corey Chiasson, who was addressing a standing-room-only crowd of officers, looked up when we walked in. He told everyone to get to work and then waved for Dawn and me to follow him into the conference room, where he kicked out a couple of officers who were studying maps of Plymouth East.

"Half of the detective bureau and a quarter of the patrol division are scouring the cane fields in Plymouth East," he said, walking around the large table and dropping into a chair. He waved for us to sit, and we did. "I've got two dozen members of the fire department and fifty reserve deputies working with them." He rubbed the sweat from his forehead. "We have to find her alive. We need to get to this bastard before he crucifies her."

"Is Ben up in the air?"

"He's doing what he can, but it's hard to penetrate the sugarcane fields at night, even with that big light he has. The state police offered to send one of their choppers up, too, and I've accepted. They'll be here at first light. Also, I got with the head of the crime lab and they're throwing everything they have on this case. They've already worked up a DNA profile on the saliva you submitted and they're running it through CODIS (Combined DNA Index System)." He paused and looked at Dawn for a long moment. "I know this'll be tough on you, but are you up for it?"

Dawn bit down hard and nodded. "I want to work this case."

"Good, that's what I want to hear. While we're out there trying to bring Debbie back home, I want you two concentrating on the case. Run down every lead you've got and use every resource you need. If you need more people, let me know. We'll do whatever it takes to resolve this before anyone else dies."

We all stood to leave, but Dawn stopped with her hand on the door. "Where is he, Sheriff?" she asked. "I want to see him before we go back out there."

The sheriff nodded and pointed down the hall. "He's in my office."

"Walk with me," Dawn whispered, and then led the way down the hall. She stopped outside the sheriff's office and knocked lightly on the door.

"Come in," called Captain Brandon Berger, his voice low and somber.

Dawn opened the door and we stepped inside to see Brandon sitting on a couch with Samantha, his fifteen-year-old daughter, and Kristen Boyd, his wife of five years. Samantha's eyes were already red, but when she saw Dawn she jumped from the couch and rushed into her arms. The two of them held each other and cried, with Samantha begging Dawn to find her mother alive and bring her back home.

CHAPTER 33

While Dawn comforted Samantha, I asked Brandon if I could have a minute of his time. He spoke briefly to Kristen and then followed me out the door. When we were alone in the hallway, I told him how sorry I was about Debbie.

"Dawn and I will do everything we can to get her back," I said. "I'm sure the sheriff told you how the case is progressing, so you're aware we're looking at this church in Plymouth East."

"He did and I am." He glanced toward the door as though making sure it was closed. "Dawn lost a bit of faith in religion when we investigated the Magnolia Life Church, and I'm worried she might let that experience skew her judgment with this case."

"She'll be fine," I said. "That case taught her a lot—*you* taught her a lot—and she'll only go where the evidence takes her."

Brandon was silent for a few seconds. When he spoke again, he sounded troubled. "If she...if they crucify her, I'll feel responsible."

"That's nonsense, Brandon, and you know it."

"I didn't have to divorce her, you know. I could've given her another chance." He leaned back against the door and folded his arms across his chest. "By divorcing her, I changed the whole course of her life. I set her on the path she's traveling now, and if that leads to her death, I'm partially to blame for Samantha losing her mother."

As I studied Brandon's face, I realized we were a lot alike, and I also realized he was right. He wasn't saying what he was saying for sympathy and he certainly wasn't feeling sorry for himself. He was stating a philosophical fact.

I nodded. "You're right about changing the course of her life, but you didn't set her on the path she took today. She's the one who decided to sneak out of bed and go meet her lover—no one else."

"I guess you're right."

"Look, while we're operating off the premise that she's been taken, do you think there's the slightest chance she ran away? I hear the church is very controlling, so she might've had enough and just wanted to be free from their clutches."

"Are you asking me if she's ever done this kind of thing before?"

"You know it."

"When I was married to her, I spent more time at work than I did at home, so you can imagine the strain that put on our relationship." He shook his head. "I messed up one night and broke our anniversary reservations to work a death investigation. When I remembered the reservations and tried to call her, she'd turned off her phone. I looked all over town for her and kept calling late into the night, but she didn't answer and she didn't come home. When I woke up the next morning, she was back and said she had kept the reservations I had made for us."

Brandon shook his head. "She's done other irrational things since then—mostly while we were going through the divorce—so we can't rule out the possibility she ran off, but it doesn't feel right. It seems she would eventually come back, and she hasn't."

"Yeah," I agreed. "You know as well as I do how bad this is, but we've got a good lead and we're not going to rest until we find her."

"Thanks." He turned and walked back into the sheriff's office, where Dawn was just standing to leave. She gave Samantha one last hug and then turned to Brandon. "We'll do everything we can to find Debbie...I promise." She then hurried out into the hallway.

It was still daylight when we stepped out into the parking lot and began the long hike to my truck, but the sun was sliding low in the distant horizon and I knew it would be dark soon.

"Who first?" I asked Dawn once we'd reached my truck and I'd cranked up the engine. "The preacher or the husband?"

Dawn chewed on her lower lip. "We need to identify the dude with the moustache, so I'm thinking Nehemiah. We also need to find out about his conversation with Kathleen and whether or not Joey knew she was having an affair."

"At this point, we don't know if Nehemiah knew about the affair," I said. "If he did, that puts him just as high on the suspect list as Joey."

Dawn nodded. "I just want to make sure I'm not being biased because of the Magnolia Life Church."

"I didn't work the Magnolia Life case, so I'm as neutral as they come, and I say Nehemiah's got some explaining to do. Especially after that sermon where he proclaimed women who cheat should get the death penalty."

"And what do men get—a door prize?" Dawn asked idly, still overcome by emotion from learning that Brandon's ex-wife was a possible victim. "I'd still like to have a word with Nehemiah's wife."

"Me, too." I twisted in my seat as I drove, wishing I had time to change out of the tight pants I'd been given at the Dark Sands Police Department. While they were better than wet clothes, it was only by a little bit.

The shadows had grown longer by the time we pulled into the Second Temple Fellowship parking lot.

"How do we get to the front door of his house?" Dawn asked, stepping out of my truck and shutting the door. "Do we go through the church, or is it around the back?"

I walked around to the side of the building and looked toward the back of the property, where a cemetery was spread out across the expansive property. A large barn was beyond the grave sites and resting up against a line of trees, and I pointed. "Maybe that's the house."

Dawn shrugged and we began walking in that direction. As we neared the corner of the church building, the side door burst open and a woman stepped out, screeching in surprise.

We spun to see Nehemiah's wife standing on the top step with a mop bucket and a terrified look on her face.

I smiled to reassure her. "Hey, we're with the sheriff's office. We were here last night—at the service."

The woman's sky-blue eyes were wide and her pale face seemed to turn even paler. "I…I'm not allowed to converse with men outside the presence of my husband."

Dawn stepped between us and nodded warmly. "You don't have to speak with him," she said softly. "You and I can have a conversation."

"I…I don't know if it's allowed."

"There's no harm in two girls talking." Dawn stepped closer to her. "I'm Dawn. What's your name?"

"Gretchen. Gretchen Masters."

"So, you must be Nehemiah's wife?"

She nodded slowly, brushing her wind-blown blonde hair out of her face. "I am his wife."

Dawn glanced around. "Is he here?"

Gretchen shook her head.

"Where is he?"

"He does not always tell me where he goes," she said. "And it is not proper for a wife to ask."

"Girlfriend," Dawn said more forcefully, "it's time someone sat you down and had a good long talk with you about the free world. But first, I need to ask you some questions about Nehemiah."

CHAPTER 34

Somewhere in Magnolia, Louisiana

Debbie had drifted in and out of sleep ever since being brought to this place. She didn't know where she was, but she got the feeling it was some kind of warehouse or workshop.

Once the law enforcement imposter had dragged her from the window of her car, he had put her in some kind of strangle hold and squeezed tightly until she had passed out. The last conscious memory she had of that moment was when warm urine poured down her leg as her body loosened up in preparation to give up the ghost.

When she regained consciousness a few moments later, she was tied up, bouncing around in the trunk of a car, and confused. What was going on? Who had taken her? She didn't allow herself to consider the possibility that she was headed for the same fate as Kathleen Bertrand. Each time her mind went there, she screamed into the gag that was strapped across her mouth and squeezed her blindfolded eyes tighter.

It had been hard to keep track of the passing time, but she figured the car had stopped after driving for thirty minutes and then the trunk had popped open. Strong arms had jerked her out of the trunk and strangled her again. She woke up stretched out on a soft surface, still gagged and blindfolded. With no one around and nothing to do, she drifted off and fell into a restless slumber that was filled with nightmares of masked men and women carrying torches and dragging her to her death.

Now awake, she lay still and tried to determine what had stirred her from her sleep. Something clicked in the distance and she twisted her head to better hear the sound. When she moved, the springs from the old mattress beneath her body squealed. She winced. She didn't want the source of the noise to know she was alert.

She felt a warm draft caressing her bare skin and she knew someone had opened a door. She didn't like being naked in front of strangers, and being tied spread-eagle on a bed made her feel especially vulnerable and helpless. Should she beg or just lie still?

Footsteps shuffled closer and she tensed up, waiting in terror for whatever would happen next. The footsteps stopped beside her bed and she could sense a presence looming over her.

"I see you are awake," said a calming male voice. He sounded vaguely familiar, but it also sounded like he was trying to disguise his voice. "This is good, because I have something for you."

Debbie involuntarily jerked away when the hands touched her face.

"Relax, Debbie Brister," the man said. "I am not going to hurt you today."

Today? Debbie gasped.

"You seem surprised. Did you think your sins would go unpunished?"

Debbie didn't utter a grunt or a moan or anything. She just lay there shivering as the man removed the gag from her mouth. The rag was filthy. It tasted like old dish water and she was happy to have it out of her mouth, if only for a short time. She flinched when the man rubbed the tips of his fingers against her lips, pushing them into her mouth.

"Ah, a strange woman's mouth is smoother than oil," he said slowly, "but her end is as bitter as wormwood."

Those words—I've heard them before!

"Father Masters?" Debbie asked hoarsely, her voice dry from lack of moisture. "Is that...is it you?"

The man laughed and she felt an unexpected stream of cold water squirt into her mouth. She hurriedly gulped it down, swallowing as fast as she could, but she was unable to keep up with the flow and had to turn her head to keep from choking. The cold liquid shot across the side of her face and down her neck and breasts, causing her to shiver.

"Drink it up," the man said. "You need to be well-hydrated for Wednesday."

"What's happening Wednesday?" Debbie asked once she'd caught her breath. "What are you going to do to me?"

"Your sins have found you out, Debbie Brister. Wednesday will be your day of reckoning."

"*Reckoning?*" Debbie's voice was shrill. "What in the hell does that even mean? Who are you and why are you doing this? Do you know who my ex-husband is? He's probably out there right now looking for me, and he'll find me—you'd better believe he will. And when he finds me, you're going to regret you ever tried to mess with me!"

"Of course, he's going to find you—I will make sure of it. However, he will not find you until the time is right and you have paid for your sins. If you are not found, your death will have been in vain and no one will benefit from the lesson to be learned."

"I've done nothing wrong! I haven't sinned!" Debbie was crying now, wailing in desperation. "Please, you've got to let me go! I have a daughter and husband who need me!"

"A daughter you never see and a husband you betrayed in the worst possible way." The man sighed. "No, Debbie Brister, the wages of sin is death, and your sin of adultery will not go unpunished. You did not heed my first warning, so you will have to suffer the consequences."

Debbie began to tremble uncontrollably as the realization of her plight registered. *I'm going to be crucified like Kathleen Bertrand!*

"Oh, God, *no!* I'm so sorry. I'll never do anything like that again. Please, just let me live and I'll serve God for the rest of my life."

"If you ask the Lord for forgiveness, He might grant it to you."

"I do! I do! I ask God for forgiveness. I'm so sorry for what I've done."

"You do sound sincere, so I think the Lord might hear your prayers."

"Thank you, God," Debbie said, relief flooding over her. "Thank you so much for hearing my prayers."

"If the Lord does, indeed, decide to forgive you, He might allow you to enter into the Kingdom of Heaven on Wednesday—"

"What?" She twisted around and jerked on the chains that bound her wrists and ankles. "I've been forgiven! You've got to let me go now."

"Oh, nonsense, Debbie Brister," the man said, shoving the dirty rag back into her mouth. "Our Lord is a just Ruler. While He may forgive you, He still must wield the rod of correction so that others might realize the benefit of your sins. Your punishment will serve as a warning to the other evil women in this community. My prayer is that they heed this warning and do not continue in their evil ways. For if they do not turn away from their sinful ways, they, too, will know the wrath of God and they will suffer greatly at the hand of His agent."

Debbie cried hysterically, but the thick rag reduced the sounds to a low muffle. No one could hear her. She couldn't escape. She was going to die.

CHAPTER 35

Second Temple Fellowship, Plymouth East, Louisiana

I'd watched for fifteen minutes as Dawn tried to get Gretchen Masters to turn on her husband, but the woman was either extremely loyal or deathly afraid to go against whom she referred to as a "man of God". She wouldn't even let us through the front door because Nehemiah wasn't home, and Dawn and I had been forced to stand on the front steps as the sun went down and the volume of mosquitoes went up. Gretchen didn't have a problem with the mosquitoes, because she was standing safely inside the screen door, which she had locked.

"Well," Dawn finally said, "do you have any idea when your husband will be home?"

"As I've already told you, he doesn't always tell me—"

"Right, right, and it's not proper for a wife to ask. Got it." Dawn shot a thumb toward my truck. "We'll be waiting right there in the parking lot. It doesn't matter what time he gets home, because we've got all night and into tomorrow if necessary."

A shoe scraped against a rocky surface somewhere in the darkness behind us and I spun, instantly dropping my hand to my pistol.

"Whoa, detective!" said Nehemiah Masters, who was approaching from the cemetery. "It would not bode well for you to shoot an unarmed reverend on the Lord's property."

I squinted suspiciously, but decided I needed to play nice with the preacher.

"You're just the man we've been looking for," I said cheerfully, extending my hand. Once we shook, I told him we needed his help. "May we come inside and talk with you for a few minutes?"

"Certainly." He walked past us and ascended the steps, stopping long enough to tell Gretchen to tend to the children before holding the screen door open and waving us inside.

We found ourselves in a simple kitchen. It was square with plain cabinets, a cheap refrigerator, an old stove, and a homemade wooden table. "Please, take a seat," Nehemiah said, pointing to the chairs shoved under each side of the table. He sat at the head of the table and placed both hands in his lap. "What is it that I can do for the Magnolia Sheriff's Department?"

"Well, some information has come to light and I was wondering if you could verify a few things for us," I began. "First, we need to ask you about Kathleen Bertrand."

"What about Sister Bertrand?"

"Well, someone said she came to you with marital issues—that she was seeking advice on whether or not she could divorce her husband."

Nehemiah nodded slowly, seemingly considering something. "I'm sure you have heard of pastoral confidentiality, detective. I am required by law to keep all private communications with my flock confidential."

"Not all communication is privileged, as I'm sure you're aware," I countered. "In this case, the church member is deceased and the information would be used to catch her killer—it would not be used against her—so I can assure you, you're on solid legal footing."

"It is not merely about legal footing. The members of my congregation must know that they can rely on me to hold their secrets sacred." He frowned and shook his head. "I am afraid I cannot indulge you."

"I respect your position, Father, but it is imperative that I find out one thing, and it's not about Kathleen." I leaned forward, resting my forearms on the table. "Did Joey Bertrand know Kathleen was having an affair?"

There was not a hint of shock in his expression. Either he was a good poker player, or he knew about Kathleen's affair.

"It is impossible for me to comment on what Mr. Bertrand knew or did not know. I am sorry, but I cannot help you."

"Fair enough, but there is something you will be able to tell me." I reached for the file folder Dawn was holding. When she handed it to me, I removed the printed screen grab of Moustache from the Dark Sands Casino surveillance video. I slid it across the table. "This guy's a member of your church. What's his name?"

Nehemiah pulled some reading glasses from his pocket and made a show of putting them on. He then pulled the photo close to his face and nodded. "Ah, yes, this is Brother Virgil Brunner. He is a member of my flock."

"Flock of what?" I wanted to ask. *"Sheep or ducks?"*

"Can you tell me where I can find him?" I asked instead.

"At his house, I imagine." Nehemiah pocketed his glasses and slid the photo back toward me.

"And where might that be?"

"Brother Virgil lives on his late father's property. Their ancestors settled the land on the eastern tip of the community, and it is here that he and his family still remain." He gave a casual wave of his hand. "Virgil is a good man, so might I ask why you are carrying around a photograph of him?"

"I'd love to indulge you, but this is police business."

If he was responsible for killing Kathleen and abducting Debbie, Nehemiah sure was being cool about it. I wanted his DNA, but I didn't think he would give it willingly. Still, it was worth a shot. Before I asked for it, I needed a firm denial from him that he had never spat in Kathleen's face—either during the murder or any time before it—so we could take away any defenses he might later have if it was proven to be his DNA.

"Father, have you ever been involved in a disagreement with Kathleen Bertrand?"

"How do you mean?"

"Have you two ever argued?" I asked. "You know, where she was yelling at you and you were yelling at her?"

"I do not raise my voice toward my sheep, and they would never argue with me."

"So, there would be no reason for you to spit in her face, is that right?"

Nehemiah revolted in horror. "I would never spit in the face of anyone."

"I expected you would say that, Father," I said in a friendly tone. "Did you talk to her at all Wednesday night—before, during, or after the service?"

"I did not even see Sister Bertrand Wednesday night. You must understand, I have a large congregation and it is not possible for me to notice every member on every day."

"Are you sure you didn't see her or talk to her?"

"I am one hundred percent certain."

Now that I had my firm denial, I asked if I could have a sample of his DNA.

His brow furrowed. "And why might you want my DNA?"

"We're asking anyone who knew Mrs. Bertrand to voluntarily submit their DNA so we can eliminate as many acquaintances as possible and move on to more plausible suspects," I explained. "Just routine police work."

Nehemiah smiled, and I detected a sense of arrogance in his expression. "I will make it easy for you and eliminate myself. I did not kill Sister Bertrand. I am the shepherd, not the wolf. I protect my sheep."

You didn't do such a great job, I thought, standing to leave. I thanked him for his time and Dawn and I made our way to the door. I stopped just before pushing through it and turned to face Nehemiah. "It's a shame about Debbie Brister, isn't it?"

"It is, indeed."

"I understand she was also a member of your church."

"Yes, she was."

"I also understand she was having an affair, just like Kathleen Bertrand."

"I was not aware." Nehemiah seemed in a hurry for us to leave, so I stayed a little longer.

"What do you know about Gerard Brister?"

"I know that Brother Gerard is a man of God and he is a faithful servant. He has been a parishioner here for many years. If you are thinking he had anything to do with his wife's disappearance, I can assure you that you are mistaken."

"Yeah..." I nodded thoughtfully. "Gerard's a man of God and Debbie—what is she?"

"Pardon me?" Nehemiah shifted his feet ever so slightly.

"Last night, you said the wages of sin is death and you said these evil and adulterous women will find their places in the pits of hell. Is that how you really feel? Do you believe Debbie deserves to die for cheating on Gerard?"

"I am sorry, detective, but you have taken my message out of context and I would appreciate it if you would leave now. There are matters to which I must attend."

"Before we go, is it okay if we search that barn in the back?"

Nehemiah cocked his head back. "Why on earth would you want to do that?"

"We're scouring the entire community in search of Debbie Brister," I explained. "Just a matter of routine."

"I assure you, Debbie Brister is not in the church barn. Now, if you will excuse me…"

With that, Nehemiah Brister pushed the door closed and switched off the outdoor light.

On the walk back to my truck, I called Jerry Allemand, who was second in command over my sniper team.

"Jerry, I want round-the-clock surveillance on a barn behind the Second Temple Fellowship Church in Plymouth East. The preacher won't give us permission to search, so I need to know why."

"Sure thing," he said. "I'm at the detective bureau with Andrew. We'll head that way now."

Andrew Hacker was a patrol deputy and one of my newer snipers, along with Rachael Bowler, who was a detective. Rachael would be busy with investigative duties, so the only other sniper I had available was Ray Sevin, a veteran who had been with Jerry and me through thick and thin. I called Ray and asked him to be on standby in the event we needed him, and then I turned to Dawn.

"Let's hang out across the street until Jerry and Andrew are in place," I suggested. "And then we can try to find this Virgil Brunner character."

Dawn was chewing her lower lip and I thought it would start bleeding. "We need to get in that barn," she said.

"We don't have enough for a warrant and he won't let us search it." I sighed. "I want to bust that door down as bad as anyone, but we can't. We'll give Jerry and Andrew some time to pull surveillance and see if they can develop probable cause for a warrant. If he's hiding something, they'll find it."

"But what if Debbie's inside the barn right at this moment?"

"What if she's not?"

Dawn looked away and was silent for a long moment. When she spoke, her voice was harder than I've ever heard it. "If I get half a chance, I'm going to kill the bastard who's torturing these women, and God help anyone who tries to stop me."

CHAPTER 36

8:47 p.m.
Virgil Brunner's Property, Plymouth East, Louisiana

While it was dark as sin outside, Virgil Brunner's property was lit up like the daytime. His house squatted at the center of a dozen—or more—acres of pristine lawn, but there was no way we were getting close to it. A solid brick fence that was ten feet high and at least two feet thick had its loving arms wrapped securely around the entire plot of land.

Dawn pointed to the large metal gate that stood between us and Brunner's mini-mansion. "How in the hell are we supposed to let him know we're here?"

I drove as close to the gate as I could and looked for a call button. I didn't see one. Perched above the large columns on either side of the gate were high-tech security cameras. I got the feeling he already knew we were there and pointed to the cameras. Dawn grunted.

"He's a private investigator, not a former president," she said, her voice dripping with sarcasm. "I swear, if he doesn't open that gate in a hurry, I'm going to—"

Before she could finish her sentence, the gate lurched and slowly parted inward, creating an opening large enough for us to drive through.

"Okay...I guess he heard you." I drove down the smooth driveway and immediately heard a loud chorus of barking from the other side of the property. "Okay...that's never a good sign."

There were at least half a dozen outbuildings situated around the property and I studied them as I drove by. They appeared to be workshops of some sort, but they were all cloaked in darkness and seemed to be out of commission. There wasn't even the slightest glow from inside, as one would expect from computer screens or smoke detectors or other power equipment.

We had run Virgil's name and learned he ran his own private investigation firm, but that didn't explain this appearance of wealth.

"What kind of PI makes this kind of loot?" Dawn asked when I pulled my truck to a stop in front of the house.

The barking grew nearer and a pack of German shepherds converged on my truck, barking as they circled us.

"I don't know, but"—I shoved the gearshift in park and opened my door—"I'm about to find out how reasonable these dogs are."

"Detective, wait!" boomed a man's voice from the front door. It was Virgil Brunner (AKA: Moustache) and he was rushing down the steps wearing nothing but gym shorts and an undershirt. "They'll bite and I don't want you shooting them."

"I won't shoot them," I replied, closing the door to my truck and standing firm as they surrounded me and barked viciously. I didn't flinch as they lunged at me, and it seemed to confuse them. I focused on the one that seemed to be the leader of the pack and spoke in a commanding voice, telling him to sit. He continued growling, but didn't advance anymore. After a few more forceful commands, he slowly lowered his back side and the other dogs followed suit.

Virgil stopped a few feet away and stared wide eyed. "Damn, you're good with dogs. The last person who stepped out of a car in my yard nearly lost a leg."

After calling off his dogs, Virgil apologized for his appearance and led us up the steps and into his house. "Make yourselves at home while I put on some clothes." He turned and hollered, "Skylar! We've got company...they're detectives."

Virgil left Dawn and I alone in the foyer and hurried up a flight of stairs. I shrugged and sauntered through the opening and we found ourselves standing in a modest living room. I was surprised by how simple the interior of the home was, given the elaborate setup on the outside.

"Hello, detectives," called a feminine voice from the opposite side of the living room. "I'm Skylar Brunner. Virgil will be down in a minute. Can I get you something to drink while waiting?"

Skylar was a few inches shorter than Dawn, but a little heavier. She carried herself well and her straight dirty blonde hair was pulled into a neat bun.

I turned down the drink and told Skylar who we were.

"Are you here about Debbie Brister?" Her face was laced with concern and her gray eyes were moist.

"Did you know Debbie?" I asked, allowing her to assume we were there for Debbie.

"No, but I mailed an invoice to her husband, Gerard, for services Virgil provided, so I figured that's why y'all wanted to talk to—"

"Hey, everyone," Virgil said, interrupting Skylar, "let's take the party to my office."

Skylar frowned, wondering if she'd said too much, and stood on her tiptoes to give Virgil a quick kiss on the cheek as he led the way out the door. The pack of German shepherds jumped to attention, but Virgil uttered a voice command and they plopped down wherever they happened to be standing. They didn't pay any more attention to us.

"You've got a nice place here," I said as we descended the steps and followed a concrete sidewalk toward one of the outbuildings. "You must have some wealthy clients."

Virgil laughed. "Not even close. I inherited the house from my dad and he inherited it from my grandpa. Had this property not already been bought and paid for, Skylar and I would be living on a small lot with a wooden picket fence—and a short one, at that. Hell, you should've seen our shitty apartment in New Orleans when we were first starting out."

"What'd your dad do for a living?" I asked.

"He ran a successful cabinet business." Virgil frowned when he stopped to open the door to his office. "Dad wanted me to go into the family business and take over when he died, but it wasn't in my blood."

I stepped back so Dawn could enter first and then I followed her inside. Virgil flipped a light switch on and took his seat behind a large metal desk. Dawn sat across from him, but I stopped and read the heading on a news article pinned to the wall behind Virgil's chair.

The caption, which was dated fifteen years earlier, read, "Off-duty detective intervenes in armed robbery, stabbed." There was a faded photo of a man lying on the ground and several people huddled around him. One person, who appeared to be a homeless man, was holding pressure on a bloody wound, and there was a young lady standing nearby chewing on her fingernails. I scanned over the article. Apparently, Virgil had saved a homeless man from being robbed, but had been stabbed in the process. It seemed that the homeless man had gone from victim to hero himself.

"As this homeless man's hero lay dying," the article read, *"the homeless man sprang into action and became a hero himself, saving the off-duty detective's life…"*

CHAPTER 37

"You were a cop," I said to Virgil as I took my seat beside Dawn.

Virgil glanced over his shoulder and grunted. "That was a lifetime ago."

I studied this man with the thick moustache. His hair was normally slicked-back and shiny, but tonight it was dull and unruly and, from this distance, I could see some gray on his upper lip.

"What happened?" I asked. "Why aren't you a cop anymore?"

"I didn't recover fast enough, that's what happened." He sighed. "I was off-duty at the time of the injury, so it wasn't covered by Workman's Comp. When I ran out of vacation time and sick leave, they terminated me."

I'd heard of that kind of thing happening before, so I wasn't surprised.

"They told me I could reapply for my job once the doctors cleared me for duty, but I was done." Virgil smirked. "You know, after firing me, the city had the nerve to invite me to their awards banquet to honor me for disrupting the armed robbery. Needless to say, I didn't show up to receive the bullshit award and I told the chief what he could do with it."

After he finished his story, I turned to the subject at hand. While we were here to talk about Kathleen, Skylar had confirmed a connection between him and Debbie, so that's the angle I pursued first.

"Your wife mentioned Gerard Brister was a client. What kind of investigative work did he request?"

"I figured you'd want to discuss my clients and, as a former cop, I'm going to respect your every request." He paused and stared into my eyes first and then Dawn's, as though trying to determine if he could trust us. "However, I have to ask that you keep everything we discuss confidential. I know you might need to use some of the information to build your case, but please be discreet and only use what's absolutely necessary."

I assured him we would and again asked why Gerard had hired him.

"Well, unfortunately, the majority of my clients suspect their spouses of cheating, and Gerard Brister was one of those clients."

"We all know he had good reason to suspect her," I said. "One of our deputies took a statement from her lover earlier today."

Virgil nodded. "I began following her two months ago and I was able to document eight meetings between her and Kim Berry."

"How'd you document the meetings?"

"Photographs, mostly."

"Were you following her early this morning when she went missing?"

"Of course not." Virgil appeared slightly offended. "She wouldn't have gone missing if I would've been following her."

"You said you documented the case *mostly* with photographs—what other methods of documentation did you use?"

"With Mr. Brister's permission, I installed a tracker on his wife's car."

"Please tell me you forgot the tracker on her car."

He frowned. "I retrieved it last week after I concluded the investigation."

I cursed silently. That would've been too good to be true, but I'd take any break I could get. I'd once solved a murder case by knocking on the wrong door, and I didn't complain one bit about it.

When I asked to see the photographs from the case, Virgil said he didn't have any, but he'd give me what he did have. He stood and walked to the far end of the room. After pulling out a key that hung from a rope around his neck, he opened the door to a closet where a giant fireproof safe was located. He entered the access code by rotating the dial back and forth and then pulled the heavy door opened. When he returned to his desk, he placed a thin file folder in front of us.

"This is my report detailing the surveillance. The cliff notes version: she'd sneak out at night, drive to Kim Berry's house, hide her car in his garage, and then leave about an hour or two later."

"Did you photograph any physical interaction between the two of them?"

"I caught them making out near the entrance a few times and once in the garage right before she backed her car out."

"What'd you do with the photographs, and why don't you have them anymore?"

"Adultery is a very private and embarrassing event," Virgil explained. "I mean, I've made my own share of mistakes—trust me, those days ended the night I got stabbed—and I know how hurtful it can be to the one you love, especially if it's made public. So, my policy is to destroy any photograph that could potentially cast an individual in an embarrassing light."

I cocked my head to the side. "Do you at least show the evidence to your client before you destroy them? I mean, how are they supposed to use it in divorce court?"

"I do better than show them." Virgil explained that his policy was to print one copy of all the photographs and present that copy to the client in a sealed envelope. "The photographs I took of Debbie Brister were hand-delivered to Gerard last week, along with a copy of my report, and he was informed that the originals were destroyed. Nowadays, with accounts being hacked and compromising photographs being put up on the 'web, it's too risky to keep digital copies floating around. Before I take on a new case, the client is aware that I don't keep copies of video footage or photographs, so if it gets out into the public somehow, it's totally on them."

As I sat there pondering this information and wondering what it meant to the case, Dawn tilted her notebook so I could see a message she'd scribbled for me.

Having had the flow of many interviews disrupted by a question from a fellow detective, Dawn and I had a habit of keeping our mouths shut while the other was conducting an interview. We usually reserved our questions or comments for the end of the interview, but she wanted me to ask him who else knew about Debbie's infidelity, and she wanted to know the same thing about Kathleen. Her note read, *"If he's so secretive, that narrows the suspect pool to him and the husbands—unless we can prove Nehemiah knew the women were 'sinners'."*

I nodded idly, as realization slowly poured over me. Virgil Brunner was the only common denominator between both women. As Dawn pointed out, if he hadn't told anyone else about the women's affairs, it left him as the one person who knew they were so-called "sinners".

I turned my attention back to Virgil, who had noticed our silent exchange. The skin around his eyes tightened. If it came down to me having to interrogate him, I knew I'd have to approach him with logic and direct evidence, rather than trickery. Games wouldn't work on him, because he had probably played all of them himself when he was a detective.

CHAPTER 38

I held my hand out to Dawn and she gave me the surveillance photo of Virgil at Dark Sands Casino. "My partner was just reminding me to ask about Kathleen Bertrand."

Virgil studied the picture I handed him. "I had to track her all the way to Mississippi," he said, "but after that, it was easy to catch her messing around. I guess she figured crossing the state line made her invisible, because she acted like that guy was her husband. She hung all over him...they made out at the poker machines...he was always grabbing her ass. It was quite a spectacle."

"Did you ever identify him?" I asked.

"No. I tried striking up a conversation with him, but he didn't care to talk to me. My boobs weren't big enough and my skirt wasn't short enough." Virgil slid the photo in my direction. "When I first heard about Kathleen, I thought Joey killed her. I saw you two sitting in church last night and I wanted to talk to you, but I didn't want to violate my confidentiality agreement with my client." He threw his hands up. "If you come to question me, I have no choice but to cooperate with an investigation, but I felt I'd be stepping over the line if I approached you without real evidence."

I grunted. "Could you tell we were cops?"

"Not her"—Virgil shot his thumb in Dawn's direction—"but you've got it written all over you."

Dawn jabbed my arm playfully. "I told you!"

I gave a fake laugh, and then asked Virgil why he suspected Joey of killing his wife.

"A few days after I send him the packet confirming his wife is cheating, she's found dead and a note's attached to her body declaring her a sinner," he said. "It made perfect sense to me, except I can't imagine him being so evil. Hell, I saw a lot as a detective, but I can't imagine *anyone* doing this to a woman. It's one thing to kill your spouse in a fit of jealous rage, but to crucify her..." He shook his head. "That's one sick bastard."

Dawn and I exchanged glances. Joey had lied to us. But why? And why hadn't he let us search his home? Was it that he didn't want us to suspect him of murdering Kathleen, or was it because he did murder her?

I turned back to Virgil and placed my hands flat on the table. "I'll be honest with you, Virgil...you're the only common denominator between Kathleen and Debbie. As of right now, we're not positive Debbie is a victim of the crucifier, but things aren't looking good for her."

"What are you saying?" Virgil looked me directly in the eyes. "Do you think I did this?"

"Did you?"

"No, I didn't."

Our eyes remained locked and he didn't waver. He appeared to be telling the truth, but he was a former detective and he knew the game, so I had to treat his reactions as suspect.

"Knowing what you know, do you still think Joey did it?" I asked.

"Initially, my money would've been on him, but I don't know anymore."

"What about Gerard? Do you think he's capable of killing Debbie?"

"Absolutely not." Virgil shook his head for emphasis. "He's a very religious man. When he first came to me, he was crying hysterically, saying how guilty he felt for thinking his wife was cheating on him."

I drummed my pen on the desk. There was still the possibility that Gerard hurt Debbie, but not in the same manner as Kathleen. The two incidents could be totally unrelated, so I decided to remain focused on Kathleen at the moment.

"Other than you and Joey, who else knew that Kathleen was having the affair?"

"No one—unless Joey told someone."

"What about your wife?"

He shook his head. "No one."

"Do you have any other investigators working for you?"

"I have one employee—his name's Keenan Tipton—but he's not

an investigator. I conduct all the investigations myself."

"What does Keenan do?"

"He runs errands for me, he'll pick up groceries for Skylar, he tends to the dogs, and he does odd jobs around the house. That's about it. He doesn't know anything about my cases."

"How can you be so sure?" I pressed, wanting him to prove to me that he was the only one who knew. If he did prove it, he would help narrow the suspect pool down to himself, Joey and Gerard—unless we could prove Nehemiah knew something.

"I handle my photographs like evidence, because that's exactly what they are," he explained. "Once I take them, I come back to the office and lock them in the safe. I'm the only one with the key to the wooden cabinet and no one knows the combination to my safe. Once the investigation is complete, I print one copy of the photographs and one copy of my report. I place the report and photographs in a large envelope that I immediately seal. I put evidence tape across the seal and affix my signature and date across the tape. I then burn the SD card that holds the photographs in the fire pit out back and the envelope is hand-delivered to the client. The original copy of my report is locked in the safe, and I destroy my records by fire every three years."

"Are you sure your wife doesn't know the results of your investigations?" I asked. "Don't you ever talk to her about the cases?"

"I don't talk to her or anyone about my cases. Look…" He leaned forward and rested his forearms on the desk. "Can you imagine how long my business would last in a small community like this if word got out that I gossiped about my cases? I'd have no choice but to start making cabinets, because no one would ever trust me to investigate their cases again."

He was absolutely correct, and I believed him when he said he didn't tell anyone, not even his wife. I was beginning to wonder if he was involved. He seemed like a straight shooter and I liked him, but that didn't mean he was clean. I just couldn't imagine what his motivation would be for killing his client's cheating spouses.

Unless…

CHAPTER 39

"Would you be willing to show me your bank records and let us have a look around your property?"

"Sure," he said smoothly, "but why do you want to see my bank records?"

"I'd like to see how much Joey and Gerard paid you for your services."

A corner of Virgil's mouth curled up into a grin, and his expression seemed to be one of respect. "I like it."

"Like what?"

"You think my clients paid me to find out their wives were having affairs, and then paid me to kill them in the most humiliating and torturous way possible." He nodded his appreciation. "That's clever, but it didn't happen. I don't have the stomach for that sort of thing."

"Do you mind proving it by showing your records?"

"Anything to help," he said, firing up his computer. While he accessed his bank accounts, he explained that he required a retainer of $500 and billed at a rate of $150 per hour. He said he offered a discount for the members of his church. "It's the Christian rate."

Just then, an ear-piercing train horn blared from somewhere nearby. It was so loud the walls seemed to shake. I glanced at the clock on the wall. "Is that the Maque Trax train?"

Virgil nodded. "It passes every night at ten and it blows the shit out of the horn. It was always waking me up as a kid. When Skylar and I moved back here, we didn't even bother going to bed until after the damn thing went by."

"Our team's conducted a lot of anti-terrorism exercises on that train," I said, standing with Dawn and moving around the desk to look over Virgil's shoulder.

"I thought I saw y'all over by the station a few times," Virgil said, scrolling through his business account. "I also saw some SWAT trucks out at the airport. It's good that your team prepares like it does. You can never be too careful."

I just nodded. As Dawn and I watched him pull up month after month of records, I began wondering if Joey had killed Kathleen and then collaborated with Gerard to kill Debbie.

"Is it possible Joey and Gerard got together and spoke about their wives cheating?"

"I'm almost sure of it," Virgil said. "Gerard told me Joey's the one who suggested he contact me."

"So, they're friends?"

Virgil shrugged. "I'm not sure how they know each other. Joey doesn't come to the services, so they must know each other outside of church."

"What about Nehemiah Masters?" I asked. "Do you think he really believes the garbage he spews about the wages of sin being death for adulterous women?"

It was very subtle, but Virgil's hand hesitated for a brief moment at the mention of Nehemiah Masters. He recovered quickly and shrugged again. "Look, I go to the church because Skylar makes me, but I'm not buying much of what that man says."

"Why does she make you attend church?" I wanted to know.

"What I'm about to say doesn't leave this room." He sighed. "Remember how I told y'all I've made my share of mistakes?"

Dawn and I nodded, and he continued.

"The night I got stabbed, I was messing around with another woman. As I lay there dying, all I could think about was getting to see Skylar one more time. When she met me at the hospital later, I admitted everything I'd done and swore to change if she would give me another chance. She agreed, but told me we'd have to start attending church if things were going to work out between us." He shrugged and continued scrolling through his bank account. "I love my wife, so I go to church with her."

While it was a good story, I knew he was deflecting. There was something about Nehemiah Masters that made him uncomfortable.

"Do you mind showing us a list of your clients?" I asked. "While we don't know much, we do know that one woman is dead and the other is missing, and you investigated both of them."

"Are you back to thinking I did this?" His voice was terse. "Even after I voluntarily let you look through my bank account and offered to let you search my property?"

"No, I'm wondering if someone is targeting the subjects of your investigation—the ones who attend Second Temple Fellowship." When I saw his face tighten again, I knew I was on to something. "How many Second Temple women have you investigated?"

Virgil leaned back in his chair and looked up at me, but didn't say anything.

I folded my arms across my chest. "Let's cut the cat and mouse game. I know you investigated Gretchen Masters, so save me some time and tell me what you know."

Virgil continued staring up at me and it was more than Dawn could stand.

"Look, you little prick," she began. "While you're sitting here stalling, Debbie Brister might be out there hanging from a cross, running out of time. Just tell us what you know and get it over with. You said you were a cop, now act like one!"

Dawn's outburst startled Virgil, but something she said hit home and he exhaled sharply.

"Look, I'm not saying Father Masters did this," he began slowly. "I would never falsely accuse a preacher of committing a sin without clear evidence, okay?"

"Sure," I said. "Just tell me what you know."

"Two months ago, he comes to me and says he needs two buccal swab kits and he wants to know if I have connections with a private lab that can test the kits. He didn't want me to open a formal investigation and he didn't want me generating any paperwork. He said it had to be completely confidential."

"And you agreed?"

"He said he'd pay me ten grand if I delivered the samples to the lab and then picked them up when they were done—what do you think?" He grunted. "That's a lot of money for such a simple task, so I figured it had to be important to him. I picked up the results two weeks ago—on a Tuesday—and hand-delivered it to his house. The following Sunday, he gave the first part of his sermon about evil and adulterous women and talked about them getting the death penalty for their sins."

I asked the obvious: "Do you think the sermon had something to do with the DNA tests?"

"I'm not positive, but Gretchen was crying throughout the sermon, so I believe it was related. She tried not to let people know she was crying, but it was obvious. Even Skylar noticed."

CHAPTER 40

After spending almost two hours searching Virgil Brunner's property, Dawn and I were satisfied Debbie wasn't there and we'd uncovered no evidence linking him to her disappearance or to Kathleen's murder. He'd also confirmed they were the only Second Temple Fellowship parishioners he'd investigated.

It was almost midnight when we left his house and I immediately borrowed Dawn's cell phone and called Jerry.

"Is there any sign of Masters?" I asked.

"Nothing. The lights in the house went out an hour ago and everything's been quiet ever since."

"Let me know if anything changes." I then called the sheriff and updated him on our progress.

"So, we don't know if the killer is Virgil Brunner, Nehemiah Masters, Joey Bertrand, Gerard Brister, or some other wacko?" he asked.

"Virgil seems clean," I explained, "and so does Gerard. I'm not so sure about Nehemiah Masters and Joey Bertrand. Hell, they might both be in on it."

Sheriff Chiasson sighed heavily. I could tell he was tired. "We've been going door-to-door throughout the community," he said. "Nearly all of the citizens out here have allowed us to search their houses, cars, barns—everything—but we've turned up nothing. A few hard-asses refused to let us go on their property, so I left deputies behind to pull surveillance just in case they're hiding something."

I told him about Jerry and Andrew staking out Nehemiah Masters' property, but he told me he already knew about it.

"Where are you two heading now?" he asked.

"Joey Bertrand's house. We're going to confront him on his lies about his wife's affair."

"Let me know if y'all need anything." Before ending the call, he told us to be careful and he wished us luck.

I handed Dawn her phone and raced down Plymouth Highway. I began to feel pressure building in my chest and I knew we were running out of time to save Debbie—if she wasn't already dead.

"I'm telling you," Dawn said, breaking the silence in the dark cab. "Nehemiah Masters stinks."

"This whole thing stinks. The only things connecting the two women are the church and the private investigator, but neither Nehemiah nor Virgil has a reason to kill the women—unless you consider Nehemiah's sermon a valid reason."

"And what's up with the DNA test Nehemiah requested?" Dawn asked. "Do you think he suspected Gretchen of cheating and he swabbed her?"

I grimaced. "I've seen some gross things in my time, but that sounds disgusting."

Dawn nodded, chewing her lower lip like she did when she was lost in thought. She didn't say another word until I turned into Joey Bertrand's driveway. "Look...is that smoke coming from the cracks in the garage door?"

I flicked my bright lights on and squinted, trying to see through the small square windows of the garage door. It did appear foggy. I drove to within a few feet of the door and stepped out.

Dawn joined me and tilted her head upward to sniff the air. "It smells like exhaust fumes—"

"Son of a bitch!" I said. "He's killing himself!"

While I pushed and kicked on the garage door in a feeble effort to break it down, Dawn raced toward the front of the house. I heard a banging sound and then wood splintered, and I knew she was inside.

I kicked at the garage door repeatedly, but it only shook and didn't break. Finally, it trembled and began to rise. I could hear Dawn coughing inside. Without waiting for it to open completely, I dropped to my belly and scooted into the garage when the crack was high enough to fit me.

"Over here," Dawn called through the fumes and smoke, gasping for air. "Help me get him out of the car."

I rushed to the sound of her voice and, through the haze, saw Joey's figure slumped over in the driver's seat of a small sports car.

CHAPTER 41

2:00 a.m., Tuesday, August 19
Magnolia General Hospital, Chateau, Louisiana

I stirred awake when I heard my name. I opened my eyes and found Dawn cuddled up against me in the waiting room chair. I glanced around to see who had spoken and saw a nurse in pink scrubs standing over us. The smile on her face seemed to say, "Aw, y'all are so cute together."

I gave Dawn a little push. "Hey, wake up. I think it's time."

The nurse nodded. "Mr. Bertrand's alert and doing fine. You can go in and see him now."

Dawn pushed lazily off of me and stretched. "That's probably the last bit of sleep we'll get for the rest of the week," she said, groaning loudly as her back cracked.

I gave her waist a subtle squeeze and followed her and the nurse down the long hallway. We went up an elevator and hooked a right on the third floor. The nurse stopped outside of a room and turned to us before pushing the door open. "Since it was a suicide attempt, we've got him strapped to the bed for his own safety."

I nodded and stepped inside after Dawn, who smiled cheerily. "Mr. Bertrand, it's good to see you alert again."

He turned to look in our direction, a sour expression on his face. "Why'd you have to show up when you did? Why couldn't you just leave well enough alone and let me die?"

When we stepped closer to him, we could smell the strong odor of beer on his breath.

"We need to ask you some questions before you go killing

yourself," Dawn said bluntly. "Why don't you start by telling us why you hired Virgil Brunner to follow your wife?"

Joey's eyes fell. "How'd you find out about that?"

"We've got our ways." Dawn slid the visitor's chair near his bed and plopped into it. "Go ahead, explain away."

"Look, I know it was wrong of me, but I felt I had no choice. She had opened a separate bank account, she started going to the gym, she was traveling...you know, all the things a woman does when she's fixing to check out of a marriage."

"Did you try talking to her?"

"I did, but she kept telling me not to worry, that everything was okay. She said she just wanted to separate the money so we wouldn't have to worry about what the other was spending. She said it would be easier, but she knew I had fallen on hard times and didn't have much work, so my account was much thinner than hers."

"You had fallen on hard times?" Dawn shook her head slowly. "I don't think that's quite how Kathleen would've characterized it, but who's counting, right? So, tell me what you did Wednesday when Kathleen left for church?"

After he explained what he did that evening, Dawn got him to describe everything he did later that night, and then she had him move through his entire weekend, ending when we showed up at his house. Either he didn't follow Kathleen and kill her, or he conveniently left that part out.

"Are you sure you never left your house to follow her?"

"No, ma'am."

"Come on, by then you knew she was cheating on you, and you just sat back at—"

"Wait a minute—how do you know she was cheating on me?"

"I saw the tape."

Joey sat upright in his hospital bed. "Virgil told me he would put one printed copy in an envelope and destroy the originals. He lied to me!"

Dawn raised her hand. "No, we didn't get anything from Virgil. We viewed the surveillance footage from the cameras at the Dark Sands Casino in Mississippi. That's actually how we tracked down Virgil, and he told us he gave you the only copy he had of the photos."

Tears flooded Joey's eyes and began dripping down his face as he sank deeper into the mattress. "So, she was really cheating on me?"

Dawn shot a confused glance in my direction and then turned back to Joey. "But you already knew it. Virgil gave you the envelope with his report and the photos."

"I never opened the envelope," he said weakly. "It's still sitting on the desk in Kathleen's office."

"So…you didn't know?"

"No, ma'am. It's why I didn't want you searching my house. I knew you would find the envelope and I was afraid of what was inside."

"I don't understand why you would hire a private investigator to follow your wife, but then you wouldn't want to know the truth."

"I did want to know the truth, but I wanted to hear it from Kathleen. I wanted her to see the envelope and I wanted her to tell me the truth—whatever that might be. If it was true, I figured she would stop once she realized she was caught, but she never made it home. Instead, you two showed up and told me she was dead…" He squeezed his eyes shut to try and stop the tears, but it was no use. When he continued talking, we could hardly understand what he was saying. "After she was gone, I didn't want to know anymore. I wanted to believe she was true to me and I wanted the world to think she was a good woman."

Dawn scrunched her face sideways. "If you didn't know she cheated on you, then why'd you try to end your life?"

"Now that Kathleen's gone, I have no more life." He turned away from us and buried his face in the pillow. "I wish you would've just left me alone and let me die!"

Dawn rose slowly and stood over Joey Bertrand. "Before we leave, I'd like to get a sample of your DNA."

"Why?" he asked without turning around.

"We need to compare it to some evidence we found at the scene—you know, just to clear you. And we'd like your permission to search your house. It might yield some clues as to Kathleen's associates."

He twisted around and stared at Dawn, his eyes bloodshot and shiny. "You have evidence that might catch the person who killed Kathleen?"

"We do."

Joey sat up again and held out his arm. "Do it—take whatever you need and search whatever you like. Just find the person who took her from me."

While Dawn explained that the procedure was as simple as swabbing the inside of his cheeks, I left the room and retrieved a buccal swab kit and *consent to search* form from my truck. When I brought them back to Dawn, she collected his DNA and had him sign the form. She then told him we'd do everything we could to find the person who killed Kathleen.

Before we turned to leave, Dawn paused. "I'll make a deal with you," she said, her voice filled with compassion. "If you agree to go on living, we'll keep the details of Kathleen's affair confidential. It does nothing to further our case, and you need to be there for your sons. Kathleen wouldn't want you leaving them alone in the world."

"I appreciate that," he quietly. "And you're right—I need to be there for my boys. I'd had so much to drink and I was so overcome with grief that I just wanted all the pain to stop."

"Stay away from the booze," Dawn warned, and then turned and led the way out the hospital and into the parking lot.

We drove to Joey's house, where Melvin and Rachael were waiting for us. We spread out to search the house, with Dawn and me going straight to Kathleen's office.

"There it is." Dawn pointed to the desk, where a large yellow envelope was propped up against the printer. There was a printed label on the face of the envelope displaying Joey Bertrand's name. Upon closer inspection, we found that it was sealed exactly as Virgil Brunner had described, with a piece of evidence tape across the flap and his signature affixed to the tape.

I pulled on some gloves while Dawn photographed it. Once she was done, I recovered it and held it up to the light, but it was too thick to see through.

"Should we open it?" Dawn asked.

I thought about it. "I think we know what's inside, but we have to be sure."

Taking out my knife, I carefully cut a slit in the bottom of the envelope—preserving the sealed end—and allowed the contents to carefully slide out into my hand. There were no surprises.

"I'm glad he didn't open it," Dawn said. "It's bad enough to think about your spouse cheating, but to actually see it…" She shuddered and turned to toss the rest of the office.

CHAPTER 42

Somewhere in Magnolia, Louisiana

Debbie Brister didn't know what time it was, but she figured it had to be morning, because the man was back and it smelled like breakfast food. As his footsteps approached her, she cringed and tried to pull her knees together. Each time he came in she feared that was the time he would assault her, but he had maintained his distance thus far.

"It's time to eat," he said in a fake British accent. The last time he'd been in here he had spoken in a flat Cajun accent, and the time before that he tried sounding Australian. Debbie didn't know if he was doing it to confuse her or torment her. Either way, it was working.

He removed the gag and she opened her mouth to stretch it. Her jaw ached and her throat was dry. It hurt when she swallowed, but she dared not complain about anything.

The man put a hand under her head and gently lifted it. Debbie's teeth chattered in fear, not knowing exactly what would happen next. She was somewhat relieved when a cup touched her bottom lip and cold orange juice flowed into her mouth. She swallowed, but groaned in pain as it burned her throat.

"What's wrong?" the man asked. "Does something hurt?"

Debbie just shook her head. She was terrified, but her stomach ached terribly from hunger. "I...can I have food? I'm hungry."

"Sure, that's why I'm here. I need to keep you strong for tomorrow. I want you to enjoy the whole experience."

Suddenly, Debbie lost her appetite. Her jaw burned and she

began bawling. "Please don't hurt me. I swear, I won't say anything if you just let me go. I won't even make a report. I'll just go home and pretend nothing happened."

"Oh, but something did happen. You committed a most unforgiveable sin, and for that you must be punished."

"No!" Debbie screamed, twisting her body, and jerking her arms and legs, trying to bust free from the chains. "Help me! Somebody help me!"

The man laughed. "No one can hear you and no one will help you. Your fate has been decided and you will surely pay for the sins you have committed."

Debbie took a breath to scream again, but the sound was shut off when the man shoved the dirty rag deep into her mouth.

CHAPTER 43

7:12 a.m.
Detective Bureau, Payneville, Louisiana

The last thing I remembered was stretching out on a cot in the first interview room at the detective bureau and closing my eyes. The next thing I remembered, which seemed like five minutes later, was the door bursting open and Dawn hollering at me that we had to go.

Dawn had been sleeping in the interview room next door to me during a quick break to recharge our batteries. The search teams were being rotated in and out to keep them fresh, but she and I had stayed out until after six in the morning. We had searched every inch of Joey Bertrand's house, but didn't locate anything of evidentiary value.

Next, we had interviewed Gerard Brister and recovered the envelope he'd received from Virgil Brunner. Gerard told us Virgil's assistant had delivered the sealed envelope to him two days before Debbie disappeared.

"After I saw the pictures, I hid the envelope in my tackle box and was going to meet with a lawyer and file for divorce, but then she disappeared." Gerard had paused to scrub some tears from his face. "When I couldn't find her, I thought she had left me first, and that's when I realized I couldn't live without her."

What a weak man, I had thought.

Once we had recovered his envelope and finished taking his statement, we returned to the detective bureau. With nothing else to do and nowhere else to turn, we had decided to catch a little sleep while we could.

"What time is it?" I asked Dawn as I pulled my boots on and shoved my holster into my waistband.

"A little after seven."

I grunted. We'd barely gotten half an hour of sleep and we were running on pure will at that point. When I stood to my feet, I looked at her and everything stopped for a moment. Her brown eyes were red from lack of sleep and her hair was a mess, but she was as beautiful as the first day I laid eyes on her.

"I love you so much," I said quietly.

She pushed her finger to my lips. "Stop it, someone will hear you."

"I don't really care anymore," I mumbled, exhaustion taking over. "When this is all over, I'm going to ask you to marry me."

Her mouth dropped open and her eyes grew wide. I suddenly realized what had just happened and cursed out loud. "That wasn't supposed to happen," I said, stammering. "I...I wasn't going to say—"

"London! Dawn!" bellowed the sheriff from the lobby. "Are y'all coming or not?"

Dawn quickly turned and called over her shoulder. "We have to go—Jerry said there's movement out at Nehemiah's barn."

Still cursing myself inwardly, I chased after her and asked what kind of movement.

The sheriff overheard me and filled me in while we hurried out to the parking lot and all piled into his Suburban. Apparently, Nehemiah Masters had been spotted bringing food to the barn.

"He's been inside for five minutes," the sheriff said. "We've got a judge on the phone who's about to give verbal authorization to search the barn, and I need a team in place before he comes out. We don't need this turning into a hostage situation and we don't want him killing her before we can take him into custody, so we need to wait until he comes out before we make our move."

I tapped Dawn on the shoulder and pointed to the sheriff's radio. "Can you hand it to me?"

When she did, I called Jerry. "Sierra Two, what's the latest?"

"He's still in the barn. No movement or sounds from inside."

The sheriff was driving as fast as his Suburban would move, swerving in and out of traffic, and we were soon shooting across the bridge that led to Plymouth Highway.

"Ten-four," I said. "We'll be there in a few."

"Unless we die first," Dawn said, grunting.

"I can still drive," Sheriff Chiasson said, taking the curves in the road smoothly. When we reached the last bend in the road before the straight run that led to the church, he backed off of the accelerator and the SUV slowed considerably. "What side do you want to be dropped on?"

"This side," I said, indicating the western side of the cemetery. From what I remembered, there were no windows on that side of the barn and we could creep up close without being seen. "Who do we have on the ground nearby?"

"Abraham Wilson is staked out in the cane fields across the highway and we've got Alpha entry team staged down the road in an undercover van."

"Great." I got on the radio and asked Abraham to start making his way to the western side of the cemetery. I then called the entry team and asked them to be prepared to move in quickly. "When we take Masters down, I want y'all hitting the barn fast."

When they acknowledged my traffic, I tossed the radio to the console and held my hand poised over the door handle. Before the sheriff's Suburban came to a complete stop, I was out the door. Dawn was right there with me and we dipped around the back of the SUV and made our way across the cemetery at a crouching run. I could see Abraham crouched behind a tombstone, his pistol in his hand and his eyes focused like a laser on the door to the barn.

The air seemed cooler than it had been earlier in the morning, and I wondered if a cold front might've blown through while we slept. Of course, during August in Louisiana, a cold front might mean going from ninety-five to ninety degrees.

When we reached Abraham's location, Dawn moved to his left and I carefully made my way across the aisle of tombs and took a kneeling position where I could see the door of the barn. My pant leg soaked up the dew and the dampness felt cool against my skin. Slipping my pistol from its holster, I studied the barn door and said a silent prayer that Debbie was alive and inside the barn, and waited for Nehemiah to come out.

The door was a metal exterior type with no windows. It opened toward the inside—great for kicking in—and there was a heavy duty deadbolt just beneath the knob. The entry team would have to hit it with the battering ram if Nehemiah locked it before we took him down.

As I scanned the pathway between the barn and the residential area of the church, I realized this was where Nehemiah had come from last night when Dawn and I were talking to his wife. He hadn't been carrying anything, but it would've been easy for him to place it down in the dark before reaching us.

A few daytime mosquitoes buzzed around my ear, but it was the only sound I heard. *Surely,* I thought. *If Nehemiah's in there hurting Debbie, we would hear it.* Most barn walls weren't insulated and even a muffled scream would be clearly noticeable. Besides, the killer planted the spikes at the scene of the discovery, so she would have to be taken to the area alive.

I checked on Dawn's position. She was crouched, looking like a tiger ready to pounce. Abraham was ready, too, and I found myself liking this kid a whole lot. While he was quick to action, he was also levelheaded and restrained.

Suddenly, the deadbolt clicked and the knob turned. I crouched lower behind the tombstone in front of me and peeked around the side. The door opened slightly and then stopped. Nehemiah stuck his face out and peered around to make sure everything was safe. None of us moved. After a few seconds, he stepped out into the opening and turned to close the door. He was too far away, so I waited for him to lock the door and begin walking toward my location.

When he was in full view, I saw an empty cup and plate in his hands, along with a fork. He hadn't taken five steps when I stood from behind the tombstone and aimed my pistol at his chest.

"Get on the ground, *now!*" I ordered, moving toward him rapidly.

He jerked in his skin and dropped what he was carrying. His head spun around to his right when he saw Abraham and Dawn approaching with their guns drawn.

"Get down!" I ordered again, this time several feet from him.

Nehemiah hurriedly dropped to his face on the sidewalk just as the entry team rushed by our position to my right and hit the barn door hard.

Dawn and Abraham held Nehemiah at gunpoint while I pressed my knee on his back, jerked his hands behind his back—left one first, and then the right—and handcuffed him.

"What is going on?" he asked. "You cannot come onto church property and assault the leader—"

"You have the right to remain silent," I said, rolling him to his back so I could stand him up. "Anything you say can and will be used against you in court—"

Before I could finish advising him of his rights, one of the entry team members reappeared in doorway to the barn and hollered for me. "Sierra One, you've got to get in here. You won't believe this."

Abraham moved up beside me and grabbed Nehemiah's arm. "I've got him, sir."

I nodded and followed Dawn, who was already on her way to the barn. When I cleared the doorway and looked inside, I gasped, not at all expecting what we found.

CHAPTER 44

After holstering her pistol, Dawn rushed to a wooden crate that was situated at the very center of the barn. There was a large spotlight beaming down on the crate, and I could see a young girl—no more than four years old—huddled against the far corner. Her round brown eyes were wide and she stared up in fear at the large SWAT cops huddled around the crate. Their eyes were wide, too, but they were shocked, not afraid.

Although nothing should surprise me anymore, I was not expecting to find a small child locked in a cage when I came through the barn door. My thoughts immediately turned to Virgil Brunner's story about Nehemiah's request for a DNA test. Virgil didn't know the specifics about the test, but what if it was a paternity test? What if Nehemiah had used the cheek swab on this small child and the results had revealed she was not his offspring?

If I was right about the paternity test, the sermon about evil and adulterous women now made perfect sense, but what was he planning to do with the child? How did this relate to Kathleen Bertrand's murder and Debbie Brister's disappearance? And was Gretchen in danger?

Dawn dropped to her knees and spoke softly to the child. "Hey, little one, my name is Dawn. How are you?"

The little girl pulled her knees up to her chin and hugged them tight.

"Hand me the hooligan tool," Dawn said to the nearest SWAT officer, holding out her hand while keeping her eyes on the little girl. "It's okay, honey, we're going to get you out of here. Everything's going to be okay. Stay where you are and I'll get this door open so you can come out and play. Is that okay? Do you want to come out and play?"

The little girl's head bobbed up and down and tears rolled down her rosy cheeks. She wore a long-sleeved all-in-one pajama, as though she had been ripped straight from her bed and shoved into this box. There was dirt and grime smudged on her face and her hair was tangled in places. While she looked well-nourished, there was sadness in her eyes that made my heart break for her.

One of the SWAT officers handed Dawn the hooligan tool and she used the claw end to rip the padlock hasp off of the door. She tossed the tool aside and smiled warmly as she opened the door and waved for the little girl to crawl out of the box. "It's safe for you to come out now."

My blood boiled as I watched the child move forward very timidly, putting one small hand forward at a time, as though worried Dawn would hurt her.

I waved the SWAT members back. "Wait for us outside," I said. "We don't want to scare her."

They snatched up their gear and retreated through the door. I backed away and watched Dawn interact with the little girl. For a fleeting moment, I forgot my anger for Nehemiah Masters and noted what a great mother Dawn would be. Her actions and words flowed naturally and the child responded favorably.

Dawn kept speaking softly and encouraging the little girl forward and she finally reached the edge of the crate. Dawn backed away and took a seat on the floor, holding her arms outstretched. "Do you want me to hold you?"

The little girl nodded and moved toward Dawn.

"You're safe now," Dawn said, holding her tight. "No one's ever going to hurt you again."

Inside, I was seething and wanted nothing more than to spend some time alone with Nehemiah, but I knew I had to keep my emotions under control in order to do my job. I owed it to this little girl. I leaned against the barn wall and watched patiently as Dawn rocked the little girl back and forth. Finally, she loosened her hug and placed the child sitting in her lap.

"What's your name?" Dawn brushed the hair off of her forehead. "I bet your name is Dawn."

The little girl's face lit up for a second as she giggled. "No! Your name is Dawn."

"Well, if I'm Dawn, then who are you?"

"Daddy said I'm not his little girl no more. He said my real daddy is a bad man. He said he's a sinner and he's going to hell." She lowered her head and pouted. "He said I'm going to hell, too, because I'm bad like my real daddy."

I saw Dawn's back stiffen. "No...no, that's not true. What does your mommy call you?"

Her face brightened up at the mention of her mom. "She calls me Isabella. My brothers and sister call me Izzy."

"That's such a beautiful name. So, how long have you been in here?"

"Daddy said—oh, I'm sorry. He's not my daddy no more. He said I have to live in here until it's time for the demons to come get me..."

I turned and rushed out of the barn. My entire surroundings were draped in a red hue and I didn't know if it was the sun or my anger. "Where'd Abraham Wilson take Nehemiah?" I asked the first SWAT officer I saw.

He shoved his thumb toward the church parking lot. "They're out front."

I stomped down the sidewalk, heading straight for Abraham's patrol car. As I passed the residential portion of the church, I saw Rachael and two female patrol deputies escorting Gretchen Masters and her other three children—the ones I'd seen in church Sunday—out onto the sidewalk. Gretchen was handcuffed and her children were crying softly.

"Bring her straight to the detective bureau and stick her in an interview room," I said as I hurried by. "She's got some explaining to do."

"Sure thing," Rachael said. "I already called the Office of Child Protective Services."

I shot my thumb in the air and continued along my mission. When I reached Abraham's patrol cruiser, I opened the back door and slid in beside Nehemiah. It was everything I could do to remain calm, but I managed.

"So, what's up with the little girl in the box?" I asked.

He sat with his shoulders pulled back, his head held high, and he looked straight ahead.

"I guess you didn't like the results of the paternity test, so you decided to take it out on your wife's child."

I could tell by his eyes and the muscles in his jaw that my comment struck a nerve, but he continued staring forward.

"Why'd you test her DNA? Was it because she looked different than your other children?" I pressed, receiving no response in return.

"Come to think of it, none of the kids look like you. They all look like your wife, but I don't see the slightest resemblance to you. They're probably all the product of an adulterous affair." I paused, hoping to incite a reaction from him, but he remained still. "If your wife committed adultery, why not just kill her? Why'd you have to kill Kathleen and Debbie?" Nothing. "Oh, I get it—your wife's still sleeping with this guy, isn't she? She can't let go of him, so you killed Kathleen and Debbie as a warning to her, but she didn't heed the warning—"

"I want a lawyer."

I clamped my mouth shut and stared through the slits in my eyes. "Very well," I finally said. "That's your right. At the moment, you're under arrest."

"For what? I did not do anything wrong."

"I'll let you know the exact charges once we complete our investigation, but, at a minimum, we're talking false imprisonment and cruelty to a juvenile."

I stepped out of the back seat just as Rachael was escorting Gretchen in front of Abraham's car. Suddenly, Nehemiah began yelling at his wife. "Woman, to speak against a man of faith is heresy! I command you to remain silent, otherwise you will know your place in the lake of fire, and your flesh will be devoured—"

"Shut your mouth," I said and slammed the door.

CHAPTER 45

Detective Bureau, Payneville, Louisiana

It was almost noon before I finally sat down to interview Gretchen Masters. Dawn was still hanging out with Isabella and agents with the Office of Child Protective Services had interviewed all of the children and they were in the process of finding a place for them to stay.

Gretchen's blue eyes were glassy from all the crying she'd been doing.

"Please, I do not want to lose my children!"

"Then you shouldn't have shoved one of them in a wooden box."

"It was not me—it was all Nehemiah's doing."

I leaned back in my chair and studied the woman in front of me. She was attractive and seemed intelligent, so why'd she put up with her husband's garbage? I posed the question to her and she shivered.

"He would kill me if I opposed him."

"How do you know that?"

She wrung her hands in front of her chest. "I do not know if I can speak against a man of faith. If I do—"

"That's nonsense," I said, thinking quickly. "If he was a man of faith, do you think we would've been able to arrest him? If he was a man of faith, do you think he would've hurt a small child—a small, innocent child who is too young to know sin?"

She considered my point, and then seemed to relax. "I think you are correct."

"I know I am." I leaned forward and rested my forearms on the desk. "Look, you're safe now. He's locked up and he won't be going anywhere for quite some time. This is your chance to break free from him, but I need you to help me keep him locked up."

"Me? How? What can I do?"

"You said he would kill you if you opposed him. How do you know that?"

She lowered her eyes. "I have not been the perfect wife. I stepped outside of my marriage and I ended up with child. I deeply regret my mistake, but I love Isabella dearly. Nehemiah insisted I give her up for adoption, but I refused. When I refused, he took her from me and said he would kill her if I did not reject her as my child."

"Why didn't you tell Dawn and me when we were out at your house?"

"I did not know where she was located and I did not know who had her. I thought if I reported him, she would surely die."

"Isabella's four years old. Why'd Nehemiah wait until just now to demand you reject her?" I asked. "Why didn't he do it much sooner?"

"It is only recently that he found out about her."

I nodded slowly. I knew the paternity test confirmed it for him, but what made him suspect she wasn't his child? I posed the question to Gretchen.

"He said the Lord spoke the words to him."

"Do you believe that?"

"I do not want to doubt a man of God, but..." Gretchen hesitated. "Isabella was sick and I had taken her to the doctor. Nehemiah always drives me places, but he usually stays in the waiting room while I bring the children in to see the doctor. This time he came in with us. While the nurse was examining Isabella, Nehemiah picked up her file and was reading through it. I did not think anything about it until he abruptly slammed the file down on the desk and left the room. When I looked at the file, it was open to Isabella's latest blood work." She lowered her head. "I knew right then that he suspected something."

"What's with the blood work?"

"Nehemiah and I are both O-negative and Isabella is A-positive."

I grunted. "That's a problem."

"It is, but he did not say anything about it when I walked out into the waiting room. He did not say anything until a couple of weeks ago, when he said the Lord told him the truth. That is when he tried to force me to give her up. When I refused, he took her away in the middle of the night and I have not seen her until earlier today." She wiped her tired eyes. "The following Sunday, he delivered the most hateful sermon. I have never heard such a vile message from the pulpit before. It felt as though the entire congregation was staring directly at me, but there was nothing I could do. I felt hopeless. He had my baby and I did not want to do anything to threaten her safety."

Gretchen was crying again. I slid a box of Kleenex in her direction.

"Do you think he killed those women?"

"I know he did."

"How's that?"

She looked up. With tears flowing freely down her face, she said Nehemiah threatened to put her where he put Kathleen if she didn't give up Isabella and confess the name of the man who was her father. "When Debbie Brister disappeared, he said he would continue taking women from the church until I signed papers giving up my rights to Isabella, and he demanded to know the name of her father."

"Did you sign the documents?"

She shook her head. "I cannot give up my baby."

"Who's the father?" I asked.

She lowered her head. "I cannot say."

I wanted to press her on it, but decided against it. I told her I'd be right back. After stepping out of the interview room, I walked around until I found Dawn.

"We don't need to take Gretchen's children from her," I said. "She's as much a victim as they are."

Dawn nodded. "I agree. We need to find a place for all of them to stay—a place Nehemiah won't be able to find them if he bonds out of jail."

While she met with the agents from the Office of Child Protective Services, I contacted the duty judge to obtain a telephonic search warrant for Nehemiah's DNA to compare against the DNA we'd recovered from Kathleen Bertrand's face. After presenting the facts I'd just uncovered, the judge gave me the authorization. He also agreed that I had probable cause for Nehemiah's arrest with regard to the child, but he told me to send him the affirmation of probable cause before he made the official determination, and he gave me a hint about the bond amount.

I retrieved a buccal swab kit from my truck and walked into the holding area, where a deputy was standing guard over Nehemiah. While I pulled on a pair of latex gloves, Nehemiah regarded me with suspicious eyes.

"You're being charged with aggravated kidnapping," I explained, "and your bond is going to be set at a million dollars."

"Kidnapping? I did not steal anyone!"

"You imprisoned Gretchen's daughter with the intent to force Gretchen to give up her parental rights to the child—that's aggravated kidnapping in Louisiana, and the penalty is life in prison."

He started to say something more, but he shut his mouth when I stepped closer to him.

"I'll be taking your DNA now." I placed the swab kit on the desk next to him and asked him to open his mouth, explaining the simple collection procedure.

His eyes narrowed and he shook his head slowly, biting down hard.

"I have a warrant to retrieve your DNA, which means I can take it forcibly," I warned. "I'm only going to ask one more time—please open your mouth."

His jaw jutted out defiantly and he shook his head.

I immediately grabbed him by the lower jaw with my left hand and jerked him out of his chair. After bending him backward over the desk, I dug my index finger and thumb into the sides of his cheeks until he groaned in pain and his mouth slowly parted.

I motioned for the deputy to hand me the packet of swabs, and then I recovered a sample from the inside of each cheek. When I was done, I stepped back and allowed him to slide off the desk and onto the floor.

I sealed the package and took one last look at him before walking out the door. "If your DNA matches the DNA we recovered from Kathleen Bertrand, you'll also be charged with first degree murder and you *will* be convicted, after which the wages of your sin will be death. I'm just sorry we can't crucify you."

CHAPTER 46

Later that evening…

After sending Nehemiah to the detention center, completing the arrest reports, and fast-tracking the DNA swabs to the crime lab for comparison, Dawn and I headed home to get a shower and some sleep. The sheriff had contacted District Attorney Ryder Crawford and made arrangements for us to meet at Crawford's office first thing in the morning to consult with Nehemiah and his attorney. The plan was for the DA's office to offer Nehemiah a deal in exchange for him leading us to Debbie.

While I felt comfortable Nehemiah was our most likely suspect, there was a nagging feeling in the pit of my stomach that we'd missed something. I went over everything in my head, but as hard as I tried, I couldn't put a finger on it.

The sheriff had decided to leave several roving patrols in Plymouth East, but he had scaled back the search for Debbie Brister. After going over most of the community twice, it was clear she was nowhere to be found—and neither was her car. We had to consider the possibility she had left on her own fruition or had been taken out of Plymouth East.

"If we don't get anywhere with Masters tomorrow," Sheriff Chiasson had told Dawn and me earlier, "we'll expand our search outward from Plymouth East. I've already gotten with dispatch and told them to put out a national alert for Debbie, just in case the killer's gone mobile."

The sheriff had then ordered Dawn and me to get some sleep so we'd be presentable for our meeting with the DA. He didn't have to tell us twice.

Now, nearly two hours after meeting with the sheriff, Dawn and I stepped out of the shower together and began toweling off in front of the mirror. I was watching her and I caught her watching me. "I can't remember the last time we—"

I didn't let her finish. I pulled her wet body to mine and kissed her like it was the first time. Our hands explored each other as I backed out of the bathroom door and into our bedroom, where we fell to the bed. The droplets of water from our bodies rubbed off on the bedspread, but we didn't care. We began making love and didn't stop until it was almost midnight. While both of us had been exhausted from lack of sleep when we first got home, we were never too tired to make love and were now fully alert—and very much into each other.

When we were done, I rolled onto my back beside Dawn and sighed heavily.

"I needed that," she said. "I feel so relaxed."

"I do, too." I closed my eyes. "I can sleep for days now."

"Hey…" Dawn suddenly popped up to her elbow and placed a cool hand on my chest. "Earlier this morning, when I woke you up in the interview room, you mumbled something that I could barely understand. What was it?"

I was instantly awake, but kept my eyes closed. I had hoped she missed it, but I knew by the look on her face that she understood what I'd said. Trying desperately to feign delirium—which shouldn't have been so hard to do considering how little rest we'd had since this investigation began—I mumbled something about DNA, murdering bastards, and German shepherd puppies, and then I pretended to be asleep.

I don't know if she bought the act, because she grunted and rested her head on my chest, seemingly frustrated. I figured she had to know I wanted to marry her, but I wanted the proposal to be a surprise. And I had worked so hard to surprise her with the perfect proposal setting, complete with real-time documentation, but then this case had happened. I sighed, knowing Dawn would've knowingly given up that perfect proposal to be here doing God's work.

Maybe I will drop down to one knee when this case is done, I thought. A crime scene proposal would probably be an original thing. I'd certainly never heard of it being done before.

CHAPTER 47

Wednesday, August 20
Magnolia Parish District Attorney's Office, Chateau, Louisiana

Red MacQuaid, a local defense attorney who had been summoned to represent Nehemiah Masters, stepped out of the secure room where Nehemiah was sitting with two prison guards. Rubbing one of his thick stubby arms, Red shook his head and addressed Assistant District Attorney Nelly Wainwright.

"He says he can't lead you to Debbie Brister, because he didn't do anything to her. He also denies knowing anything about Kathleen Bertrand's murder."

Nelly Wainwright was a great prosecutor and was well respected in the law enforcement circle. Tragically, she had lost two brothers—one of them a former captain with the sheriff's office—within a span of four years, but she had found the strength to press on.

"Did you tell him we'd take the death penalty off the table on Kathleen Bertrand's case if he leads us to Debbie Brister?" Nelly asked Red. "Dead or alive—we want her body."

"I told him all of it." Red wiped sweat from his forehead and, when he raised his arm, I couldn't help but notice the dark wet spot under his armpit. The man definitely had a perspiration problem. I didn't know if it was his nerves or a medical condition, but despite how cold it was in the building, sweat seemed to be draining from every pore in his body.

"Did you tell him Detective Carter has sent his DNA off to be compared against the DNA found on the victim?" she asked. "If it matches, he's a dead man."

"I told him." Red nodded for emphasis. "He swears he didn't do it. He said he can't give me what he doesn't have."

Nelly walked briskly toward the room where Nehemiah was being held and instructed the guards to get him out of her building. When she turned back toward us, she folded her arms across her chest and regarded Red with a cold stare. "If your guy killed Kathleen Bertrand and Debbie Brister, I'll make sure he dies twice for his crimes."

Red shrugged his shoulders as though to say he tried, and then he gathered up his briefcase and trudged out the door.

I turned to Sheriff Chiasson. "I guess we expand the search parameters now."

He nodded and, after thanking Nelly, Dawn and I followed him out onto the sidewalk. The morning sun was shining bright and a cool breeze was blowing in from the north. It was a beautiful day, but the fact that Debbie was still missing cast a dark cloud over our mood.

Dawn's phone rang and she answered, then handed it to me. "I'm not your secretary," she joked. "It's time for you to replace your phone."

It was Melvin. He had hand-delivered the buccal swab kit to the crime lab yesterday and they had just called him with the results.

"The analyst worked through the night on this, and it was her daughter's birthday," he said, "so we owe her big time. Anyway, it's not Joey and it's not Nehemiah."

My shoulders fell. I felt deflated. I could tell by Dawn's expression that she had accurately interpreted my reaction to the news. She cursed and turned to let the sheriff know.

"Are they sure it's not Nehemiah?" Even as the words left my mouth, I knew how foolish it sounded. They were the best at what they did, and they were certain.

"Yeah…it's not him."

I thanked Melvin and ended the call, absently handing Dawn her phone. "If the killer's not Nehemiah or Joey, then who in the hell could it be?"

"What about this Virgil Brunner fellow?" the sheriff asked.

I shook my head. "We interviewed him and he was very cooperative. I think he's clean."

"I agree. He let us look into his bank records and search his property," Dawn said. "He didn't act like a person with something to hide."

"Then who the hell's doing this?" The frustration was evident in the sheriff's voice. "And how do we know he won't take another woman?"

"I really thought Nehemiah did this," Dawn mused aloud. "He gave that sermon about adulterous woman deserving to die and..."

Her voice trailed off and I cocked my head sideways. "What are you thinking?"

"What if one of the church members thought Nehemiah was speaking literally, rather than metaphorically, about adulterous women needing to die for their sins?"

"I thought he *was* speaking literally," I said, "which was why I thought he killed Kathleen."

"Exactly, but *you* wouldn't go out and kill anyone just because he said they deserved to die. Instead, you'd think he's a lunatic." She paused and held up a finger. "But what if someone in the church thought it was a call to action? What if that person knew Kathleen and Debbie were cheaters, and they did what they thought was God's work?"

"We need to find out if there are any other cheaters in the church," the sheriff said. "They could be potential targets. If we ran surveillance on every possible victim, we might be able to catch this monster in the act."

"We already know one of them," I said slowly, extending my hand toward Dawn. "Gretchen Masters, but she's on the way to a safe house."

Knowing I wanted her phone again, Dawn handed it over and reminded me again that I needed to replace mine. "How am I supposed to call you when we're not together?" she asked.

I grunted and called Virgil Brunner. When he answered, I asked him if he was sure he hadn't investigated any other women for adultery in the church.

"No," he said. "The only women I've investigated from the church were Debbie Brister and Kathleen Bertrand, and, of course, what I told you about Gretchen Masters."

I ended the call and tossed the phone to Dawn. "We need to pick up Gerard Brister."

"Why?" Sheriff Chiasson asked. "He seems like a sincere and simple man."

"He does, but he knew Joey suspected Kathleen of cheating and he knew his own wife was cheating," I explained. "He's also a very religious man and he's devoted to the church. If Jim Jones can convince almost a thousand people to commit suicide, then Nehemiah Masters can surely convince one simple man that cheating women deserve to die—even if it wasn't Nehemiah's intent."

"We might as well pick him up, then," Dawn said. "We've got nothing else."

"When we get back to the bureau, I've got to give a briefing to the press. I just got a call and there're a dozen reporters already waiting in the conference room." The sheriff rubbed his face and sighed. He looked haggard and I knew he'd gotten as little sleep as we had. "I'd like you two to stand with me in case they have some questions I can't answer. After we're done, y'all can pick up Gerard Brister and see what he's got to say."

I grumbled silently, not liking the idea of being in the limelight, but I didn't want to be difficult. We'd all had a long week, and there was no use complaining about something so trivial.

CHAPTER 48

The lights from the reporters' cameras were bright and the questions came fast and furious. I stood to one side of the sheriff while Dawn stood to the other, and we waited patiently as he fielded question after question. Word of the *Crucifix Killer* was spreading across Louisiana and a sense of panic was starting to set in. The reporters were not making it better.

"While I won't divulge too much information," Sheriff Chiasson said calmly, "I will say that we believe the incidents are isolated to Plymouth East."

"Is it true that the Crucifix Killer has struck again?"

"We don't know that for sure," the sheriff said. "We're still searching for Debbie Brister, who went missing early Monday morning, but there's no real evidence to indicate that…"

When the rest of the sheriff's sentence didn't materialize, I glanced sideways to see what was wrong. He was staring down at his phone and his face was twisting into a scowl. I looked past him at Dawn. While she was doing a better job of masking her expression, she was also reading her phone.

What in the hell is going on? I wondered to myself, wishing we'd stopped long enough to get me a new phone. I looked up when the door at the back of the conference room opened. It was Rachael and she was waving for us to go now.

Sheriff Chiasson turned first to Dawn and then to me and nodded. "Get going."

"What's happening, Sheriff?" one of the reporters asked as we hurried toward the door.

"It's nothing, really." I glanced over my shoulder and saw him smile in a feeble attempt to reassure them. "They've got work to do. So, who has another question?"

"What's going on?" I asked Rachael when Dawn and I met her out in the parking lot.

"They found Debbie's car in an old cane shed off of Highway Eighty between here and Seasville." She jogged toward her cruiser. "Follow me!"

Dawn and I jumped in my truck and we raced out of the parking lot and onto Highway Three, heading south.

Dawn glanced over her shoulder and cursed. "The news vans are following us."

I checked my rearview mirror and, sure enough, there were three of them hot on our trail. I could've radioed some patrol deputies to pick them off and issue them citations for speeding, but we didn't have time for that. We'd just have to keep them back if we found Debbie's body.

I turned onto the first bridge we came to, crossed Bayou Magnolia, and then headed south on Highway Eighty. Although there wasn't much traffic on that stretch of highway, Rachael was running lights and siren. We traveled for about ten minutes before I saw flashing blue lights on the shoulder of the road about a mile ahead.

"That's the building," Dawn said, pointing to a wide tractor shed that was nestled under some ancient oak trees. "We passed it this morning and I didn't notice a car inside."

I stopped about a hundred yards from the tractor shed and turned my truck sideways in the road, blocking the news vans behind me. Once I'd shut off my engine, I grabbed some crime scene tape and Dawn and I quickly strung it across the highway, tying one end to a tree on the bayou side and the other end to a telephone pole. The news vans screeched up and reporters piled out, but Rachael lifted her hand to stop them.

"The tape is as far as y'all go," she said firmly. "This area's a crime scene and anyone who violates the integrity of the scene will be arrested."

While the cameramen began setting up, the reporters fired several questions in our direction, but we ignored them and hurried to the tractor shed, where Deputy Arlene Eiland was standing near the car. Her shoulder-length blonde hair was pulled back into a ponytail and she was talking on her cell phone. She looked up when we approached and ended the call.

I'd first met Deputy Eiland three years earlier when she'd responded to a body found under a bridge. Since then, she had been averaging the highest number of DWI arrests per year in all of Magnolia. Having lost my family to a drunk driver, I was an instant fan of her work.

"Hey, detectives, I only walked up to make sure no one was inside, but, other than that, I haven't touched anything."

"Good job," I said, examining the car from where I stood while Dawn and Rachael approached it. It was a gray Nissan Sentra and it was backed into a dark corner of the shed, deep in the shadows. "How'd you find it?"

"Just driving by," she said simply. "They stuck me working south while everyone else was searching Plymouth East, and I got bored working the day shift. I started making the rounds of the bridges, patrolling every neighborhood I came across, when I drove by this tractor shed. At first, I drove right on by, but then I remembered they told us at this morning's briefing that Captain Berger's ex-wife was still missing, so I decided to check it out. I thought it would be a good place to hide a body."

Dawn and Rachael had gotten the trunk open and turned to where I was standing. "It's empty," Dawn said. "Let's check around back."

"Should I stay here and keep the reporters at bay?" Arlene asked.

I glanced in their direction. They were behaving, so I shook my head and told her she could come along if she wanted. She and I caught up to Dawn and Rachael, who were making their way around the side of the shed, and the four of us squeezed between the metal shed and the tall cane until we reached the back of the shed.

"What's that?" Dawn pointed north along the back of the structure.

I squinted, but it was hard to see because the sun above was bright and the shadows of the large oak trees below were dark. I waved to them. "Let's go look."

I shielded my eyes as I walked along the narrow pathway between the sugarcane and the shed, but it wasn't until we were immersed in the shadows of the giant oaks that the image came into view. It was only a silhouette in the shadows, but there was no mistaking what it was—a naked woman nailed to another cross.

CHAPTER 49

"Oh, no!" Rachael said when she realized what we were seeing.

Dawn cupped a hand over her forehead to shield her eyes. "Please tell me that's not Debbie…"

I ran the last hundred feet to the cross, which was attached to the back of the shed. A ladder was propped up against the structure and I wondered if Arlene had interrupted the killer. My head was on a swivel as I ran. I didn't see any hostiles, but I didn't want to take a chance. I pointed toward the fields beyond the oak trees. "Arlene, keep an eye out there! The killer might be close by."

As I rushed to the ladder, I heard Arlene calling it in over the radio. She requested an ambulance for the victim and a K-9 officer to track a possible killer. While I knew we would need the K-9, I wasn't so sure about the ambulance.

Debbie had been nailed to the cross in the same manner as Kathleen, but she was in the shade, so her lips weren't as parched. I felt a surge of hope as I climbed the ladder. It was much cooler here and she could survive much longer. I called her name as I climbed.

"Debbie, can you hear me?" I pulled on some latex gloves when I reached the top of the cross and shook her arm gently. Her flesh was still warm. "What the hell?"

Her head was slumped forward and her eyes closed. I shoved my fingers up under her jaw, searching for a pulse, but there was none. When I pulled my hand back, the glove was wet with blood. I slowly tilted her head back and sighed when I saw the hole in her throat. She had suffered greatly, but the killer had eventually ended her suffering—either through pity or because he heard Arlene drive up and he didn't want her to be found alive. Either reason could mean she knew her killer. Someone familiar with her might not want her to suffer for an extended period of time, or it could simply mean she was able to identify the killer.

I called down to Rachael, who was on the phone with the sheriff, and let her know Debbie was gone and we could cancel the paramedics. I then climbed wearily down the ladder and walked over to where Dawn was sitting on the ground. She was leaning against the shed and her face was pale.

"Debbie's fingers and jaw are loose and she's still warm. She hasn't been dead long."

"What am I going to tell Samantha?" Dawn asked weakly. "The last time they talked it ended in an argument. The poor kid will never have a chance to make up with her mom. She'll be plagued by guilt for the rest of her life."

I sat beside her and put my arm around her shoulders. "I'll take care of the scene if you want to go make the notification. Arlene can drive you."

"You sure?" she asked.

"Positive. If anyone can console Samantha, it's you." I shot my thumb toward the cross. "I'll call for some help to get the cross down, but it'll be easier than last time because of the way it's attached to the shed."

Dawn stared at her hands for a long moment. When she looked up, her brow was furrowed. "Why here?"

I looked around and shrugged. "I have no clue."

"I know there were cops crawling all over Plymouth East, but there are so many other locations up and down the bayou that would be better than here." She nodded slowly. "I feel like the locations are a message in and of themselves. If we figure out what that message is, then we find the killer."

"Hey, get back!"

I jumped to my feet and looked toward the northern end of the shed where the voice had originated. It was Arlene and she was hollering at a cameraman who had snuck through the fields to get a shot of the back of the shed. Before the cameraman could get away, Arlene had reached him and tackled him to the ground.

"You can't do this," the cameraman said. "I'm with the media."

"You're under arrest for crossing a police cordon," Arlene said calmly, cuffing his hands behind his back. "And I'm confiscating your camera, because you've obtained unlawful footage."

"I'll sue all of your asses, just you wait and see!"

I'd walked up and retrieved the camera from the ground. While

Rachael stayed with Debbie's body, Dawn, Arlene, and I walked the cameraman to Arlene's marked cruiser. We allowed the cameraman to lead the way north through the thick cane that rubbed up against the shed and it helped to clear a path for us. I didn't want to take him to the south—the direction from which we'd approached the cross—because I didn't want him seeing Debbie that way.

When we reached the back corner of the shed, we made better time along the side and then Arlene took him to her car. He began yelling at the other reporters to let them know the Crucifix Killer had struck again and that there was a nude woman hanging from a cross in the back of the shed. He also encouraged his fellow cameramen to film his illegal arrest.

"I'll go ahead and leave with her," Dawn said to me once the cameraman was locked in the backseat. I nodded and she hugged me tight. "I love you so much."

"I love you, too," I said slowly, squeezing her back. There was something in her voice that troubled me. "Are you okay?"

"For the first time in my life, I'm really terrified. I don't know who the killer is or where he'll strike next—and that scares the shit out of me. Not for me, but for all the women we can't protect. What if we never catch him and he keeps torturing women? I'll feel responsible for every murder that happens from here on out."

"I don't need to tell you it's not your fault, because you already know it." I kissed the top of her head. "I'll come find you as soon as I'm done here."

She nodded and hurried off, wiping a tear from her eye as she walked away. As I watched her walk, I hoped she wasn't right. We were going to find the bastard—we *had* to find him, and hopefully sooner rather than later.

One thing was certain—no one who worked this case would be the same afterward.

CHAPTER 50

Five hours later…
Detective Bureau, Payneville, Louisiana

Along with Rachael and Melvin, a team of us had processed the scene of Debbie's murder. I'd located the same snail tracks of saliva across her face as we'd found on Kathleen's, and I'd collected a sample. Melvin had volunteered to take it straight to the crime lab and Rachael had volunteered to attend the autopsy. I'd readily agreed with both of them.

A K-9 officer had worked his dog around the area and he'd picked up a scent, which tracked from the car to the cross and into the cane fields north of the shed. They had tracked it for six miles through the cane rows and then it veered sharply to the west until it reached Highway Eighty.

"It looks like the suspect got into a vehicle," the K-9 officer told me later. "Either that or the son of a bitch grew wings and flew away."

I had gotten with the sheriff and he immediately put out a press release asking for information from anyone who might have picked up a hitchhiker along that stretch of Highway Eighty.

On the way back to the bureau, I had stopped at the cell phone shop and swapped my dead phone and six hundred dollars for a new phone. It was bigger and fancier, with more gadgets, and I hated it.

Dawn was the first person I called and she was happy to see I was back online. She told me her conversation with Samantha had been tough, but Samantha had handled it better than could've been expected. "When are you getting here?" she had asked, sounding impatient.

I had answered by walking through the door. We were now in the conference room with the notes from every officer involved in the case scattered across the large table. We began pouring over canvas sheets from the recent search for Debbie, as well as past complaints and traffic stops that occurred in Plymouth East within the last year, but we kept coming up dry—until we received the anonymous tip.

A seasoned dispatcher named Julie called Dawn's phone and told her they'd received an anonymous call from a female stating Virgil Brunner was the killer.

"Did she say what proof she has?" Dawn asked, waving for me to get close so I could hear the answer.

I put my ear right next to Dawn's, but I couldn't hear anything. I was beginning to think the years and years of shooting my three-oh-eight rifle were starting to take a toll on my hearing.

Dawn nodded and then asked Julie to send the audio file to her phone. "The lady didn't leave a name," Dawn said as she activated her text messages, waiting for the file to arrive. When it did, she played it and held the phone up so I could hear.

"Hello," said an oddly familiar voice. *"I'm calling to say I think...um, I believe the killer of those women is Virgil...I believe it's Virgil Brunner. I know he did it and I have proof, but I can't give it until he's arrested. I'm scared for my safety."*

The mystery woman's voice was quivering and she was speaking low, but I realized almost immediately who she was.

"It's Skylar Brunner," I said. "I'm positive!"

"I agree it's her." Dawn was frowning. "What the hell does she have on him?"

"We need to interview Skylar and find out what it is."

"She won't talk until he's arrested, but we've got nothing unless she talks." She stood and paced back and forth in the conference room. "What do you think she's got on him?"

I'd been wondering that very thing since we got the call, but I couldn't imagine what evidence she could possibly have.

"What if he took pictures of the women when he killed them and she found those pictures?"

Dawn stopped pacing. "You mean, took the pictures as trophies?"

"Could be...or he might want to relive the incident over and over. Reenact the fantasy or some crazy shit." I raised an eyebrow. "Or it could've been proof to his employers that he completed the job."

"Are we back to thinking Gerard and Joey paid him?"

"They could've paid him cash. Virgil's no fool, after all."

As we continued to bounce ideas off of each other, a thought suddenly popped into my head and exploded. "I've got it!"

My outburst startled Dawn and she clutched at her chest. "Damn it, you scared the hell out of me!"

"Follow me." I rushed from the conference room and hurried to my desk, where I unlocked the door to the locker box hanging from my wall. Dawn stood behind me and looked over my shoulder as I pulled out two large plastic evidence bags. When I turned around, I held them up so she could see the yellow envelopes Virgil had sealed and then gotten hand-delivered to Gerard and Joey. "Virgil's DNA is on these envelopes. If he did it, it'll match the DNA we recovered from the victims."

"This is great!" Dawn's eyes widened with excitement, but then narrowed. "What if it doesn't match?"

I didn't have an answer, so I didn't give one. I heard talking on the other side of my cubicle wall and I hollered, "Melvin, do you feel like heading back to New Orleans?"

"Can I shoot your sniper rifle?"

"Only after I'm dead," I said.

"Then it's a deal."

After handing the envelopes to Melvin and calling in a rush order to the lab, Dawn and I met with the sheriff in his office and briefed him on the new developments.

"I thought we weren't looking at him as a suspect?" he asked.

"We weren't until we got this tip," I explained. "I also think we should pull surveillance on his house until we get the results."

"How long will it take to get the results?"

"Melvin's leaving now and the lab said they'll get on it right away. We should have the results by tonight."

"I've got everyone stretched thin doing roving patrols throughout the parish, but I guess we can spare a couple of officers—"

"Dawn and I will do it," I said quickly. "We'll take Rachael and Warren with us." Warren was a solid guy and I'd take Rachael anywhere.

"Very well," the sheriff said. "Take whoever you like, just as long as you solve this damn case. I don't want another woman being tortured in my parish."

CHAPTER 51

Dawn and I met Warren and Rachael in the parking lot of the detective bureau, and Rachael and I shrugged into our ghillie suits. I instructed Warren to drop Rachael off on the western side of Virgil's property. I turned to Rachael, who had just zipped up her suit and shoved her rifle into her drag bag.

"Skirt his property line to the west and try to find high ground on the northwest corner. You should be able to have a good visual of his house from there." I turned to Warren. "After you drop her off, disappear somewhere along the highway to the west, but be ready to move at a moment's notice."

They both nodded. Before heading toward Warren's unmarked Charger, Rachael asked, "Where will you be?"

"I'm going to set up in the woods across the highway from his house where I can watch his front gate. We need to see who comes or goes." I then grabbed my drag bag and cradled it in my arms as I slipped into the front passenger's seat of Dawn's Charger.

As Dawn drove down Plymouth Highway, I stared out the window and wondered if this case was finally coming to a head. It was the most disturbing homicide case I'd ever worked and I wanted to put it to bed. I couldn't imagine the pain our victims had endured at the hands of this beast before they died, and I knew we couldn't allow him—or her—to kill again.

Dawn gently applied her brakes and rolled to a stop on the shoulder of the highway two hundred yards from the front gate to Virgil's property, which was on the left side of the highway. She leaned over and kissed me. "Please be safe."

"You, too." I slipped out of her car and jumped the ditch that ran parallel to the right side of Plymouth Highway. Hitting the ground at a smooth running pace, I dodged palmetto bushes and jumped over cypress knees as I faded into the heavy shadows of the surrounding trees. Thick, low-lying branches slapped at my face and ripped at my ghillie suit as I plunged deeper into the Louisiana jungle, but I didn't let it slow me down.

After traveling about two hundred feet, I changed course and began heading east, counting my paces so I would know when I was directly across from Virgil's gate. I was hoping to find a tall tree to climb that would provide adequate concealment and a view of the front of his property, but I stopped dead in my tracks and dropped to my knees when I approached the two-hundred-yard mark.

Before me, there was a tiny clearing with overgrown weeds and a smattering of trees, but the most remarkable thing was the two-story wooden house squatting at the center of the property. The siding was weathered and splintery. The house was clearly abandoned. There were places where the cedar shingles had lost their grip over time and left gaping holes in the roof. A four-by-four treated post at one corner of the front porch had long-ago slipped off the foundation and stabbed into the ground. It was the only thing keeping that part of the awning from collapsing.

I studied the house for several long moments. There were no sounds from inside and no movement that I could see anywhere on the property. Keeping my eyes on the three windows that I could see, I felt around on the ground until I found a stout stick. It had a little weight to it, so I lifted it and launched it into the air, aiming it for the roof of the house. It landed with a sharp crack, but it brought no reaction from inside.

It was an old plantation style home. A wide dirt path—overgrown with weeds—extended northward from the side of the house toward Plymouth Highway. I hadn't remembered seeing a driveway across from Virgil's house, but we had come during the night and it was so overgrown that it probably blended with the shoulder of the highway.

I scurried to my right until I could see the back of the structure better. An old dilapidated garage came into view and my heart started to race. *Could this be where Debbie and her car had been concealed?*

There was a large outdoor wooden stairway leading to the upper level of the home. If I could ascend the stairs and gain access to the inside, I should have a partially obstructed view of Virgil's gate— and I could do a lot with a partial view.

Although I was confident no one was inside, I pulled out my

pistol. As I made my approach, I kept at least one tree positioned between myself and the house. When I ran out of trees, I hurried to the back door of the lower level first, because I wanted to clear the house before I set up a hide upstairs.

I tried the rusted door handle, but it was locked. It was a flimsy knob, so I twisted it forcefully and it snapped. I scowled when the door still didn't open. I leaned my shoulder firmly against the door and took a breath. With a quick motion, I pushed off explosively with my legs and the door popped inward.

I took a forward step to catch myself and immediately stepped out of the doorway. I slid along the wall as my eyes adjusted to the dim interior. The musky smell of mold greeted my nostrils and made me want to sneeze, but I stifled it. When the room started coming into view, I noticed it was void of furniture and the walls had apparently been ripped out to form one large room.

Wait a minute...

I squinted and made my way toward the far end of the room, where there appeared to be one piece of furniture. As I drew nearer, I realized it was an old metal-framed cot with a dirty iron spring mattress. What alarmed me the most was seeing chains attached to all four corners of the bed. It looked like a torture chamber. I took a step closer and my right foot brushed against something on the floor. Squatting low so I could see in the darkness, I took a sharp breath when I saw a leather bag containing a small sledgehammer, a handful of railroad spikes, and a wood chisel. Next to the bag was a pile of chain and a pair of come-alongs. I pulled my flashlight from a pouch attached to the outside of my drag bag and turned it on. There was a small pile of women's clothes in the corner of the room and some empty plates and cups strewn about.

I'd found the killer's lair!

CHAPTER 52

After clearing the lower level of the abandoned home, I holstered my pistol and released my drag bag from my shoulders to pull out my sniper rifle. Next, I dropped to a prone position on the floor about ten feet from the back door and peered through my scope, scanning the trees for any sign of the suspect. I knew I would be exposed once I made my way up the back staircase, so I needed to be sure there were no threats out there.

The sun was going down and the back yard was cloaked in shadows, but it wasn't completely dark yet. Darkness was a sniper's close friend and it would be better for me to wait, but I didn't have that luxury. I had to get up top and get eyes on the front gate to Virgil's property.

As I lay there trying to penetrate the forest behind the house, I heard Rachael's voice drone over my earpiece.

"Sierra One, I'm in position on the western side of the Brunner property. There's movement between the house and an office building." Rachael paused for a second before giving a description of a white female and a white male. The description matched Virgil and Skylar.

Since she could account for Virgil's location, I knew I was clear to go upstairs. I quickly scrambled to my feet and exited the lower level, but then stopped when I saw a pile of weathered planks on the ground beside the building. There were six-by-sixes, four-by-fours, and six-by-fours of varying lengths. Several of the boards had already been notched out in preparation for making more crosses.

Shaking my head in anger, I ascended the staircase two steps at a time—careful to skip over the ones that were too rotten to bear my weight. When I reached the door to the top level, it was already open. Holding my rifle in a hip-shooting position, I pushed the door inward with my foot. The hinges squealed and cobwebs hung like moss from the door frame. No one had been up there in quite a while.

Once inside, I moved down a long corridor that was lined with small, empty rooms, heading for a window at the opposite end. I stared toward the north when I reached the window, but the trees were too thick to see Virgil's gate. I did notice faint tire tracks in the overgrown driveway that led to Plymouth Highway.

I pulled out my cell phone and called Dawn to let her know I'd found the killer's hideout.

"You *what?*"

Although she couldn't see me, I nodded. "Everything was right here under our noses. He was too smart to do anything on his property, so he used this abandoned place as his dungeon."

She bristled on the other end. "When I get my hands on that prick…"

"I have to move into a better position so I can get a visual on Virgil's house," I said. "I'm sending you the coordinates to this location. Can you get Jerry and Andrew out here to secure the scene?"

"Sure." She ended the call and I hurried down the back staircase. I was wrapping around the house when my radio scratched to life in my earpiece.

"Sierra One, they're on the move!" Rachael called. "Both parties just entered a vehicle—a dark blue Chevy Tahoe—and they're heading toward the gate."

Warren checked in and said he had backed into a sugarcane road west of Virgil's property and was out of sight, and Dawn was farther west of his position in one of the neighborhoods.

I asked Dawn to begin tailing Virgil and his wife once they passed her location. I then called Warren on the radio.

"Once Dawn's got them, head this way and pick up Rachael and me." I then called Jerry on my cell phone.

"Did you hear what's going on?" I asked when he answered.

"Yep," he said. "We'll park by the church and wait until y'all are clear before we move in. I've got Abraham Wilson driving us out there. Once he drops us off, he's going to float around the area in case we need something."

"Sounds great." I shoved my phone inside the front of my ghillie suit and hurried through the trees, making my way toward Plymouth Highway. I was still fifty feet away when I saw headlights zoom by heading west, and I figured that had to be Virgil and his wife. About two minutes later, Dawn radioed that she was tailing them.

When I reached the highway, I remained in the heavy bushes at the edge of the shoulder and waited for Warren. Darkness was falling fast and the area was already alive with the sounds of the Louisiana night life. Cicadas began screaming their death cries and nearly drowned out the other noises. I scowled, wondering if that was how loud our victims had screamed when they were being nailed to the crosses.

CHAPTER 53

I stretched out across the back seat of Warren's unmarked cruiser and fought to free myself of my ghillie suit. Rachael had shrugged out of hers before jumping into the front seat.

Once I was down to my jeans and shirt, I put on my seatbelt and held on while Warren raced down Plymouth Highway, trying to catch up to Dawn and Virgil. Dawn gave frequent updates about her location and the last we'd heard from her was that they were pulling up to a seafood restaurant in Gracetown. Since then, the radio traffic had been quiet.

"Are you sure Skylar's the one who called?" Rachael asked me as Warren turned off of Plymouth Highway and we headed north on Highway Three. "It looks like they're having a date night and she didn't seem to have a problem with him."

I couldn't argue the point. My guess was that she was carrying on as normal until she could make a break from him, or until he was taken into custody. We couldn't arrest him without evidence, so we had to hope the DNA results came back soon.

"Virgil seemed like a credible guy," I mused aloud.

"He cheated on his wife—there's nothing credible about the man," Rachael countered.

"Cheating doesn't make you a killer," Warren said, chiming in as though he had a guilty conscience.

"No, but it makes you a liar," Rachael retorted. "So we can't believe anything he says."

"Just because he lied about an affair doesn't mean he would lie about everything," Warren continued. "Covering up an affair is survival. You can do that and still be honest about everything else."

"Is there something you need to get off your chest?" Rachael asked, raising an eyebrow.

"What're you talking about?"

Rachael grunted. "It's starting to sound like your wife needs to hire Virgil to follow you around."

Warren started to stammer and Rachael smiled triumphantly, knowing she'd pegged him.

I glanced at my phone when Warren pulled into the parking lot of the seafood restaurant. It was almost seven-thirty and I hadn't heard from Melvin yet. I pointed to Dawn's car, which was parked in the shadows on the northern end of the lot.

"Drop me off with Dawn," I said to Warren, "and then set up on the south side, where you can confess your sins to Rachael."

Rachael giggled as Warren began stammering again. "I didn't...I'm not cheating!" he insisted.

"Tell it to the priest," Rachael said, turning away from him.

I slipped out of the back seat and lugged my drag bag and ghillie suit with me. The parking lot was full of cars, but there wasn't a person around. The smell of fried seafood clung heavily to the night air and my stomach growled. I couldn't remember the last time I'd eaten.

I shoved everything into the back of Dawn's Charger and slipped into the front passenger's seat.

"Nothing, eh?" I asked.

She shook her head. "They've been inside ever since we got here. You know this place—their food's the best, but it's slow."

I nodded and leaned back in my seat, figuring it was going to be a long night. I was wrong.

A few minutes later Dawn nudged me. "Your phone's vibrating."

I reached for my pocket and pulled it out. "I didn't feel it."

"Couldn't you hear it?"

I shook my head.

"I think you're going deaf," she said. "All that shooting is messing up your—"

"It's Melvin!" I quickly answered the call. "What's the news?"

"It's him, London—it's Virgil Brunner."

"No kidding?"

"The technician extracted DNA from the seal on both envelopes and it matched the DNA from the saliva on both victims. He's our guy."

I sighed heavily, wondering how I could've missed the signs. Was I so wrapped up in the horrific nature of the case that it threw me off my game? Or was my personal life—the fact that I wanted to wrap this case up so I could propose to Dawn—clouding my judgment?

"Do you want me to type up arrest warrants for two counts of first degree murder? I could have them approved within thirty minutes."

"Go ahead and get them ready, but wait before getting them signed," I said. "I want to give Virgil a chance to explain himself first. If he knows we have arrest warrants, he might lawyer up and we'll lose any chances of obtaining a confession from him."

"Are you sure?"

"Yeah, I'm sure." I shoved my phone back in my pocket and turned to Dawn. There was a tortured look on her face.

"I can't believe we missed it," she said slowly.

I knew what she was thinking and I told her not to go there.

"I can't help it." Her voice was low. "If we would've sniffed him out when we first interviewed him, Debbie would still be alive."

"But there were no warning signs—no red flags."

That didn't seem to comfort Dawn. She turned and stared out the window as we waited for Virgil and his wife to finish eating. I did the same.

Forty minutes later the front door to the restaurant opened and Virgil and Skylar walked out holding hands. They were talking about something and Skylar was laughing. Either she was a good actress or we were wrong about her being the tipster.

I keyed up my police radio and called Warren and Rachael. "Let's move in."

Dawn and I stepped out of her Charger and made our way casually across the parking lot, just as Warren and Rachael approached from the south. Virgil noticed us and missed a step.

"Detective Carter—is that you?" he asked, craning his neck to see in the dark.

His keys were in his right hand and his left hand was in plain view. Even in the dim light from a nearby lamppost, I could see the color drain from Skylar's face. I smiled to put Virgil at ease.

"Did you save some food for us?" I asked.

He laughed and nodded, but his face fell when he caught movement behind him. He glanced over his shoulder and saw Warren and Rachael spreading out behind him. When he turned back toward me, there was a quizzical expression on his face. "You're not here to eat, are you?"

I frowned and shook my head. "I need to ask you more questions about the murders. I think you have some information that might prove helpful."

He shrugged. "Sure. I'll follow you to the bureau."

I stepped forward. "I'd appreciate it if you rode with us."

He studied my face and I knew he was working through all the possible scenarios in his mind. "Am I under arrest?"

"You'd already be in cuffs if you were under arrest, and we would've taken you down at gunpoint."

He nodded and glanced back over his shoulder. He finally took a breath and exhaled. "Is it okay if Skylar follows us in my Tahoe?"

"Absolutely," I said, relieved he was willing to come voluntarily. If he would've refused, I would've gotten the warrant and taken him by force if necessary, but that might've caused him to shut down.

We waited while he turned to Skylar, who was trembling and crying, and reassured her that everything was going to be okay. While he thought she was afraid, I knew her emotions were a mixture of fear and guilt as she watched the results of her anonymous tip play out in front of her very eyes.

Rachael stepped forward and offered to drive the Tahoe for her. Virgil agreed and handed Rachael the keys. He then turned toward me and raised his hands. "I guess you'll want to frisk me before I get in your car?"

CHAPTER 54

While Rachael and Warren kept an eye on Virgil in one of the interview rooms, Dawn and I sat with Skylar in the conference room and recorded her statement.

"How'd you know it was me?" Skylar asked Dawn.

Skylar wore tight jeans and a form-fitting shirt that was low-cut in the front. As though she felt self-conscience about it, she kept pulling the front of her shirt higher on her chest.

"We recognized your voice," Dawn explained.

"I didn't want Virgil to be arrested like that in public." Tears rolled down her cheeks. "I...I just thought someone would come out to the house and get him. To be honest, I'm not even sure he did it."

"Well, let's start with what you do know." Dawn opened a drawer and removed a box of tissues from inside. She slid it toward Skylar. "When you're feeling up to it, tell us why you called the tip line."

Skylar nodded and jerked a tissue from the box. After wiping her eyes, she took a deep breath. "But I don't know if he did it. I was frightened when I made the call and I think I might've overreacted."

Dawn reached across the desk and patted her forearm. "Would it make you feel better to know you're not the sole reason we picked him up?"

Her eyes widened. "I'm not?"

Dawn shook her head. "We've got evidence on him. I can't get into it, but you're not the only reason he's sitting down the hall from us."

Skylar began trembling even more. "Dear Lord, I can't believe he would be capable of something like this!"

"It's okay." Dawn was patient and allowed her to calm down before pressing her for information. When she thought Skylar was ready, she coaxed her on. "Go ahead and tell us why you believe he did this."

"I think it was a warning to me."

I looked at Dawn and then back at Skylar, puzzled.

"Why do you think that?" Dawn asked.

"I've been unfaithful." She lowered her head and cried silently. "Years ago, Virgil put me through hell. He was always going to New Orleans to party with his old buddies—or so he told me. I learned the truth the night he got stabbed. That's when he finally came clean and told me about all the women he'd slept with. Strangers—all of them. He'd meet tourists on the street and sleep with them in public places, just like we used to do." She rubbed tears from her face and continued. "I loved him and was really worried he would die that night. He begged me to give him another chance. He promised he'd change and that he would be completely devoted to me.

"Well, I agreed to stay with him if only he'd come to church with me." She grunted. "That was a mistake, but I would've never dreamed people would go to church to hookup."

I grunted, not surprised at all, but wondering to whom she was referring.

"Go on…" Dawn coaxed.

"Well, about five years ago I suspected him of having an affair with Gretchen Masters."

I noticed Dawn's hand freeze in place.

"I confronted him, but he denied it. I continued suspecting something was going on and then she ended up pregnant. Nine months later, she has a baby who looks nothing like Father Masters. In fact, the child looks like Virgil's baby picture. He swore up and down it wasn't his child, even offered to take a paternity test." She sighed. "I never told a soul, but I was bitter. I hated him but I loved him at the same time, so I couldn't leave him."

Skylar paused for a long moment, staring at her feet. "About a year ago, I started seeing this guy. He's a farmer who works the fields behind our property. I met him in the grocery store and he was so nice to me. I began running into him more often and then I noticed him on a tractor behind my house one day. One thing led to another and—while Virgil was out on a stakeout one night—I met him at the abandoned house across the street from our property. It used to belong to Virgil's uncle. No one ever goes there anymore, so it was a safe place to meet. After that first time, I began meeting him at his house down the road. He lives a mile from us. I was very careful to never get caught and I thought I was getting away with it, until…"

"Until what?" Dawn pressed when her voice trailed off.

"Until Kathleen's body showed up." Skylar looked up, her eyes glassy. "She was nailed to a cross in the exact spot where Virgil and I made love for the first time."

Dawn nodded slowly, taking it in. "Could it have been a coincidence?"

"I thought so, until Debbie was found—in the very spot where we had sex for the second time." Skylar lowered her head again. "I feel responsible for Debbie's murder, because I didn't heed the warning that was left on Kathleen's body. It was calling me a sinner and telling me to stop what I was doing, but I didn't. I kept seeing my boyfriend and then Debbie was killed. When I saw that reporter on the news getting arrested behind that tractor shed—*our* tractor shed…" She shook her head. "That's when I knew it was Virgil."

"Have you seen your boyfriend since Debbie was found?"

She shook her head, tears flowing down her face again. "I was too scared someone else would die. I kept wondering why he didn't just kill me. Why go after other women who had nothing to do with anything?"

Dawn was thoughtful. "This was a barbaric way to kill someone. Why do you think he chose it?"

"I think he got the idea from Father Masters' sermons, because Father Masters often preaches about sinners being crucified in the olden days. And then when he started preaching about adulterous women"—she shook her head—"I knew he was talking directly to me, and I think Virgil suspected it, too."

"Why didn't he just divorce you?" Dawn asked. "Why go through all this trouble to get you to stop cheating?"

"Oh, he'd never divorce me." She shook her head from side to side. "He knows I'd get everything and his business would be destroyed. His life would be ruined. He told me many times he didn't want to end up like Keenan."

"How's that?"

"Keenan used to be a surgeon. He had a mansion, four cars, two boats, and his own golf course, but he lost it all when his wife divorced him. He turned to alcohol and drugs and his life took a dive. He ended up homeless on the streets of New Orleans, sleeping in a box."

"Oh," Dawn said, "is he the homeless guy in the newspaper article above Virgil's desk?"

Skylar nodded. "He saved Virgil's life, so Virgil took him in and lets him do work around the house. He's really gotten his act together and he wants to go back to being a doctor, but his mind isn't what it used to be. I think his former drug use has caused some permanent brain damage."

Dawn continued questioning Skylar for several minutes, getting more details about her relationship with the farmer and the goings-on at the church, and then we stepped out into the hallway.

"What do you think?" Dawn asked.

I sighed. "How do we argue with the DNA results and this new information?"

"That's what I thought."

I followed Dawn back into the conference room and she told Skylar we would be holding the Tahoe as evidence. "Do you need a ride back home?"

Skylar shook her head. "I'll call Keenan to come get me."

CHAPTER 55

I flipped the switch to activate the audio and video recorder before Dawn and I stepped into the room with Virgil. He looked up and lifted his hands in objection as Rachael and Warren stepped out.

"I told them I wanted to see Skylar, but they said I couldn't. What's going on here?"

I placed my file folder on the floor near my chair and took the seat directly across from him. Dawn sat to my left.

"We need to talk some more about Kathleen Bertrand and Debbie Brister," I began.

"I told you everything I know." He said it with finality.

"Well, some things have come up that we need to discuss." I placed my notebook on the desk in front of me and leaned back. "You know the drill...can you start by telling us where you were when Kathleen disappeared?"

"I'd love to, but I don't know when she disappeared."

I gave him the date and time ranges, and he asked if he could refer to his phone. I nodded and, once he did, he ran through his activities for the entire week. When I asked if he had witnesses who could verify the information he'd provided, he just looked up with a scowl on his face.

"I didn't know I'd need to provide proof of every move I made...but I'm sure Skylar and Keenan can verify most of it."

"What about when Debbie disappeared?"

He accessed the calendar on his phone and began listing everything he did beginning on the day she disappeared up until yesterday, and it included the time we visited his house. It all sounded legit, but he'd left out the parts where he'd spat in

Kathleen's and Debbie's faces. If he expected us to believe he didn't kill the women, he'd have to offer up an explanation about how his saliva got on their faces.

"Did you speak to Kathleen at church on the night she disappeared?"

He shrugged. "I might have."

"What about Debbie?"

"I don't usually speak to Debbie. I might've spoken to Gerard, but I can't be sure."

"Is there a reason why your saliva would've ended up on their faces?"

I saw his expression fall and his color drain. He used to be a detective. He knew the implication of such evidence—he just wasn't sure if I was bluffing or not.

"If my saliva's on their faces, someone planted it."

I smiled wryly. "You do know how ridiculous that sounds, right?"

"From where I'm sitting, what you're saying is ridiculous."

I opened my mouth to respond when a sharp knock sounded on the door to the interview room. Dawn and I exchanged glances. Every deputy in the sheriff's office knew we were in with the crucifix murder suspect, so if they were knocking, it had to be important.

I asked Virgil to excuse us and we stepped out into the hallway. Sheriff Chiasson was waiting for us.

"The fellow who came to pick up Skylar—a Keenan Tipton—is demanding to speak with you. He says he's been in contact with Virgil's attorney and they are demanding that all interrogations cease."

I handed the sheriff my investigative file and Dawn and I headed for the front lobby, which was on the opposite side of the building from the detective bureau. Warren was waiting with Skylar and Keenan. Keenan was pacing back and forth in the lobby and he whirled around when I opened the door.

"Detective, you've got to release Virgil," he pleaded. "I swear to you, he didn't do this. I know this man better than anyone and he would never hurt an innocent person."

I recognized Keenan from church. He had been the guy sitting next to Virgil when Dawn and I visited on Sunday night. His beady eyes were swollen, as though he had been crying.

"The sheriff said you were on the phone with his lawyer."

Keenan sighed. "I called for him, but he didn't answer. I'm sorry for lying to your sheriff, but I had to speak with you immediately. Virgil Brunner is a decent man—a law-abiding man. Please, you've got to believe me when I say he didn't do this."

"How do you know he didn't do this?" I challenged.

"Because I'm with him every single day. If he would've been involved in something like this, I would certainly know about it."

Skylar reached out and took Keenan by the arm. "Come on, Keen," she said soothingly. "Let's go home and allow them to do their jobs."

Keenan turned slowly to fix Skylar with a knowing glare. "You—it was you who accused him of this, wasn't it?"

"No, they have their own evidence. Look, if Virgil didn't do it, they'll release him tonight." She turned toward me and nodded. "Isn't that right, Detective Carter?"

"It's true that he's not under arrest," I admitted. "Once we finish interviewing him we'll know more."

Keenan sighed deeply. "Thank God! I thought he was under arrest."

"You know, if you believe you have some information that would exonerate Virgil, I want to hear it." I knew the importance of pinning defense witnesses down early, and I wanted to hear everything Keenan had to say and I wanted it on record. That way, if we ended up arresting Virgil—and I was certain it was about to happen—Keenan couldn't modify his story later to try and help his boss and friend. "Just hang out here in the lobby and we'll be with you as soon as we finish with Virgil."

Keenan nodded, seemingly satisfied. "I appreciate it."

Skylar grumbled under her breath. She didn't seem happy, but she plopped into a chair to wait.

I asked Warren if he could keep an eye on Skylar and Keenan, and he grumbled even more than Skylar did, cursing good-naturedly about being reduced to a babysitter.

"He's a loyal little soldier, isn't he?" Dawn said about Keenan as we made our way back to the interview room. "I can't wait to hear what he's got to say."

"If he tries to lie for Virgil, it'll be easy to trip him up."

CHAPTER 56

The sheriff handed me the case file and Dawn and I reclaimed our seats in the interview room. I apologized to Virgil and asked if he remembered where we were.

"I do." He pursed his lips and nodded. "You were apologizing for wasting my time."

I gently placed the case file on the desk in front of me and rested my hands on it. "Look, you were a detective at one time, so I'm going to shoot straight with you. We've got direct evidence that links you to both victims."

"Because I investigated them?" He scoffed. "I work cases on hundreds of people every year. That doesn't make me responsible if something bad happens to them."

I decided to change gears on him.

"Can I trust that you're going to be completely honest with me—as I've been with you—or should I assume you're going to play cat and mouse games all night?"

"I'm not playing any games. I've been honest about everything and I'll continue to be honest."

"Even when it comes to your daughter?"

He scowled. "Skylar and I don't have any children. We've tried for years, but one of us can't get our shit together down there."

"I didn't say anything about Skylar," I said, noting what he did there. "I'm asking about *your* daughter."

"I don't have a daughter." His eyes were level as he met my gaze, and I knew right then he was too good of a liar to trust.

"Then you won't mind giving me a sample of your DNA to compare against Gretchen Masters' brown-haired daughter?"

Virgil's face fell just a little. "I'm not consenting to anything."

"You don't have to." I reached into the case file and pulled out the photographs I'd taken of the yellow envelopes we'd recovered from Joey and Gerard. I spread them out on the table. "Do you recognize these?"

He glanced at them and shrugged. "Yeah. What about it?"

"We recovered your DNA from the lick-and-seal part of both envelopes." I paused to let that information sink in. "And then we compared it to DNA evidence we recovered from the victims, and it was a match."

Virgil stared at me for a long moment. "What did you just say?"

"You heard me. Your DNA is on the dead victims."

"Is this a bluff?" he asked. "Some kind of bait?"

I shook my head. "It's as real as it gets."

"That's impossible." He folded his arms across his chest. "If you're telling the truth, someone planted my DNA because I didn't do anything to either of those women."

"Really?" I leaned forward and rested my forearms on the table. "Where'd you and your wife have sex for the first time?"

"Why is that any of your business?"

"Just answer the question."

"That's all I'm saying about it."

I dug in the file folder again and flipped through the crime scene photos from 1711 Plymouth Highway until I found one depicting the bayou behind where we'd located Kathleen Bertrand's body. I pulled it out and placed it on the desk in front of Virgil.

"Does this jog any memories?" I asked.

"What's that got to do with this case?" Virgil was clearly agitated.

"This is where we found Kathleen Bertrand." I pulled out a photo of the tractor shed where we'd found Debbie Brister, and plopped that one on top of the last photograph. "And this is where we found Debbie Brister—the exact spot you and Skylar had sex for the second time."

Virgil's expression was quite telling—he knew he was screwed.

"Look, if what you're saying is true—and I still think you're bluffing—I can't explain the locations or the DNA, but I guarantee you I had nothing to do with any of it."

"I'd love to believe you," I said, "but the evidence is too damning."

Dawn and I sat and watched as Virgil lifted each picture and studied it, as though he were looking for a way out of his predicament through the images. When he lifted the picture of the envelope we'd recovered from Joey, his brow furrowed and he pulled the picture close. Scowling, he looked up at me and asked if I had a digital copy of the photograph.

"Sure," I said simply.

"Can I see it?"

I pulled the flash drive out of the file folder and shoved it into the USB port on the desktop computer. Once it was up, I scrolled through the photos until I found the one he was looking at. "Here it is," I said, turning the monitor so he could view it.

"Enlarge the signature across the evidence tape—please."

When I did, he gasped and stabbed at the monitor. "That's not my signature!"

I forced a chuckle. "Of course it's not your signature. It's also not your DNA and it's not where you and Skylar had sex."

"No, it is where we had sex, but that's not my signature, it's not my DNA, and it's not my handwriting on the front of the envelope. Granted, it's a good forgery attempt, but it's not my handwriting." He leaned back and nodded his head vigorously. "Take my DNA and handwriting samples and test them—you'll discover you've got the wrong guy."

He seemed so confident that I found myself doubting our evidence. While I hadn't suspected him initially, I didn't know how we could explain away the mountain of evidence we now possessed. "You said you sealed the envelopes, secured them with evidence tape, and then hand-delivered them to the clients. How on earth is it not your DNA and handwriting?"

"I said I *had* them hand-delivered, not that I did it personally."

"You expect me to believe someone switched envelopes and recreated your method of sealing them? To what end? Why would someone go through all that trouble to frame you?"

"I don't know," he said, "but it wasn't me."

I leaned back, thoughtful. What if they weren't trying to frame him? What if they simply wanted to see what was inside of the envelope? The killer had no clue we would eventually end up with the envelopes, so there was no reason to try and frame Virgil. In fact, if what Virgil was saying was true, we'd recovered the killer's DNA from the envelope, not Virgil's.

"We'll need your DNA and I'm holding you until the results come back," I said. "In the meantime, I need to know who delivered those envelopes."

Virgil hesitated. "I can't believe it would be…"

"Who, damn it?" I needed the name.

"Keenan Tipton…he does most of my deliveries." He shook his head. "But I can't see him hurting anyone. He's a gentle guy. His own wife cheated on him and left him for his best friend, but he did nothing about it. He didn't try to fight the other guy…he didn't beat his wife over it…nothing. He turned to drinking and drugs and lost everything because of it."

"Did he deliver the envelope containing the paternity results to Nehemiah?"

"No, I delivered that one myself." Virgil sighed heavily. "Gretchen found me in a moment of weakness. She was miserable with Nehemiah and she was looking for a way out. She wanted me to take her away from Nehemiah—for both of us to leave our spouses and run off together. I tried explaining to her that I couldn't leave Skylar. We had too much going on. I'd lose everything if we got divorced. Hell, in this economy, I'd be living in a cardboard box somewhere if I got divorced. Gretchen was desperate. The last time we were together, she told me she was pregnant and the baby was mine. When I told her I couldn't have kids, she ran off crying and we haven't been together since."

"Don't you mean you'd lose half of everything if you got divorced?" I asked, remembering how Skylar had also said she'd get everything.

"Like a fool, I signed a postnuptial agreement while I was in the hospital recovering from my knife wounds. At the time, I was terrified of losing Skylar and would've done anything to keep her." He shook his head and frowned. "She gets everything if I commit adultery."

"What if she commits adultery?"

"She wouldn't do something like that. She's too good of a person."

I nodded slowly, studying Virgil's face closely. The man had no clue about his wife cheating on him. "If she cheated on you and decided to divorce you, who else might be affected by that decision?"

"What do you mean?"

"Let's say she knew about you and the preacher's wife. Let's say she decides to get revenge on you for all of your past indiscretions and she starts sleeping with some random guy. She falls for this guy and realizes there's life after you, so she decides to go through with the divorce, citing your relationship with Gretchen as cause." I paused while he mulled over the scenario I laid out. "If that were to happen, who else would lose everything?"

"I mean, Keenan would be out of a job unless she kept him on, but she can't run the investigative business."

"So, Keenan would be back in a cardboard box, too?"

"I guess so."

I looked at Dawn and she nodded. We needed Keenan's DNA.

After telling Virgil to sit tight, Dawn and I walked into the lobby, where Warren was sitting in a chair playing on his phone.

"Where'd Keenan and Skylar go?" I asked.

He shot a thumb over his shoulder. "They're outside smoking."

Dawn and I rushed out the door and scanned the parking lot. It was empty. They were gone.

CHAPTER 57

"Did Keenan know about the postnuptial?" I asked Virgil when I burst through the door to the interview room.

"Yeah, I mentioned it to him."

"Did you also mention where you and Skylar had sex?"

He hesitated, then said, "I mean, sure…we talked shop from time to time."

"Where'd you and Skylar have sex for the third time?"

"Why?" There was a confused expression on Virgil's face. "Where's Skylar?"

"She left with Keenan and only God knows where they're heading."

"Do you think…?"

"Yeah, I think Keenan switched the envelopes and began killing women as a warning to Skylar to stop cheating, but she didn't."

"Cheating?" Virgil instantly deflated. "Was she really? But with who?"

"That doesn't matter right now—what matters is finding Keenan before he crucifies Skylar. Where'd y'all have sex for the third time?"

Virgil jumped to his feet and began pacing in the small space behind the desk. "Um…we had sex in New Orleans that third time, but Keenan wouldn't know about it. I never told him."

"Well, what did you tell him?" I asked pointedly. "I need to know all of it."

"I told him about our first time in the boat and our second time behind the tractor shed, but…" He licked his dry lips and stopped walking. "Our third time was in the alley where I got cut, but I didn't want to tell him about it because it was disrespectful of me to bring a strange girl to the same spot where Skylar and I made love, so I never mentioned it."

"Well, what did you tell him?" Dawn asked, chiming in impatiently.

"I told him about the railroad tracks behind Plymouth East." Virgil's face turned pale as he glanced at the clock on the wall. "I told him we had sex on the tracks as the train was barreling down on us and we took some railroad spikes as souvenirs."

"Where exactly on the tracks were y'all?" I asked, already heading toward the door.

"It was a hundred yards north of where the tracks intersect with Plymouth Highway."

"Stay here!" I ordered Virgil and waved for Dawn to follow me. As we hurried to the parking lot, I got on my phone and called the sheriff to let him know what was going on. He was inside the building and I had run right by him, but I wasn't wasting time to stop and tell him. If we were right about Keenan, we might already be too late. The train passed at ten o'clock every night, and it was already nine-thirty.

I was ending the call with the sheriff just as Dawn and I got into her car and she sped out of the parking lot. I called Rachael next and told her to head to the end of Plymouth Highway as fast as she could. I accessed Dawn's onboard computer and pulled up a driver's license photo of Keenan Tipton.

"If you see Tipton on the railroad tracks with a woman, shoot him immediately." I ended the call and glanced at the dash clock. "We've got to move it!"

Dawn was already traveling as fast as she could along Highway Three without crashing. While she was concentrating on the road, it didn't stop her from issuing a warning. "If you ever 'talk shop' to one of your buddies about our sex life, I'll cut you off for two days."

"Only two days?" I asked, relieved.

"Yeah—that's about as long as I can go without being with you."

We both laughed, but it was a hollow laughter. We knew the danger Skylar was in and we knew we couldn't predict how this night would end. It was a terrifying prospect. I didn't want this bastard putting his hands on another woman, but I didn't know if I could stop him in time.

Dawn slowed down just enough to turn onto the bridge. We zipped across and nearly went airborne as we got onto Plymouth Highway.

"Do you really think Keenan knows about Skylar, and he killed Kathleen and Debbie as a warning to her?" Dawn asked.

"I think he killed Kathleen and Debbie because they were supposed to die for their sins—at least, according to his spiritual leader—and he used their deaths as a warning to Skylar." I shook my head. "I don't think he would've spared Debbie if Skylar would've stopped seeing the farmer, and I don't think he'll spare her even though she did stop sleeping with the dude. In his warped mind, she sinned against God and her husband, and there's only one just outcome—death. And by killing Skylar, he protects Virgil's assets forever."

Dawn was quiet for a long moment and I glanced at her. She was staring straight ahead, gripping the steering wheel with both hands. I knew she was thinking about more than this case, so I asked what was on her mind.

"Please don't ever cheat on me."

I reached over and squeezed her arm. "That's something you'll never have to worry about."

"Did Bethany worry about it?" Dawn asked quietly.

"That was one of many mistakes I've made in my life," I said, "and I'm not proud of it. But I can tell you this—I learn from past mistakes and don't repeat them."

After sitting quiet for a while, she smiled and her brown eyes glistened in the blue police lights. "I believe you."

"Besides, I'm too afraid to piss you off," I said as we plunged deeper into Plymouth East. "You might slice off my balls and drop them in a garbage disposal."

She grunted and I got on the radio to ask for all the responding officers' locations. When they radioed me back, I realized Dawn and I were going to be the first unit on the scene.

CHAPTER 58

Dawn shut off her blue emergency strobes and headlights and pulled to the side of the road as we neared the end of Plymouth Highway. I pointed to a pickup truck parked across the railroad tracks about twenty yards ahead of us. "That's them."

There was a first quarter moon shining above and it painted our surroundings in an eerie glow. While I didn't like how much it illuminated us, I knew my scope would be able to gather enough light to clearly see Keenan and Skylar. I was also encouraged by the fact that there had not been enough time for Keenan to erect a cross yet, so we were in time to save Skylar, unless—

The thought that popped into my head spurred me into action. While Dawn grabbed her flashlight and drew her pistol, I snatched my Accuracy International sniper rifle from my drag bag and slipped out of the car. Keeping our heads on swivels, we made our way quickly but quietly toward the truck, keeping to the darker shadows of the trees.

Dawn went straight to the truck to search it. As she did that, I flipped the legs on my bipod down and stretched out on the ground in a prone position, facing north. From somewhere off in the distance came the blaring horn of the train, but it was immediately drowned out by a bloodcurdling scream.

I'd never heard such pain and terror ripped from the vocal chords of a human being before and it made my skin crawl. I took a deep breath to calm my racing heart and peered through my scope, searching the length of railroad track ahead of me. The backdrop of thick trees and shadows made it difficult to see. I lowered my view, using the lighter backdrop of gray rocks to try and discern human figures along the way.

The train horn blared again. It was drawing closer, but was still miles away.

Blinking sweat from my right eye and ignoring the mosquitoes buzzing around my head, I focused on the area from which the screams were emitting, and suddenly saw movement close to the ground between the rails. I tightened the focus on my scope and saw the shadow of an arm rise and fall. A few seconds after it fell, I heard a metallic *ding* and a new chorus of tortured screams coming from the female voice. I couldn't recognize it as Skylar's, but knew it had to be.

The arm rose again and I quickly traced it back to where the head should be. As soon as my crosshairs hovered over the dark circular shadow that was the bad guy's head, I squeezed the trigger.

The dark figure collapsed forward and muffled the screams of our victim.

"Go! Go!" I hollered to Dawn as I scrambled from my position and rushed forward, taking my sniper rifle with me. "We need to get her off the tracks before the train gets here!"

The tracks were situated atop a levee of rocks that plunged steeply into the trees below us. It was impossible to drive a vehicle beside the tracks, so we had to go by foot. We rushed the hundred yards to the victim and dropped beside her. I pulled the bad guy roughly off of her and confirmed that it was Keenan. Dawn began assessing Skylar's condition.

Skylar was screaming out in pain. Dawn shined her light over the woman, not knowing where to start. I winced when I saw that Keenan had nailed her spread-eagle and naked to the railroad ties. Large railroad spikes had punched large holes in her wrists and feet.

"Take a deep breath," Dawn warned, and then tried to jerk Skylar's left wrist free of the spike. Skylar screamed louder than earlier and Dawn quickly apologized, glancing north toward a bend in the track where the train would soon appear. "We won't be able to jerk her free."

I tried to wiggle the spikes loose, but they were too deeply imbedded in the railroad ties. We didn't have the tools to remove them and we couldn't rip her arms and feet over the head of the spikes. I cursed silently and glanced in the direction from which the train was coming. It had to be traveling around sixty miles per hour and, at that speed, it would need more than a mile to stop. The bend in the tracks was about two hundred yards away. Even if the conductor applied the emergency brakes immediately upon rounding the curve, the train would stop long after mowing us all down.

Realizing there was only one option, I snatched up my rifle and broke into an unsteady run, heading north as fast as my legs could carry me. On a flat surface and wearing full sniper gear, I could run a mile in eight minutes—not even close on these loose rocks.

Dawn began hollering from behind me, telling me I was on a suicide mission and begging me to come back.

I ignored her cries, drawing closer and closer to the oncoming train. I held my breath as I rounded the first bend in the tracks, and breathed a sigh of release when I was met with an empty length of tracks. In the dim glow from the moon, it looked like the next bend in the railway was about a thousand yards away. I leaned into my run and pushed my legs as hard as I could.

When I rounded that corner, I heard the horn's blare and realized it was almost reckoning time. I could actually see a glow through the trees and knew I was running out of real estate. I had to get at least a mile away from Skylar and I had to exercise my plan before the train got to within 440 yards of me. If the train was traveling sixty miles per hour, I'd have about fifteen seconds to get my ass off the tracks. If it was traveling much faster…well, I was in trouble.

My legs burned and I could feel them slowing down. I gritted my teeth and forced myself forward. I had gone at least a mile, but I needed more room. I was pushing on when the bright eyes of the train appeared out of the darkness around the next curve up ahead. My heart raced as I continued running toward the train. It felt unnatural. I should've been running away from it, not toward it.

I tried to gauge the distance as I continued on a collision course with this steel monster, its two eyes beaming ominously as it barreled down on me. I knew I'd only get one shot at this, and I'd have to fire four rounds—one at each of the headlights and the crossing lights.

One mile…half a mile…a quarter mile…

I skidded to my left knee and shouldered my rifle. I panned from left to right, taking out the left crossing light first, then the left headlight, the right headlight, and the right crossing light. I fired the rounds as fast as I could, working the bolt like a machine. When I'd pulled the trigger for the fourth time, I threw myself toward the side of the rails. All of the lights blinked out and the conductor—his visibility now gone—instantly applied the emergency brakes.

CHAPTER 59

Dawn's head jerked up from Skylar when she heard four gunshots in rapid succession. They were booming reports and she knew it was London's sniper rifle. "What in the hell did you do, London?" she wondered aloud.

Immediately following the gunshots, brakes screamed and loud hissing sounds emitted from the darkness to the north. *The train was trying to stop—London's plan worked!*

As she continued listening, she realized the train was moving way too fast. *Will it stop in time?*

Her eyes wild and her heart racing in her chest, she stared blindly into the darkness. The ground shook. Somewhere off in the distance, the train skidded toward her location, the wheels screeching in protest.

As the sound grew nearer, she held her breath and stared. Within seconds, she caught sight of an ominous shadow cloaked in smoke rounding the bend and heading straight for them. It didn't look like it would stop in time. It was still going too fast.

"God, help us!" Dawn hollered, throwing her body on top of Skylar and holding her tight. Skylar screamed when Dawn's weight fell over her. She was so blinded by pain that she didn't realize they were both about to die.

Dawn's eyes were squeezed shut as many things raced through her mind at once. The biggest regret she had as the metal beast bore down on her was that she'd never live to be called Mrs. Dawn Carter—

Dawn suddenly opened her eyes and took a breath. The rumbling had stopped. She was still alive. She looked up and saw the front of the locomotive mere feet away from where she lay.

"Dawn! London! Are y'all okay?" It was Sheriff Chiasson.

Dawn spun around to see a dozen beams of light jostling as the sheriff and his deputies converged on her location. Her mind was whirling. She stood slowly, but felt unsteady on her feet. Someone was cursing from behind her and she turned to see the conductor walk up carrying a large lamp. When his light fell on Skylar's nude body nailed to the railroad ties, he revolted in horror and vomited on the rocks.

Dawn didn't wait for the sheriff to reach her. She snatched her flashlight from the ground and began running north along the side of the train, screaming for London as she ran. Knowing London as well as she did, she knew he would stand strong in the pocket and take the shot even if it meant he'd have to sacrifice his own life.

"Please be okay!" she wailed. "Please be okay!"

Tears spilled from her eyes and blurred her vision. She stumbled often and fell twice. The second time she fell, she was trying to push herself to her feet when she heard some noise up ahead.

"Dawn? Is that you?"

"London!" She pushed off the ground just as London reached her and wrapped her in his arms. They both collapsed to the sharp rocks and clung to each other, thanking God and each other that they were still alive.

"I didn't think it would stop in time," London said, out of breath. "I thought it would run over you and Skylar. It seemed to be going too fast."

"And I thought it plowed over you." Dawn felt for his face in the dark and pulled his lips to hers.

CHAPTER 60

A week later...

"I still can't believe you shot at a moving train," Dawn said as we approached Skylar's hospital room.

I grunted. "And I can't believe I got away with it."

The federal investigators were not amused that I'd shot out the headlights and the crossing lights on their train, and there was talk of "reckless endangerment" and "criminal negligence". However, the fact that I was familiar with the Maque Trax train and knew that the conductor was seated high above the lights and out of danger, immediately dispelled their accusations.

It had taken days for us to complete the investigative report, use of force reports, and crime scene sketches. Expedited DNA tests confirmed that Keenan Tipton was the real killer, and a citizen had come forward to say he'd picked up a hitchhiker in the area of the tractor shed on the day Debbie Brister's body was found. He later identified Keenan from a photographic lineup.

We also confirmed Keenan was the one who leaked the information about the "sinner" note. Two days after his mug appeared on the local news, a cashier who worked at Plymouth Shop—the only grocery store in Plymouth East—identified Keenan as the person who mentioned the "sinner" note in the store.

"I wondered how he knew so much about the case," the young girl had said when we interviewed her. "Now I know!"

When we re-interviewed Shelby Rove and showed her a photographic lineup containing a picture of Keenan, she immediately picked him out as the one who mentioned the "sinner" note to her.

After we had wrapped up the case and presented the file to the district attorney's office for review, the sheriff urged Dawn and me to take some time off.

"When you get back," he told me in confidence, "I want you and Dawn to start training Abraham Wilson. I'm transferring him to the detective bureau immediately. That boy's the future of this department."

I was thrilled the sheriff had recognized his talent and drive, and that his self-initiative and hard work on this case had paid off for him. Dawn was equally excited and we couldn't wait to get back to start working with him.

But for now, we wanted to visit with Skylar before finally heading to Tennessee.

Skylar lifted her head when we ducked into her room. She smiled and waved a bandaged hand. "I'm so glad I get to see you two again."

Dawn smiled warmly, pulling the stool close to Skylar's bed. "We'd never think of leaving without saying goodbye."

I stood at the foot of the bed and smiled down at her. The woman had courage…that was for sure. Even while nailed to the railroad ties waiting to be cut loose, she had given a coherent statement. The sheriff had covered her nude body with a blanket and she explained how Keenan had flashed out when she told him she thought Virgil was the killer.

"Are you the reason Virgil's in jail?" Keenan had asked.

When she told him about the tip she'd called in, he went berserk and began beating her while he was driving. His back-fist had busted her nose and dazed her. "You're the reason those women are dead!" he had yelled. "The Lord wanted *you* dead, but I decided to spare you—to give you a chance to walk away from your sins. Not once, but *twice* did I warn you. But did you listen? No! You betrayed God and you betrayed the very man who gives you everything! You're a sinful woman and the wages of sin is death!"

Dawn had interrupted her to point out that she told us she had stopped seeing the farmer after Debbie's body was found. She had tearfully admitted she lied to us.

"I thought I was being careful, but when Virgil came home early and caught me on the phone, I thought he knew about us, and I thought he would kill me next. That's why I called the tip line—to protect myself. But when he took me to dinner, I began to think I had misjudged him and that it was all a coincidence.

"Come to think of it, I put a target on my back by calling in the tip line. Keenan said he was going to punish Gretchen next for cheating on Father Masters and he was saving me for last, but…"

When she hadn't continued, Dawn had finished for her. "But then you added insult to injury by having Virgil arrested."

"Yeah." She shook her head. "He loved Virgil and was extremely loyal to him, but I would've never thought he'd do something like this."

"Do you know why he decided to start killing these women?"

"He said God told him to do it. He said God was talking to him through Father Masters and directing him to purify the church." She had stopped when the paramedics had arrived and gave her something for the pain. When she continued, she said Keenan had been opening Virgil's envelopes for a while. "He said he began opening the packages over a year ago to read for entertainment, but he realized God had placed the envelopes in his hands. He knew about a lot of adulteries, so I asked him why he only killed the women from the church. He said that's all God told him to kill. He said we were held to a higher standard and he had to purify the flock for Father Masters."

"How'd he know about Gretchen?" Dawn had asked. "Virgil personally delivered that envelope to Nehemiah."

"He saw them together one night in Virgil's office. I was at the grocery store and Virgil didn't know Keenan was at the house."

Dawn scowled. "Then why didn't he kill Virgil? He committed adultery, too."

Skylar had grunted, and then winced in pain. After taking a few breaths, she explained that the standards were different for men and women in Nehemiah's church. "I know it's not like that everywhere," she had explained, "but Nehemiah believes the women in the church are second-class citizens."

"Well, he'll enjoy being a second-class prisoner," Dawn had said as we stepped aside so the medics could begin working on Skylar. After watching them in silence for a few minutes, Dawn had said, "You know, this case was so bizarre that Keenan would've probably been found not guilty by reason of insanity."

I couldn't argue.

Now, I stood watching Dawn tell Skylar how much of a fighter she was. "You've got true grit, girl."

Skylar smiled and wiped a tear from her eyes. "Did you hear Virgil and me are calling it quits? And I'm not going to take his business. He worked too hard for it, you know?"

"To be honest, I think it's the best thing. There's been too much damage in your relationship. It's time both of you started off fresh with someone new." Dawn glanced at me and winked, then turned back toward Skylar. "Just make sure you learn from your mistakes."

"I will." Skylar took a breath and exhaled, tears clouding her eyes. "Virgil told me he and Gretchen are going to make a run at it. He wants to help her raise their child, and he can protect her from Nehemiah—*if* the man ever gets out of prison."

"I know it's hard, but you'll be fine." Dawn frowned and brushed the hair off of Skylar's forehead. "It sounds like you've got a good man now, and you two can always adopt some children."

Skylar nodded, cheering up a bit. "I've actually been thinking about that for a while. I mentioned it to him and he's open to the idea."

"Well, I'll always be around if you need anything."

CHAPTER 61

After leaving the hospital, Dawn and I drove the ten hours to Gatlinburg, Tennessee, arriving just after three o'clock their time. When the supervisor at Blue Summit Mountain Rental had found out why we'd missed our reservations, she put us up in a better cabin free of charge. Even the photographer had moved her schedule around to accommodate me.

After an amazing dinner at a place called The Peddler, Dawn and I retired to the cabin, got the first real sleep we'd had in weeks, and then woke up the next morning and headed for Cades Cove. I'd decided to drive to the Abrams Falls trailhead instead of making Dawn hike it, and we enjoyed the Loop Road immensely. We saw two black bears cross the road—a mother and a cub—before we even reached the trail, and Dawn was itching to see more.

"Do you think we'll see some along the trail?" she asked when we parked and unloaded our rucksacks.

"I hope so," I said idly, scanning the faces of the people scattered across the grassy parking area. I sighed with relief when I saw the photographer—I recognized her from the picture on her website—fiddling with her camera, pretending not to notice us. Pleased that everything was coming together, I hoisted my pack and said, "Let's do this!"

We crossed a weathered wooden bridge and hit the trail with the gusto of two people who had never had a vacation before. We had been so surprised our phones hadn't rung on the drive up here that we kept checking to see if our batteries had died. And once we hit the mountains, we'd lost service. For that, I was secretly thankful.

The trail was rocky and rugged and we stared in awe at the

beauty that surrounded us. We did see a bear, but it was too far away and hidden in the bushes, so we only caught a fleeting glimpse of it. Two hundred yards farther, we began hearing the roar of the waterfall.

"It sounds so big!" Dawn said as we drew nearer.

"It should—it's the most voluminous waterfall in the Smoky Mountains." I said it with my chest puffed out a little, proud of the research I'd done.

Of course, none of the pictures I'd found compared to seeing it in person for the first time. I gasped out loud when we rounded a turn in the trail and the waterfall came into full view. It was majestic and powerful. A mysterious-looking fog floated over the pool of water at its base. I stood staring—I even think my mouth was hanging open— and didn't look away until Dawn tugged at my arm.

I turned to look at her and she shot a thumb over her shoulder. "I think that woman's following us. She's been on our trail since we left the parking area."

I glanced over and saw the photographer pretending to mess with the buttons on her camera. She was ten feet away and we were all aligned perfectly for her to get a picture of the waterfall behind us. I quickly dropped to one knee and looked up into Dawn's eyes.

"What the hell are you doing?" she asked.

I had spent countless hours rehearsing what I was going to say to her at that moment, but, suddenly, the words wouldn't come. Her eyes melted me. The significance of the moment rendered me speechless.

Her eyes slowly widened. "Are you...?"

"I am." I had to holler above the roar of the waterfall. "You're the first and only women I've ever met who could get me down on one knee—and I'm not getting up until you agree to marry me."

The photographer began snapping pictures and Dawn turned in her direction, her mouth agape. She then slowly took in our surroundings, from the thick forest to the waterfall. "You did all of this? You set this up?"

I grinned and nodded.

"I had no clue what you were up to." She shook her head and giggled. "I didn't think you had it in you."

I cocked my head sideways, not sure how to take her comment. "What do you mean?"

"This is so romantic. I didn't expect it."

"What'd you expect?"

"I don't know—maybe for you to propose at the shooting range or a crime scene. Maybe have me place my left hand on your sniper rifle and raise my right hand and swear to love and cherish you for all of my days."

I laughed, but the sharp rock I was kneeling on was beginning to tear into my kneecap.

"So...your answer?" I asked.

She feigned surprise. "What...are you still down there?" She bent and kissed me fully on the mouth, cupping my face in her cool hands as she did. When she pulled away, her eyes were glistening. "You already know my answer, London Carter. I wouldn't be standing here if I didn't want to spend the rest of my life with you."

BJ BOURG

BJ Bourg is an award-winning mystery writer and former professional boxer who hails from the swamps of Louisiana. Dubbed the "real deal" by other mystery writers, he has spent his entire adult life solving crimes as a patrol cop, detective sergeant, and chief investigator for a district attorney's office. Not only does he know his way around crime scenes, interrogations, and courtrooms, but he also served as a police sniper commander (earning the title of "Top Shooter" at an FBI sniper school) and a police academy instructor.

BJ is a four-time traditionally-published novelist (his debut novel, JAMES 516, won the 2016 EPIC eBook Award for Best Mystery) and dozens of his articles and stories have been published in national magazines such as Woman's World, Boys' Life, and Writer's Digest. He is a regular contributor to two of the nation's leading law enforcement magazines, Law and Order and Tactical Response, and he has taught at conferences for law enforcement officers, tactical police officers, and writers. Above all else, he is a father and husband, and the highlight of his life is spending time with his beautiful wife and wonderful children.

Made in the USA
Las Vegas, NV
23 May 2024

90286602R00132